PRAISE FOR LACEY BAKER

"Lacey Baker has written a heartwarming and inspiring novel about Christmas magic and a second chance at love."

—BRENDA JACKSON, *NEW YORK TIMES* AND
USA TODAY BESTSELLING AUTHOR

"*Snow Place Like Home* is an authentic look at managing the merry and bright of the holidays when your heart isn't in it, only to find happiness and joy are just around the corner."

—NANCY NAIGLE, *USA TODAY* BESTSELLING AUTHOR

"Lacey Baker is a premier author of holiday stories that leave readers with a warm, fuzzy feeling and a smile that lingers long after the story ends. *Snow Place Like Home* is a wonderful, heartfelt story of two people who truly belong together. Baker delves deeply into her characters, sending a message that will resonate with us all: It's never too late for anyone willing to take a chance."

—JACQUELIN THOMAS, AWARD-WINNING AUTHOR

"*Snow Place Like Home* by Lacey Baker is a heart-warming treat just in time for the holidays! Readers will be hooked from page one and won't stop until they reach the end. Brew a cup of hot chocolate, grab your favorite blanket, and curl up by the fire for this charming story filled with Christmas cheer as well as faith, family, second-chance love, and more."

—AMY CLIPSTON, BESTSELLING AUTHOR OF *STARSTRUCK*

"As I cozied up to read *Snow Place Like Home*, I instantly got small-town Christmas movie vibes, as in, this should be a movie! I felt the need for a warm blanket and hot cocoa. And fell completely in love with Seth and Ella's second chance love story."

—VANESSA MILLER, AUTHOR OF *THE AMERICAN QUEEN*

snow place like home

A Novel

LACEY BAKER

THOMAS NELSON
Since 1798

Snow Place Like Home

Published in Nashville, Tennessee, by Thomas Nelson. Thomas Nelson is a registered trademark of HarperCollins Christian Publishing, Inc.

Thomas Nelson titles may be purchased in bulk for educational, business, fundraising, or sales promotional use. For information, please email SpecialMarkets@ThomasNelson.com.

Scripture quotations are taken from the King James Version. Public domain.

Publisher's Note: This novel is a work of fiction. Names, characters, places, and incidents are either products of the author's imagination or used fictitiously. All characters are fictional, and any similarity to people living or dead is purely coincidental.

Any internet addresses (websites, blogs, etc.) in this book are offered as a resource. They are not intended in any way to be or imply an endorsement by Thomas Nelson, nor does Thomas Nelson vouch for the content of these sites for the life of this book.

Library of Congress Cataloging-in-Publication Data

Names: Baker, Lacey, author.
Title: Snow place like home / Lacey Baker.
Description: Nashville, Tennessee: Thomas Nelson, 2023. | Series: A Christmas novel
Identifiers: LCCN 2023021530 (print) | LCCN 2023021531 (ebook) | ISBN 9780840716774 (paperback) | ISBN 9780840716781 (epub) | ISBN 9780840716781
Subjects: LCGFT: Christian fiction. | Romance fiction. | Christmas fiction. | Novels.
Classification: LCC PS3601.R763 S66 2023 (print) | LCC PS3601.R763 (ebook) | DDC 813/.6--dc23/eng/20230505
LC record available at https://lccn.loc.gov/2023021530
LC ebook record available at https://lccn.loc.gov/2023021531

Printed in the United States of America

23 24 25 26 27 LBC 5 4 3 2 1

*To Ms. Addie Rebecca Bagley (1943–2020). We were
not related by blood, but you made us feel like family.
Your kindness and loving spirit are truly missed.*

CHAPTER 1

Mama was singing, her lovely soprano voice reciting the lyrics to "Silent Night" as if she were an award-winning soloist. Ella sat on the couch, her little legs tucked under her as she watched the most beautiful woman in the world reach out to hang yet another bulb on the Christmas tree.

"We still need more, Mama?" The tree seemed so full to her already. Red, gold, and green bulbs hung from every branch. Santa, shiny gold reindeer, big and small bells, and other ornaments were tucked alongside them. White lights that blinked like starbursts and gold ribbon had been wrapped around the tree too. It was beautiful, just like every year, and Ella was tired, just like every year, after they'd been decorating the tree for what felt like hours and hours.

Mama paused her singing and looked lovingly at her child. "Yes, baby. The more the merrier."

Her smile was as bright as those lights on the tree, and it made Ella smile too. With a burst of energy, she got off the couch and took another bulb from one of the many boxes scattered around the living room. Going over to the tree, she found the tiniest available spot and placed the bulb there.

Mama continued to sing until the song was over, and Ella

1

found a few more places to add a bulb or ornament. "It's all done now, Mama."

"Not quite, baby," Mama said. "You know what's the last very special part of decorating the tree?"

Ella did know and she hurried over to the bin that held a red velvet box. Ella knew to handle the box with care and she lifted it out of the bin, moving as slowly as she possibly could. She took a deep breath, then let it out in a whoosh as she eased the top from the box. The gold star inside glittered and glistened as if it were brand new. Her fingers moved over it, going from one pointed peak to the next.

"Do you know why the Christmas star is so important, Ella?"

Mama had come up behind her, touching a hand lightly to her shoulder as Ella nodded. "Yup. It's where all the wishes come from."

"That's right." Mama smiled down as Ella turned to look up at her. When she grew up, Ella hoped she'd be as pretty as her mother, and as nice too. "And when we put this star on the very top of our tree, we can make a wish."

Ella eased the star out of the box, still being careful not to hold it so tight that it broke or so loose that it dropped to the floor. Mama clasped her hand and walked her over to the tree.

"And when we make that wish, it'll come true in the next year," Ella said, reciting what Mama had been telling her every year since she was two years old.

"Right again. You're such a brilliant girl, Ella."

Mama had used a stool to get the bulbs up high on the tree because she wasn't very tall, like Mr. Randolph next door.

"Okay, let's get this star up there so we can make our wishes." Mama eased the star out of Ella's hand and gingerly stepped onto the ladder again. She reached her arm up to place the star on the tallest part of the tree. "There," she said. "Isn't it lovely?"

"Yes, Mama." Ella stared up at that gold star as if it were the most perfect thing she'd ever seen. And Mama stepped down off the ladder and stood beside her.

"Okay, now close your eyes and make a wish."

Ella did as Mama instructed, clamping her lips down tight, too, because if anyone else heard the wish, it wouldn't come true.

I wish for a pony so I can ride like the wind the way we did in summer camp.

She opened her eyes.

Mama still had hers closed. She was still wishing. For what seemed like a long time, Ella stared at Mama, at the way her black hair was styled in big, fat glossy curls that bounced on her shoulders when she walked. She marveled at the smooth skin of her mother's cheeks, the color of Ella's favorite caramel candies. And her scent. Mama always smelled like roses and rain, but no matter how much soap Ella used, she'd never been able to get that same scent on her skin.

When Mama finally opened her eyes, her lips spread into another smile before she leaned in and kissed Ella on the tip of her nose. They had the same nose—a little wide and pudgy—but as Mama always said, still cute. Ella wanted to ask Mama what she'd wished for because it had taken so very long—it must've been something big—but she didn't ask. Another song was playing now, "Christmas Island," and her mother began singing again. This time, Ella sang along too.

They sang and packed up all the empty boxes, putting them into bins and stacking them against the wall. Tomorrow, Mama would carry them up to the third bedroom where they'd stay until

January, and then they'd pack all the Christmas stuff into them again. It seemed like they sang for hours that night, one song after another, after another. All the Christmas songs with all the Christmas joy that Mama loved to fill the house with. It was the best time of Ella's life.

And six months later, after the new year, when Ella was waiting for her wish to come true, it became the worst time of her life.

Bolting up in her bed, Ella breathed heavily, a hand going to her chest in an attempt to still her thumping heart. "It was just a dream," she reminded herself. "Just a silly dream."

But it was the dream that had haunted her for the last nineteen years because it was the first time that Ella had wished upon the Christmas star and that wish hadn't come true. She hadn't gotten that pony she wanted. Instead, her mother had succumbed to complications from lupus, and Ella knew from that moment on that her life would never be the same.

For a few moments she remained still in the bed, taking one steadying breath after another in an attempt to reacclimate her thoughts to the here and now. Light peeped through the partially closed blinds at her window, and she eventually turned her attention to the nightstand in search of the time. What she found, right next to her digital alarm clock, was the stack of mail she'd brought into the bedroom with her last night but had neglected to open. With an inward groan she stared at the red envelope on top of the small stack. The Christmas card from Ben.

His handwriting was all too familiar—the festive Peanuts-themed stamp in the corner way more jovial than she felt upon seeing it—and her heart had plummeted . . . then and now. How dare he. Not after all this time. Not after what he'd done.

After being forced to grow up without her mother—accepting the reality that life wasn't always her friend—and finding a career path that gave her a purpose, last year Ella had finally thought she'd found some happiness again. She was in love last Christmas, and that love had opened her heart to the joy of the season, the wonder of this time of year that her mother always talked about. Her first wish since she was that hopeful ten-year-old girl had been for a fairy-tale wedding. On New Year's Day, Ben told her he'd accepted a job in Honduras and would be leaving without her.

Overwhelmed with emotion, she shook her head before bringing her hands up to cover her face. She held back the tears that always threatened to come after the dream and the memories of those thwarted hopes.

Wishes don't come true, she reminded herself. *There's no such thing as Christmas magic or a powerful star. No such things at all.*

And she was fine with that. Since losing her mother, she'd decided to put away childish things and expectations—namely, Christmas. It was for the best.

Ella flopped back down on the bed. She pulled the blankets up to her neck and closed her eyes tightly, trying to force herself to claim the forty-five minutes she had left to sleep. Moments later, she was still awake and with a heavy sigh, she opened her eyes again.

"Might as well get up and get this day over with," she mumbled and then pushed the blankets away.

An hour and a half later she walked out of her town house wearing a sage-green pantsuit, beige wedge-heeled booties, and an ivory wool coat. With the strap of her leather purse over one shoulder, she fumbled with the keys in her hand until she could press the fob to disengage the automatic locks on her car door. She'd just tossed her purse onto the passenger seat and slid behind the steering wheel when her phone rang. She'd stuffed that into her coat pocket after downing a quick cup of tea and now retrieved it. "Ella Wilson," she answered.

"I can't believe this is really happening! What are we going to do? This was too fast; I haven't had enough time to process and there's so much to be done. How're we ever going to be ready in time and what happens if we're not? I cannot do this alone, Ella. Are you there? Are you taking care of everything?" A very high-pitched, emotionally charged voice chattered in her ear.

Ella closed her car door and let her head rest back on the seat. "Yes," she replied. "I'm here, Claire. And I've taken care of everything. All seven of your paintings that we were showing were packed—meticulously, I might add—and put onto the truck for delivery first thing Monday morning. You have to sign for the delivery, so make sure you're up and have had your requisite three cups of coffee. The delivery will go a lot smoother if you're at least polite to the drivers."

Claire Castille was an amazing artist whose use of bold and vibrant colors conveyed strength, courage, and resilience. She was also an impatient woman who'd been one of Ella's top sellers in the last few years.

"But this still feels so surreal. We've been doing so well—things have been running so smoothly. And then, out of nowhere, we get hit with . . . this!"

"I know, Claire." Ella sighed and eased her key into the ignition.

"And after today I'll have to find someone else to work with.

Someone new who won't understand me like you do. Who won't know the things you know."

"I know," Ella continued and nodded to herself. "This is our last day. I've really enjoyed working with you and getting your paintings in front of as many people as possible. I'm sure your agent will book you in other galleries. Thanks to your last two shows, your name is on everyone's radar."

Claire's paintings paid homage to her Afro-Caribbean roots and were nothing short of brilliant. Ella had purchased one for her dining room last year. They'd been planning a new exhibit to launch in the spring. Unfortunately, that was now canceled.

A heavy sigh filtered through the phone and Ella had to resist the urge to follow it up with one of her own. She couldn't blame Claire for being a bit wound up this morning—today was the start of a big change for a lot of people. Ella included.

"I'm going to miss you," Claire said in a rare whisper.

"I'm going to miss you too." Ella cleared her throat as the lump of despair and sadness formed once more.

She'd known this day was coming. Everyone at the Liberty Art Gallery in Philadelphia had known. There were just too many richer galleries in the area taking their business for the small boutique space she'd come to know and love to remain open. In the past few weeks there'd been many calls and meetings as she worked to return paintings and sculptures to their creators or transfer them to other galleries. She'd spent days packing up shipments and talking to agents. Trying to smooth the waters for everyone she'd ever worked with, to keep them calm and encouraged, all while she slowly fell apart.

"Can I call you when everything arrives? You know, so you'll know that they're safe and sound?" Claire asked.

Ella nodded and clasped her seat belt. "Absolutely. And hey, listen, we'll keep in touch, and wherever I land I'll be sure to let you and your agent know."

"Thanks, Ella," Claire said. "I mean, really, thank you for everything. Even all the things that really didn't pertain to work—like having my favorite coffee delivered from the café down the street whenever I was working on a new project. I've never worked with anyone like you and I want you to know that I really appreciate you. Oh, and have a merry Christmas!"

Claire's voice had lifted slightly with those final words as if no matter what was happening around them, she wasn't going to forget that cheerful proclamation.

Ella started the car and waited while it warmed up. "Thanks so much," she replied. "That's very nice of you to say. You've been one of my very favorites to work with too, Claire. And merry Christmas to you too."

Claire couldn't see Ella rolling her eyes as she disconnected the call and tossed her phone onto the passenger seat with her purse. There was absolutely nothing merry about being unemployed, regardless of what time of year it was.

"Deck the halls with boughs of holly. Fa-la-la-la-la, la-la-la-la. 'Tis the season to be jolly . . ."

No, it wasn't.

At five forty-five, Ella closed the top drawer of her desk with a resounding *click* before sitting back heavily in her chair. The cream-colored ergonomic chair had taken her a year and a half to get used to, and now she had to accept that she wouldn't be sitting in it tomorrow, or any other day for that matter. She rubbed her hands along its arms and closed her eyes. And then she sent a silent wish to the heavens that the loud singing coming from outside her office would stop.

It wouldn't. She'd been chanting that same wish all afternoon, since the very early holiday party began at noon. Normally the annual gallery party would be held a few days before Christmas, but this year—since they would be closed by then—it was taking place on December 8. Today.

She checked her watch. *Fifteen minutes to go.*

That's how much longer she had in this office where she'd spent the majority of her time for the last seven years. It was a nice office, with soft beige walls and built-in shelves on one side. Shelves that used to hold photos of her and Mama or her and her aunt, and figurines she'd collected from other galleries she'd visited. Sighing deeply once more, she dropped her arm and sat up.

Get it together, Wilson. Worrying is a waste of time.

Giving herself directives was much easier than actually carrying them out—although when those directives included sage advice from her mother, that made them all the more worth listening to.

"I can't believe you really ditched the whole party." Josie, one of the interns, came into Ella's office wearing a reindeer antler headband with flashing red lights. It complemented her thick green sweater with a Christmas tree—complete with jingling bell ornaments—on the front. "You're missing Rudy in the Santa outfit. He's totally rockin' it," Josie continued.

"Of course he is," Ella replied, trying really hard to find just a little bit of cheer to appease her coworker one last time. "Nobody's as jovial as Rudy at Christmastime." That wasn't an exaggeration. Rudy—the gallery manager—loved any holiday, but especially Christmas, and he cultivated his thick white beard throughout the year so it'd be perfect when it was time to put on the red suit.

Ella thought it was all silly—from the ropes of garland draped around the back of the office space to the tasteful white twinkle lights in the gallery's front window. There was just too much holiday in this space. A couple of weeks ago, Josie had even plopped a slightly annoyed-looking elf on the corner of Ella's desk to remind her of the time of year. But Ella didn't need reminding. She liked ignoring Christmas and all the festive trimmings that came along with it. Her peace of mind depended on it.

Besides, they were adults working in a professional space. Making their offices look like a Christmas shop exploded inside was pointless. But Mama used to do the same thing. Nell Wilson would begin decorating the day after Thanksgiving, going through each room of their two-story house and adding what she called "a touch of Christmas magic" to each space. Then, like clockwork, on January 2 Nell would walk around the house taking everything down, packing each bulb, string of lights, roll of garland, red ribbon, miniature train set, and everything else ever so neatly into plastic bins that would then be stored in their third bedroom.

And for what? So that on the twenty-fifth of December, the two of them could sit at the table and enjoy a huge meal together? They did that most Sundays anyway, so looking back on it, it seemed all that decorating and singing and hoopla once a year had been just a waste of time and energy.

"Anyway, I'm all packed," Ella continued, not wanting to take that trip down memory lane or talk anymore about the party going on, when there was absolutely nothing to celebrate. To show rather than tell Josie this was how she felt, Ella picked up a box that had been behind her desk and walked to one of the guest chairs in her office. She set the box down on the chair next to the bag she'd finished packing this morning. "Since I started taking some of my things home earlier this week, I won't have to come back and make another trip over the weekend. I know Rudy said we'd still be able to use our keys until Monday, but I'd rather not. I'm ready to leave."

"Really?" The quiet sadness in Josie's tone made Ella stop and look more closely at her. Josie's sandy-brown hair was pulled back into a low puff that rested at the base of her neck, her cocoa-brown eyes filled with questions. "I mean, just like that? You're ready to leave this place where you've spent so many long hours and had so many successes?"

"You don't know about any of that." The response was a little snappier than she'd intended, and that annoyed Ella more. She wasn't normally so easily agitated, even at this time of year. She'd learned to ignore most of the festiveness that engulfed the world during the holidays, but this year felt different—or rather, it was turning out to be so similar to a couple of other years past that she was afraid of what else might happen in the next few weeks.

Taking a deep breath and releasing it quickly, she attempted to start again. "What I mean is, you've been here for only six months, so you haven't witnessed that many of the ups and downs."

"I know, but I've followed your shows since I was in high school. It's what made me want to go to school here in the city and to seek out this internship."

Ella had been flattered by Josie's similar words in her interview, and while that wasn't the only reason she'd hired her, it had made Ella feel good to know that her work was being noticed. "There'll be more shows, Josie. Just not here at Liberty. And listen, you've got a great eye and your cataloging and research skills have grown exponentially since you've started. You're going to snag a new position in no time. Remember to put me down as a reference."

Ella was moving again, this time going back behind her desk to have a second look around. She didn't want to leave anything, didn't want to have a reason to come back.

"What about you? Where will you go?" Josie picked up the moody elf she'd insisted Ella keep on her desk, rubbing her fingers absently over the ridiculous red hat it wore.

"As soon as Rudy made the announcement, I put some feelers out to other galleries, so we'll see." Ella hoped she'd hear back from someone soon, but in the meantime, she wasn't entertaining any pity parties. Not her own, nor anyone else's.

Certain she had everything now, Ella retrieved her purse from the desk drawer and returned to where Josie stood, touching her arm lightly. She really did believe in Josie's potential and wanted her to achieve all her goals. It wasn't that long ago that Ella had been this eager and excited to make her mark in the art world. She was hit with a pang of sadness at the realization that she wouldn't get to see all her goals come to fruition here at Liberty, and she hurriedly pushed it away.

"You're graduating this spring, so another full internship isn't necessary," she told Josie. "You're more than ready to walk into any gallery and handle whatever job they offer you."

"I really liked working here." Josie frowned. "I liked working with you, Ella. You made me feel seen in a way I never have in that fancy art school. Like I really belonged here instead of just being the recipient of what was basically a hardship scholarship. Like I could really do this job, and one day I could become a curator at another gallery. And in these past months, everyone has welcomed me. I've learned so much . . ." There was a pause and then an exaggerated sigh. "I don't really like change."

Ella grinned. "Can't say that I blame you, but you know you'll never grow if you stay in the same place forever." Warmth spread instantly through her chest at the memory of her aunt Addie saying those very words to her the morning she graduated from high school. That seemed like so long ago, and yet she recalled the day and that advice so clearly. It always amazed her how seamlessly Mama's older sister had slid into the parental role when Ella was eleven and had become an orphan.

"See," Josie said, pulling Ella into a hug. "It's when you say stuff like that, I know I'm going to miss you so much. Who's going to give me great advice at some new gallery?"

Josie was hugging her so tight that Ella could barely breathe, but she didn't pull away. Instead, she held on for a few seconds too, letting the reality of tonight really sink in. For the past two weeks since Rudy had announced the gallery closing, she'd been busy trying to arrange new commissions for some of her artists, packing and shipping paintings and sculptures to other galleries, and making sure all her records were in order for the person who would see them next. According to her "no pity party" mantra, she hadn't taken one second to absorb the magnitude of leaving the place where she'd worked for the last seven years. Or how her life might drastically change because of it.

"I'm gonna miss you too," she told Josie and meant it. The

girl was so much like Ella when she'd been in her last year at college. Bright, enthusiastic, and ready to take the art world by storm. Now they'd both have to channel that energy in a new direction.

"Well, if you're trying to ditch this party for real, you'd better head out the side door. And you can't forget Mr. Elf," Josie said when they parted, and she dropped the elf into Ella's bag.

Ella stared down at the silly elf and couldn't resist a small smile. It was fleeting, and seconds later she set her purse on the edge of the desk and grabbed her coat from the second guest chair to put it on. "I wouldn't exactly call it ditching," she said. "Laurie from accounting brought me a gingerbread cupcake earlier, but she didn't know what I wanted to drink so I had to go out there and grab a cup of festive punch."

"And how long did you stay out there?" Josie asked with a smirk. "Right. About as long as it took you to get that punch and hustle your way back to your office."

Unable to argue, Ella shrugged and slid her purse strap onto her arm. She picked up the box and Josie put her other bag on top of it. "No lies detected," she said. "But really, this just isn't my favorite time of year. And that doesn't totally rest on the fact that the gallery is closing. I haven't enjoyed Christmas in a very long time."

They were both at the door now, and Josie turned to give Ella a quizzical look. "Honestly?"

Ella nodded. "It's just another month to get through, and some years it's a little harder than others. This," she said, "I can tell is shaping up to be one of those years."

As if the universe were determined to prove her point, a different song drifted from the party down the hall to Ella's office.

All Christmas carols were familiar to her, but this one had her stopping, her heart pounding as she listened to the lyrics about spending Christmas away across the sea.

"Christmas Island" by Ella Fitzgerald, the jazz singer Mama had adored so much she'd named Ella after her, was playing just loud enough to hear. Memories of last night's dream slammed into her, and Ella tried to steady her breathing to keep the pain from resurfacing.

"Hey, you okay?" Josie came to stand next to her again.

The movement had those bells on Josie's sweater clinking together, and Ella gave a little chuckle. "Yeah." She cleared her throat. "I'm fine. And your sweater's jingling," she said.

Josie laughed. "That's right," she said and shook her shoulders so the jingling would continue. "That's the sound of Christmas joy!"

Ella began walking again, leaving the song and the memories it evoked behind. With Josie's help, she was able to skirt around the other partygoers undetected and made her way out the side door of the gallery.

Holding a box under one arm and a bag with the goofy elf sticking out of it in the other hand, she went through the glass doors of the Liberty Art Gallery one last time. And stepped outside right into a torrential rainfall.

Grumbling, she broke into a run, hopping over a puddle and barely making the light to get across the street to the parking lot. She was soaked by the time she made it to her car and fumbled to pull her keys out of her coat pocket. Of course they fell, and she had to put the box on the roof of her car before bending down to get them. When she did, Mr. Elf fell out of her bag and she hurriedly picked him up. He had a smudge of wet on his face now, and she shook her head. "See, you should've stayed in the office with the rest of the festive folk."

With a rueful sigh, she tucked the elf back inside the bag and stood to unlock the car. Once she had the box and everything else inside, Ella slid into the driver's seat and closed the door. She dripped water onto her leather seats and the steering wheel, and she groaned at the sight. This day was just getting worse and what she really wanted was to eat something, grab a cup of hot tea, and go to bed. Clenching her teeth and fighting off a shiver, she started the car and headed home.

Twenty minutes later—thanks to traffic—she was making another trip out into the rain. This time, she left the box in the car but grabbed her purse and the bag and ran into the house. Her phone had started to ring along the way, so as soon as she was inside, she dropped the bag on the floor and reached into her purse to pluck it out before it stopped. Praying it was about a job, she answered without looking at the screen to check the caller ID.

"Hello?"

"Hey, Ella Bee! How's my sweet niece doing?"

The smile that came immediately reflected the warmth that had spread through her chest at her earlier memory of her aunt. "Hey, Aunt Addie. It's so nice to hear from you."

Ella closed the door and continued to walk through the narrow foyer of her town house. Along the way she passed several pictures hanging on the dove-gray walls. One was of Mama and Aunt Addie as little girls—bows held their freshly pressed hair into two ponytails and also topped the white patent leather shoes they each wore with pastel-colored dresses. It was probably Easter and they were on their way to church. Another picture was of her and Mama when Ella was just a baby—Mama's smile was bright and beautiful while Ella displayed a soft, toothless grin. And the last was of her and Mama on Ella's eleventh birthday, two months before her mother passed away. Ella stopped at that one, staring as she often did at their smiles, recalling the happiness she'd felt in that moment so long ago and yearning for just one more of Mama's warm hugs.

"Oh, how I miss hearing your voice, Ella Bee."

Her aunt's cheerful tone pulled Ella back into the present. Aunt Addie had been calling her by that nickname since Ella won the spelling bee three years straight in middle school. That seemed like so long ago, and she was an adult now. Ella was sure the nickname could be dropped. Yet she never said that to her aunt, the woman she'd grown to love just as much as she'd loved Mama.

"I'm really glad you called. How are you?" Aunt Addie was the closest relative Ella had, in proximity and relationship. Her father had passed away before Ella's second birthday and his family hadn't kept in touch with Mama after the funeral. Then, when Mama became sick and passed so quickly, Aunt Addie took the two-hour drive to Philadelphia, handled all the funeral arrangements, and brought Ella back to live in Bellepoint, Pennsylvania, with her.

"Not too good, baby." Aunt Addie sighed. Ella was about to ask her what was wrong, but her aunt continued, "You know I miss you most at this time of year. This is a time for family and reflection."

Ella rolled her eyes—thankful that Aunt Addie wasn't there to see her doing such a disrespectful thing—and pulled one arm out of her wet jacket, water dripping onto her glossed hardwood floors. "I miss you too, Aunt Addie. I always miss you."

Aunt Addie was all Ella had in this world. She was the rock that kept Ella tethered to her foundation—at least she had been before Ella left Bellepoint to attend Temple University. Then Ella, like every other eighteen-year-old, had thought she could handle life on her own. Oh, how wrong she'd been. Not that she wasn't handling her life. It was more like she didn't think she was doing that great a job of it.

"Well, then, that means we should be together this Christmas. Now, I know you've got your fancy job and house there in the city, but I'd love to have you home for the holidays this year, Ella Bee. It's been almost ten years since you've been back. We could do all the things we used to do, like bake cookies—well, I bake and you eat." Aunt Addie chuckled. "We can get out the stockings and hang them on the mantel, go out and buy a tree and get it all dressed up. And you could go to church with me. You know Phyllis asks about you every year at the Christmas pageant. Said she never had another student create such perfect scenery as you did for the play."

While her aunt talked, Ella eased the other arm out of her jacket and walked over to hang it on the banister. She hadn't returned to the small town where her aunt had raised her since that one week in the summer before she'd entered her junior year of college. After that, internships, accelerated course loads, and then landing the job at the gallery had kept her busy in the city. Too busy to return to a place that held so many tough memories.

"Ms. Phyllis was a fantastic art teacher," she said. Since fifth grade when Ella first sat in the back of her classroom, Phyllis DeShields had taken Ella under her wing, spending time with her after school at the community center and at church whenever they were doing arts and crafts. Ms. Phyllis was also the first person to encourage Ella to go to college and study art. For that, Ella would always be grateful to the sweet woman.

"Yes, she was. You know she retired a couple years back. But she's still active in the church and at the school from time to time. So what do you say? Think you can take off Christmas week and come home?"

"I don't know, Aunt Addie," Ella said and took another step before staring down at her feet. She was tracking water across the floor with her wet boots. Annoyed, she eased them off and walked the remaining distance from the hallway to her kitchen in her stocking-clad feet.

"You know, baby, even Jesus set aside a day for rest," her aunt continued. "Working yourself to death doesn't fill in the gaps left vacant by those we've loved and lost."

Leave it to her aunt to go right for the jugular. Ella entered the kitchen and tucked the phone between her ear and her shoulder. "I really have a lot to do in the next few weeks." Namely, look for a job so she'd be able to keep the lights on in this fancy city house, as her aunt had called it.

Rolling her eyes skyward, Ella realized she still hadn't gotten around to telling her aunt about the gallery closing. To be honest, she'd hoped she would find another job right after the first of the year and therefore wouldn't ever have to share her disappointment and moderate despair with her aunt. The last thing she'd ever want was to cause her aunt to worry.

"Busyness isn't a substitute for living." It was a solemn statement, one that Ella had heard many times before. Mostly during this same conversation when her aunt would ask her to come home and she'd decline.

"Now, I'm not gonna preach," Aunt Addie continued as Ella

pulled open the refrigerator door with a knowing smirk. The woman was definitely getting ready to preach.

"But I will tell you that life goes by fast and you only get one. You gotta stop and smell the roses. Sit still and let life happen. It's what my mama always used to tell me and Nell. Just be still." Aunt Addie released a heavy breath.

Ella grabbed a water bottle and closed the refrigerator door. She could imagine her aunt sitting in the recliner that was positioned just so in her living room, so that she could stare directly out the window and see everyone turning onto her block. It was her favorite place to sit in the dusty-blue craftsman-style house she'd lived in all of Ella's life.

"I'd love to come, Aunt Addie. It's just that—"

"Every year you come up with more and more excuses," her aunt interrupted. "And Lord knows I won't be here forever to listen to them. So I'm not gonna push either. You do what you feel is best for you, baby."

If not pushing meant she'd slide in a layer of guilt instead, then Aunt Addie was a pro at this. And this time, she was also right.

Each year her aunt called and invited Ella to come home for Christmas, or for the Easter parade and worship services at the church. Or for Aunt Addie's birthday, which her aunt celebrated the entire month of August because she said she never knew which one would be her last. Or for Mama's birthday, when Aunt Addie always went to the cemetery to take Ella's mother a bouquet of her favorite tulips. But every year, Ella really did have something to do.

This year, she didn't. Or at least nothing she couldn't do in Bellepoint. Looking for a job would consist of combing the online job sites for openings and contacting every connection she had in the art world. All of which required only her laptop, a comfortable place to sit, and tea to keep her pumped while undertaking the dreary task. Each of those things was possible in the small college town where Ella had grown up and where Mama had sung in the church choir.

"Do you still make those chocolate chip pancakes?" Ella asked before she could talk herself out of it.

Her aunt paused only a beat before replying, "Only when my best girl is here to eat them."

"Good, because I'm gonna need plenty of those and a whole pot of that Earl Grey tea you make with cinnamon sticks and honey." She shook her head because she couldn't believe she was actually doing this. "I'll be there in the morning, Aunt Addie."

"Bless the Lord! So soon? Well, no, I'm not gonna question it." She could hear her aunt clapping through the phone and it made Ella smile. "I'll have breakfast all ready for you and then we can sit and talk awhile and catch up on everything. Oh, we're gonna have such a great time."

"Yeah, a great time," Ella added as she opened the bottle of water and took a gulp.

"Ella? Are you all right? You sound a little off."

Because she was way off. Her life had just taken a tumble that Ella wasn't sure she'd be able to rebound from and she didn't know what to do next. Still, she replied, "I'm fine. I'm gonna go start packing now and then get to bed so I can get an early start in the morning."

"Oh, okay then. I'll see you in the morning."

"Good night, Aunt Addie," she whispered, and after her aunt had said the same, Ella disconnected the call.

She set the phone on the island and took another drink of water, trying her best to hold back the tears of disappointment that threatened to fall. "The Christmas jinx," she mumbled. "That's what this is. That relentless Christmas jinx."

Frowning, she closed her eyes and vowed that the bad luck she swore came into her life at this time of year wasn't going to get the best of her. She was going to get through the next few weeks regardless of the downward spiral she felt she was in, and then, in the new year, she'd start all over again.

CHAPTER 2

On Friday morning, Ella ditched the idea of getting an early start, opting to lie in her bed longer than usual. It was her attempt at giving herself the time and space alone to contemplate once again her next steps and this impromptu trip she'd committed to. By the time she finally got herself together and made it out of the house, there was some midmorning traffic on the highway, extending the roughly two-hour drive from the city to Bellepoint so that it was a little after one o'clock in the afternoon when she stepped out of her car and onto the curb.

The blue craftsman-style house on the corner of Tenderleaf Lane still looked the same. Three steps and a wide walkway led up to another trio of stairs and the large porch. Huge hunter-green planters were filled with violas in brilliant shades of blue, yellow, and Aunt Addie's favorite, violet. Mama had loved to garden, which meant Ella used to help her, and even now she could recall the names and best seasons for some flowers. The lawn was cut low, and the flower beds along the front of the porch had been weeded and waited for the winter to skitter along before bright and beautiful spring blooms would take center stage.

Staring down at the sidewalk where she stood, Ella recalled drawing on these cement squares with sidewalk chalk. She'd create a different scene in each block just like she'd seen in one of her favorite childhood movies, *Mary Poppins*. A brilliant rainbow with a pot of gold at the end, a grinning puppy because neither Mama nor Aunt Addie had allowed her to get a dog, and two little girls on swings because she'd always wanted a sister. The memory somehow filled her with a cheer and optimism she hadn't felt in the last few weeks.

Deciding she would return to the car later to get her bags, she climbed the stairs, feeling a bit giddier about being home with each step she took. Even so, she still had to admit it was odd being back here after staying away so long. Not that her absence had been on purpose—it hadn't. She'd simply been focused on building her career and trying to find the woman she was meant to be. Mama had done the same when she married and left Bellepoint. The stories Mama told about growing up in this small town had entertained Ella often, but the light that came into her mother's eyes when she spoke of the joy she found working in the elementary school cafeteria was all pride for what she was doing—what she'd built for her life. Ella had wanted the same, and for a while she'd had it. Then she lost at love, and now in her career too. In the last year she'd gotten over Ben, but the closing of Liberty had hit her hard and no matter how much time she'd taken this morning to ruminate over it, she couldn't quite explain why. There'd been a sense of finality as she walked out of the gallery last night, and she was afraid of what that might ultimately mean for her future.

But standing here on the porch in Bellepoint, at this moment, pushed that unexplainable despair to the back seat in favor of better memories. She let out a sigh as visions of her dolls sitting in the cushioned Adirondack chairs came flooding back. As a little girl, she loved dolls—collectible porcelain ones that sat on a shelf in her bedroom, and baby dolls that she could play with. On rainy days when she wasn't allowed to leave the cover of the porch, she would bring them all out and line them up while she taught school or directed them in the choir the way she'd often seen Aunt Addie do at church.

She hadn't realized a sheen of tears coated her eyes until she tried to blink, and then she waved her hands in front of her face, willing the tears not to fall. The onslaught of memories was more intense than she'd anticipated, replacing her previously vivid feelings with a strange mixture of melancholy and joy. Who was she kidding? Her emotions were clearly all over the place. She had to get it together before she saw her aunt. Growing up, Ella always swore her aunt could read her like a crystal ball, seeing everything Ella thought or felt, even things Ella hadn't admitted to herself. Rolling her shoulders and shaking her head, Ella forced herself to push all the conflicting emotions back into a corner and put a smile on her face. She stepped up to the brown door with its frosted window center and almost rang the bell, but then recalled she had a key. She fumbled with her key ring for a few seconds trying to find the correct, barely used key before slipping it into the door and stepping inside.

The house smelled the same—like lemons and brewing coffee. As she recalled, Aunt Addie liked her coffee with lots of cream and sugar from the time she got up in the morning—which was usually around six—until just after lunch. In the evenings, her beverage of choice was hot tea—which was when she'd fix that delicious, spiced Earl Grey Ella loved in the fall and winter, and sweet tea with lots of lemon (of course!) in the spring and summer.

"Ella!"

25

Ella turned her attention to the left just in time to see her aunt reaching for a box on top of a tall stack of other boxes. She immediately went to her, setting her purse and keys on an end table before reaching up to retrieve the box herself.

"Oh, Aunt Addie," Ella said. "What are you doing? Packing up to move?" Setting the box on the carpeted floor of the living room, Ella turned back just in time to be pulled into a tight hug.

"My sweet baby! My sweet, sweet baby girl is home!" Aunt Addie did that thing where she rocked, hugged, and sighed all at the same time.

Left without much of a choice, Ella hugged her aunt in return and for just a moment closed her eyes to the familiarity of the squeeze. There was nothing like a warm and comforting hug from her aunt. Absolutely nothing in the world. Ella hadn't known how much she missed these hugs in the ten years she'd been away until Aunt Addie finally eased back from the embrace.

"Let me look at you," her aunt said, holding her at arm's length now.

But it was Ella who took this opportunity to look at the woman who'd meant so much to her in the years following her mother's death.

Addie Suellen Gibbs was a woman of medium height and slim build. What was once a head full of fluffy black curls was now cut into a cute cap of salt-and-pepper that highlighted her hazel eyes and bright smile. Her aunt shared the same caramel-brown complexion that Mama had, and when Ella leaned in quickly to kiss Aunt Addie's slightly weathered cheek, she immediately wished she could kiss her mother again as well.

"You look amazing," Ella said, fighting back the lump of emotion that had formed in the back of her throat.

Aunt Addie waved a hand. "Don't take my words," she said playfully. "Look at you. All grown up and wearing that smart suit. Turn around and let me get a good look."

As Ella dropped her arms to her sides, memories of going through the "Aunt Addie inspection" every Sunday morning when she came downstairs dressed for church flitted through her mind, and she turned around slowly. As a little girl she'd often lift the hem of the dress or skirt she wore, adding a flourish to the part of Sunday mornings where her aunt made sure her outfit wasn't wrinkled, her tights weren't twisted at the ankles, her shoes were shined or buffed to perfection, and the hairstyle her aunt had painstakingly worked to create the night before had survived. It usually did since Aunt Addie would tie that scarf around Ella's head so tight after sitting in the kitchen, either curling Ella's thick tresses or styling them into neat ponytails.

Ella hadn't bothered to tie the belt of her black drape-front wool coat she'd grabbed from the passenger seat and slid on before climbing out of the car. And now her aunt reached for one lapel, holding it open farther as she surveyed her outfit.

"Yeah, that's a sharp suit," Aunt Addie said. "I like that gray color and that crisp white shirt. And those boots. Whew, chile, you look like a million bucks."

Ella chuckled and eased out of the coat when her aunt stepped back once more. "Thanks, Aunt Addie. As I said, you look great too." She folded her coat and draped it over the arm of the chair behind her, then turned back to her aunt.

Aunt Addie wore dark brown pants, a beige sweater, and what looked like comfortable brown leather loafers on her feet. Her nails, which her aunt had always kept manicured and polished, were a calming neutral tone, and at her neck was the thin gold necklace with the gold cross pendant that Ella had never seen her without.

"Well, I'm blessed," Aunt Addie said. "Blessed and tickled pink to have you here." Before Ella could say another word, she was once again pulled into a hug.

This time, instead of closing her eyes to the waves of nostalgia that had been steadily hitting her since she'd parked her car out front, Ella looked around the living room. The recliner was still in its same place facing the wide front window, and she grinned as she eased out of the hug. A thick gray-blue and white rug covered the weathered, wood-planked floors. The remaining furniture consisted of a navy-blue couch with coordinating throw pillows, a matching love seat, cherrywood coffee and end tables, and a plaid ottoman that had definitely seen better days.

"Everything looks exactly the same," she whispered and shook her head. "Like the day I came down those stairs carrying my bags, ready to leave for college." She vaguely recalled the house being the same when she was home that summer before junior year as well, but for some reason, the memory of that day she left for college was more prevalent in her mind.

Aunt Addie nodded. "That was a day, wasn't it? You were so excited and so filled with hope. And I was bursting with pride." Ella's aunt stepped closer and grasped a few of the long passion twists that had fallen from the messy bun Ella had pulled her hair up into, tucking them back behind her shoulders. "I watched you walk out that door, and my chest filled with pride and misery. I said, 'Nell, look at our girl go.' And then you went." She sighed wistfully, a thin smile on her face.

"But I came back," Ella countered as a lump of something grew in her throat. This was it. These were the emotions that had begun building in her the moment she passed the huge royal-blue-and-white wooden sign welcoming her to Bellepoint. It was exactly the reason she'd allowed herself to believe that staying busy in the city was better than coming back here.

Aunt Addie nodded. "You did, at first," she said.

Ella recognized that the lump in her throat was guilt—something she'd always known her aunt was good at dishing out. She blinked rapidly and prayed she didn't actually start bawling. But she couldn't help the tears that sprang to her eyes at the memory, and the sound of Mama's name in Aunt Addie's voice. Hadn't she already told herself to push all those overwhelming feelings away? This, of all things, wasn't what she needed right now. Getting lost in the past certainly wasn't going to help her future. She took a deep breath and reminded herself that she could do this—she could stay focused on the present because now was the only moment that mattered.

"What's all this stuff?" Ella walked toward the tower of boxes she'd almost forgotten about in this trip down memory lane. "And how'd you even get it in here?"

"Oh, those are my Christmas decorations. Don't you remember? I bring them all up from the back of the basement the first week of December."

Unlike Mama, Aunt Addie always waited until the calendar officially read *December* before opening her house and mind to the hustle and bustle of the Christmas season.

"Yeah, I remember," she said, glancing at the boxes again. "I guess that means you'll want me to help you decorate." A thought that held very little appeal.

"Well, not at this moment," Aunt Addie replied. "C'mon into the kitchen and let's have some chocolate chip pancakes for lunch. I've got a meeting over at the church later this evening, but we'll have a couple hours to go through the decorations first." Then her aunt's eyes widened. "You can go to church with me tonight and see Phyllis. She'll be there for choir rehearsal. It'll be a lovely reunion for you two." Aunt Addie didn't give Ella a second to respond before she turned and started walking toward the kitchen. "In the meantime, you can tell me what's going on in your life while we eat."

"There's nothing going on," Ella said, falling into step behind her. "Just the same ol', same ol'." That couldn't be further from the truth, but her aunt was in such a good mood, and despite Ella's topsy-turvy emotions, this welcome home was taking her mind off her unemployment situation. Sort of.

Once they were in the spacious kitchen with its butter-yellow walls and cheery white table and chairs, Ella took a seat and immediately reached for an apple. There was always a bowl of fruit at the center of the kitchen table. In the dining room, there were two candleholders—which held candles only during Easter and Christmas—and a vase of fresh flowers. She opted for the Granny Smith apple because it was so shiny, she wanted to make sure it wasn't fake.

"I keep buying those bitter apples even though you're not here to eat them all," Aunt Addie said as she tied an apron around her waist and headed toward the stove. "After a few days, I end up making caramel apples and taking them over to the church. The kids love 'em after Sunday school, and as long as I wrap them up real nice, their mamas don't mind them having them either."

Her aunt chuckled just as Ella took a bite. She'd always loved fruit and kept a full stock of it in her refrigerator. Now, if she could manage to enjoy vegetables with the same vigor, her doctor would be much happier.

"How's work?" Aunt Addie asked just as Ella finished chewing.

She swallowed with a big gulp and sighed before saying, "Fine."

Her aunt spun around, one hand on her hip while the other pointed a metal spatula. "Ella Claudine Wilson, you know better than to sit at my table and lie to me."

Ella's next sigh was much deeper as one word rattled in her mind: *caught.*

Clearing her throat, she sat up straighter and glanced down at the apple seconds before gathering the courage to look at her aunt again. "I'm sorry," she said, and then before she convinced herself it was okay to tell a half truth, she admitted, "I lost my job."

"What?" It was a good thing Aunt Addie hadn't poured any of the already prepared pancake batter into the skillet, because she walked quickly to take a seat across the table from Ella. "How'd that happen? You were the best curator they've ever had."

Wow, she'd forgotten how good Aunt Addie was for her ego. If there was anything her aunt believed in, it was building Ella up to trust she could be anything she wanted, and to be the best at it. That was just one of the many things that had stuck with her throughout her adult life. The other was the importance of being optimistic, even though truthfully, it had been tough reminding herself of this one.

"To be fair, the gallery is closing. So no gallery, no need for a curator." Because it was still in her hand, she took another bite of the apple and chewed thoughtfully. "I'm gonna find another job," she continued. "I've already got some feelers out there and I know something's gonna come through soon."

Aunt Addie nodded. "That's right. Keep your head up," she told her. "Everything happens for a reason. The Lord has a plan for everyone and He always makes a way."

More great advice from her favorite person in the whole world. But truthfully, it had been years since Ella had stepped into a church, let alone allowed herself to ponder any spiritually ordained plans for her life. She was still angry that part of her mother's divine plan had been to leave Ella. But that was neither here nor there. Right now her aunt was trying to make her feel better and—to her surprise—it was working. She reached across the table to touch her aunt's arm with her free hand. "I know," she said. "I'm so glad to be home, Aunt Addie."

"Whoa! Hold on, boy. We're going, we're going," Seth told his two-year-old retriever-poodle-whatever mix that Rhonda had suggested they rescue to help prepare them for having children.

He held the leash tighter as his feet moved along the sidewalk. Late afternoon had brought a drop in the already cool winter temperatures, and he silently chastised himself for forgetting his hat. Although his waist-length, black wool trench coat was buttoned and the collar turned up at his neck, the brisk air coming off the mountains wasn't friendly this evening, and the last thing he wanted was to have to chase his big, curly-haired dog down the block.

The dog that Rhonda had wanted before sickness ravaged her body and took her life. Seth was never convinced about Rhonda's rationalization that taking care of a dog would prepare them for raising their future children, but Teddy had certainly trained *him* to be his perfect human in the years since coming to them after his previous owners left him hungry and cold on the side of the road. Hence the reason they were now walking—well, Teddy was pulling against Seth's hold on the leash, ready to break out into a run—toward Primp & PawPrints on a Friday evening.

"Hey, Teddy! Aren't you a handsome boy? Yes, you are, cutie pie!" Seth's sister, Max—short for Maxine—crooned as she turned from cleaning the front door of her pet adoption, grooming, and boarding facility and saw them coming down the street.

Giving up the battle with his dog, Seth released the leash and let Teddy forge his way toward Max, the younger of the two Hamil children. She bent down to clasp both hands to either side of Teddy's face, giving him a scrub behind his ears that had the dog vibrating with glee. Her straight black hair was pulled into a sleek high ponytail, and she stood, offering Seth the same grin she'd given his dog.

The family had been bursting with pride three years ago when Max leased this building on the high-traffic Academy Drive. From the cheerful turquoise-and-green awning out front to the white picket fence gate at the store's entrance where new adoptees were on display every Tuesday and Thursday mornings, the place was a pet lover's dream.

It was no surprise that opening Primp & PawPrints was her calling—Max had always loved animals and at one time had dreamed of becoming a veterinarian. After the incident that changed Max's life when she was in college, Seth and his parents thought they'd never see Max this happy again. *Grateful* and *blessed* didn't begin to describe how he felt each time he saw his sister. And despite how she shamelessly spoiled his dog, he couldn't help but grin at the way she once again leaned in for all the doggie cuddles and Teddy's sloppy kisses. The special treatment was exactly what the rambunctious pooch craved.

"Oh come on, you're always acting like you don't get any attention at home," Seth said as he came to stand right next to Max and knelt down to unhook the leash from Teddy's collar. He gave his dog a quick tummy rub, then forced himself to stand. "I won't be long," he told Max. "I just have a quick meeting at the church and then I'll be back to get him."

Dressed in tattered jeans and a kelly-green Primp & PawPrints hoodie, Max had already reached for the door and held it open. Teddy didn't waste a moment, immediately bolting into the facility and crossing the lobby to scratch at another door on the other side of the space. Max stepped inside before Seth followed. "That's fine," she said with a wave of her hand. "Lucky for you, Mama has to be at the church tonight too, so we rescheduled the Mix 'n Mingle at the restaurant."

One of Max's staff members opened the second door, most likely in response to Teddy's request for entry, and Seth watched his dog head happily for the play area with the other barking pooches.

He shook his head and returned his attention to Max. "Not sure how that makes me lucky since I hadn't planned on coming to that anyway."

Max tilted her head and folded her arms across her chest. "Oh really? Then what were you planning to eat for dinner tonight?"

"Oh, I still intended to stop by like I do every night to get my dinner. But then I was gonna get outta there before any of the desperate singles started to file in looking for good food and a hook-up." He was going to get in and out of Beaumont's, the restaurant his parents took ownership of after his father was injured and honorably discharged from the Navy, without any run-ins with the single-looking-to-be-married crowd of Bellepoint.

"Nah, I was never gonna let that happen. And neither was Mama." Max grinned. She looked just like their mother with her cinnamon-brown complexion, high cheekbones, and bright, infectious smile. "You have to come next week. I've handpicked three women that I know you'll like who will be there."

"Would you listen to yourself? You're really trying to set me up with three different women? What kind of sister are you?" His tone was teasing, but really, the last thing Seth wanted was to be set up by his sister—or mother, for that matter.

Max stepped closer to him and reached up to touch a hand to his shoulder. The action magnified how much shorter her five-foot-one stature was compared to his six feet, two inches. "I'm the kind who worries that her older brother is taking too long to get back on the wagon." Her eyes had gone soft, her brow slightly furrowed into what was her worried face.

Seth sighed because worrying his family was the last thing he ever wanted to do, but after his wife's death a little over a year ago, it seemed to be their preferred pastime. As for Max, he got the impression that it was a lot easier for her to worry about him than to deal with her own trauma, and a part of him ached for her. That was the part that had him responding gently. "I didn't know it was a race," he said as he pushed his hands into the side pockets of his coat.

Max eased one of his hands free, twining her fingers with his the way she used to do when they were young and needed to cross the street. "It's not. And I'm sorry, that's not what I meant. I just want you to be happy."

"I am happy," he told her. "I love my job teaching music. This year's class is full of talented eleven-year-olds. I mean, they can really sing, and a few of them are extremely talented with the instruments." He hoped he sounded convincing because the last thing he needed was for his sister to continue playing matchmaker, or to feel sorry for him. The latter was the bigger issue. "Listen, I know you mean well, but trust me, I'm good."

He squeezed her hand to solidify his words, but when she tilted her head and arched a brow at him, he knew she was still skeptical. "You'd tell me if you weren't good?" she asked.

That was a hard question, one he didn't want to answer. Lying to his family wasn't something Seth considered doing. But keeping things from them that were his alone to deal with was another matter. "Let's put it this way—when I'm ready to start dating again, you'll know." He released her hand and tweaked her nose before turning toward the door.

"You could still stick around when you come to the restaurant tonight. I'm sure somebody'll hop onstage for some karaoke. We could do our famous BeBe and CeCe Winans tribute. You know Daddy insists we get our money's worth out of the machine I convinced them to buy." Max held up a hand like it was a microphone and did a few dance moves. She grinned, and because he really loved seeing her happy, he did too.

She was three years younger than him, and since they often were each other's only friends in whichever new place their father was stationed during their early childhood, they were very close.

"Now you want me to do karaoke in front of a bunch of strangers?" He shook his head. "You're not presenting a very good case here."

"Ah, c'mon, you love singing . . . off-key, that is. But you still like it and you know all the best music because, well, you're a music teacher."

"Not the same thing," he said and continued his trek toward the door. "I might stick around for a while after I drop Teddy off. But just to have dinner, no karaoke."

"Aw, that's no fun," she joked. "But I'll take it."

"I'll be back in a couple hours to get Teddy," he replied and left before his tenacious sister could throw out a different suggestion. He couldn't help another grin as he started to walk down the street.

The church wasn't too far and this evening was beautiful, even if his ears were probably red from the cold, so he'd opted to walk instead of drive to the charity auction meeting. Besides, Teddy needed the exercise and his dog loved walking the streets of Bellepoint. Just about everyone in town knew Teddy and often asked about him when they saw Seth alone. The dog was more popular than he was, and Seth had lived here since he was eight years old. As strange as it seemed, that thought made him happy as he crossed the street.

His stomach growled as the sweet scent of whatever muffins, rolls, cookies, cakes, or pastries Stella was cooking up in the corner storefront housing Sweets Bakery circled in the air. Through the window, Ned Harrington, who taught English at the middle school, spotted Seth and waved. Seth waved in return before making a gesture to rub his stomach when Ned held up one of Stella's famous bear claws.

The sounds of a few cars driving by mixed with the faint lyrics of a Christmas tune that drifted down from the Valley Christmas Closet about a block away. There was also some banging as the crew hired by the town council to hang the Christmas decorations finished up their day's work. So far, they had the garland light structures hanging from one lamppost to the next all the way down Main Street and on a few of the side streets as well. At every traffic light there were snowflake light fixtures, and colorful garland wrapped around all the lampposts and every other railing in town. Shop owners were responsible for their own decorations, and as Seth continued on his walk, he noticed the different themes each storefront displayed.

"Hi there, Seth! You taking an evening stroll without Teddy?"

Walking over to where Ms. Cora was leaning into the back of her truck, Seth couldn't help but sigh at the thoughts he was having about his hyperactive dog's popularity. "He's over at Max's hanging out with his friends. Here, let me get that for you."

Seth reached into the back of the truck and lifted the box into his arms.

"Oh, aren't you a dear. I'm just taking these over to the post office since they've started their extended holiday hours. Gotta get my Christmas cards out early," she said.

Cora Langford had been a teacher at the elementary school when Seth was there. She'd actually taught Max math. Now she was retired, spending a few afternoons a week as the receptionist at her daughter Katy's beauty salon. That meant Cora's snow-white hair was always styled to perfection. Her cheery smile and soft gray eyes suited her pleasant personality, which was probably why everyone in town felt comfortable talking to her about anything and everything.

"Are your cards all ready to go?" she asked.

The post office was on the other side of the street and they walked over together. "Nah, but I don't have as many as you, so I'll be okay sending them out next week or the week after."

Ms. Cora shook her head. "Nonsense. You don't want to be late. Who wants to receive a Christmas card after Christmas? Not me, that's for sure. You get those cards together and get over to this post office as soon as possible. That's how you do it. Punctuality is a virtue."

Seth had never heard that before, but everyone in town knew it was pointless to argue with Ms. Cora.

They walked into the post office and he stood in line with her while they waited to get the envelopes processed. It helped that she had each one stamped and ready to go.

"Thanks so much for your help, Seth," Ms. Cora said when they were back on the other side of the street.

"It was no problem. Have a good evening."

"Oh, wait, if you're not in a hurry, come on in to BB's and I'll buy you a cup of coffee or cocoa, whichever you like best."

"That's not necessary, Ms. Cora. Besides, I've got to get down to the church for a meeting."

She waved a hand and started toward the storefront with the Bellepoint Beans sign in the window. "Oh yeah, the charity auction. Well, Nancy can wait a few minutes until you get there. She's probably got everything all worked out anyway. You know how she likes to be in charge."

For a split second Seth recalled that he'd skipped lunch in lieu of spending some extra time with Sunni at her piano lesson. BB's had delicious warm croissants that went well with their dark roast coffee. They also had a nice moist coffee cake that was phenomenal—something he'd never mention to Stella over at the bakery—with a cup of hot cocoa. Besides, trying to argue with Ms. Cora was unthinkable.

"Yes, ma'am," he finally replied and skipped around her so

he could open the door and let her walk into the coffee shop first.

Ten minutes later, Seth had decided on a compromise with his coffee cake in a bag as he went to the counter to pick up his coffee. He found the cup marked with his name, waved to Ms. Cora and Mona, the barista, and headed out the front door. Only to be stopped by a yelling woman about thirty seconds later.

"Hey, I think you've got my coffee!"

She looked vaguely familiar in her black jogging suit and white puffy jacket. Seth knew he was running late now, so he glanced down at his cup, saw his name, and shrugged. "No. This one's mine. It says Seth." He pointed to the cup as he met her gaze again.

With a frown affixed to a face Seth was certain he'd seen somewhere before, she turned her cup toward him. "Mine says the same."

He glanced at it. "Well, look at that," he replied. "It sure does."

"Lucky for us I'm very particular about my coffee, so I was watching as both were made."

He wasn't sure whether "very particular" also meant a tiny bit controlling but decided it didn't really matter. "Okay, so you think mine is yours and yours is mine?"

"Mine should be dark roast, heavy cream, caramel, and two sugars. Yours is dark roast, black, heavy sugar. Take your top off," she told him and then motioned her head toward his drink.

Her hair was black, styled in long twists that were pulled over her right shoulder. She wasn't smiling at the moment, but he wondered if he'd seen her smile before. Shaking his head to remove the persistent thought that he knew this woman, he did as she said and removed the top from his cup. The cream-colored liquid was an odd surprise.

"And you are correct—this isn't mine." Placing the top back on the cup, he handed it to her. She handed off the cup she held at the same time and smiled when they both took the correct beverages.

He definitely recognized that smile.

"Ella?" The name burst into his mind. "Ella Wilson from Mr. Dobson's chemistry class."

She took a step back, the smile slipping slowly from her face. "Seth Hamil, the guy who spilled acid on my book bag, burning a hole straight through."

Scrunching his face in reaction to that memory, he nodded and she frowned.

"I didn't know there was a hole until class was over and I picked up my bag, only to have everything, including my change of clothes for dance class, fall out in the hallway."

Seth remembered that too. James Pritchard had picked up her pink polka-dot leotard she'd packed for dance rehearsal at church later and run down the hall waving it in the air. James was always a jerk, agitating any girl he probably liked and didn't know how to communicate with, as if he were still in elementary school. He'd spent a good portion of their senior year taunting Ella until Seth pulled him aside for a stern conversation that may or may not have resulted in a threat. So he was baffled at the fact that Ella might still be irritated by what happened—but then again, he hadn't broadcasted the fact that he was the one who stopped James from bothering her. He was just happy to see that some of the tension Ella always seemed to carry had abated.

"Yeah, but I apologized like a million times," he said, hoping that was enough just as he had all those years ago. At one point, he'd considered just telling her about his confrontation with James, but in his mind, that was just between the guys, and explaining why he'd felt the need to defend her was more complicated than eighteen-year-old Seth had wanted to deal with. He'd often wondered if her ire was directed toward him for another reason, but he never had the guts to ask her that question. Or any of the other questions he'd secretly held for her.

"I just would've appreciated you giving me a heads-up about the hole so I wouldn't have been caught off guard." She rubbed her forehead with her free hand. "I could've made sure none of my things fell out."

"I was actually more worried about Mr. Dobson's reaction to what I'd done than yours."

He thought he saw a fleeting smirk, as if she were resisting a slight smile. He couldn't tell, but he also couldn't take his eyes off her.

"That didn't come out right. I mean, yeah, I was worried about you when all your stuff fell out, but how was I supposed to know what James was going to do? And I needed to pass Dobson's class. You were the smartest girl in the room—that's why I sat next to you." He shook his head when he realized the possibility of her actually smiling was dwindling. "I'm not making this any better, am I?"

"No," she replied with a half-hearted chuckle. "But that was a long time ago. It's no big deal now." She glanced over her shoulder before briefly making eye contact one more time. "Glad we got the drink thing situated. Have a nice evening, Seth Hamil."

She'd spoken quickly, and her tone shifted from the irritation of recalling their high school episode to one that seemed as awkward as he felt. "Bye, Ella Wilson," he murmured, unsure how to respond. He frowned when he realized he was definitely going to be late for the meeting now.

CHAPTER 3

"Y ou're late, Seth. We've already started," Nancy O'Riley stated in a clipped tone while staring at him over the rim of her red-framed glasses.

Seth walked the rest of the way into the small meeting room that doubled as the young adult Sunday school classroom. "I know. I'm sorry." He pulled out the chair across from Ms. Nancy and set his cup down on the table before taking a seat. He'd hurriedly eaten the coffee cake during his speed walk the few blocks he had left to get to the church.

Ms. Nancy resumed her focus on the yellow legal pad in front of her. She'd worked as a legal secretary at her husband's law firm for more than thirty years and tended to conduct all her meetings as if they were formal legal proceedings. "Helen's keeping track of our time and taking notes. We'll continue with discussions about the theme."

"Well," Helen Merch, who owned the town's only souvenir shop, began in her softer voice. "We were actually just mentioning that, once again, Cal Jefferson will be blessing us with his former theater talents by directing the Christmas play. Now, that's on Friday night . . ." She paused and tapped the eraser end of a pencil against her cheek.

Ms. Nancy took that as her cue to begin speaking again. "That's all the normal stuff, Helen. We have the order of activities for the week leading up to the morning service on Christmas Day. What we're specifically here to talk about this evening is the auction. That has to be different this year and bigger than ever if we want to raise enough money for the playground renovations and to add an after-school program. I, for one, think we need to offer additional items in the auction. Trees just aren't enough."

Seth had pulled out his tablet and took a sip from his coffee while he waited for it to boot up. Rhonda had been on the committee that came up with the idea to open the church's kitchen and fellowship hall every morning to feed the school-age children. She'd been a latchkey kid growing up in Cincinnati, and her parents always left for work long before she needed to be at school. Most mornings she'd skipped breakfast in lieu of having more time to watch cartoons before needing to be at school on time. Of course, life in Bellepoint was a lot slower than life in the city—something Rhonda had mentioned many times during their college courtship. Still, she'd been adamant that children needed a nutritious meal to get their minds and bodies prepared to learn, and many of the women at the church had agreed. The Christmas tree auction was their blockbuster fundraiser that year and the Morning Munchies program had begun the following year. Now, two years later, the plan was to add afternoon snacks and homework assistance for those same children, and more if need be. Rhonda would've been elated that the church was building on her original plan. So Seth pushed aside his aversion to meetings and pulled his tablet closer so he could begin to take notes.

"The auction has always been about the trees," Addie Gibbs said. She directed the choir and made snacks for the Sunday school children. Seth knew because he'd often received some of those snacks in cute little bags or bowls that were discreetly left on the edge of his keyboard in the sanctuary. "Following the tradition of our annual tree lighting, which will take place next weekend, the tree is the focal point that starts and wraps up our festivities."

Ms. Nancy huffed. "We all know what the real focus of this holiday season is. I mean, just take a minute to observe where we are."

Ms. Addie shook her head. "Yes, Nancy, we all know the reason for the season. I'm just saying that for the purposes of raising money, whether it be for the church or the businesses throughout the town, the tree auction has become a prominent part of people's new year budgets. Besides, the local store owners love having the chance to sponsor and decorate their trees."

"I think Ms. Addie makes a good point," Seth said, breaking his staunch rule not to speak at any of the meetings he was forced to attend.

He hadn't been obliged to join this committee. He just hadn't countered Ms. Helen's suggestion after Rhonda passed. At the time it seemed like the right thing to do, to keep the things that were important to Rhonda alive. Now, as Ms. Nancy glared at him for the second time in less than fifteen minutes, he was rethinking that decision.

"Well, referring to Addie's point," Ms. Nancy said as she finally looked away from Seth, "that's been fine up till now. But what are we going to do to make this year bigger and better? We should always be looking to step things up a notch, especially when we need more money."

"I have the perfect idea," Ms. Addie said, and then she hopped up from the table and left the room.

"Now where's she running off to?" Ms. Nancy scribbled something on her notepad.

Seth wondered if it was the equivalent of a note he might write to a misbehaving student's parent. The thought made him chuckle inwardly just as he heard Hilliard, the senior musician at the church, begin playing "Hark! The Herald Angels Sing." It was one of the songs that would probably be heard during some of the Sunday services throughout the month and most likely again at the Christmas concert, which would take place just before the auction. Since he was a teenager, Seth had played the keyboard and sometimes the drums at the church. After college, he was named associate musician, and so he also helped with the concerts, in addition to playing exclusively for the youth and young adult choirs on the second Sunday of each month. He loved working with the children, whether in school or at the church. Rhonda had said that was a sign that he was meant to be a father. But now that she was gone . . .

"This is my niece, Ella," Ms. Addie said as she came back into the room.

The sound of her name snapped Seth right out of his thoughts and he looked up to see Ms. Addie entering the room, holding a very confused-looking Ella by the hand.

"She's here for the holidays and she has lots of experience selling stuff and making a lot of money." Ms. Addie took her seat again and motioned for Ella to pull up one of the other chairs to join them.

Ella had removed her coat but now carried it tucked under her arm. She adjusted her purse strap on one shoulder as she slid a chair over to the table. After she sat, she hung the coat on the back of the chair and placed her purse on the table, all while the members of the committee stared at her in silent anticipation.

"Hey, Ella," Seth said when she glanced down to the end of the table where he sat. What looked like irritation flashed quickly in her eyes before she turned to the other women sitting around the table and offered them a smile.

"Good evening," she said. "I apologize if I'm intruding."

"Nonsense," Ms. Addie declared and reached over to pat her niece's hand. "You're here just in time. Tell everyone how you go out and select the best pieces of art and then sell them to other folks for loads of money. Tell 'em." Ms. Addie encouraged her with a nod.

"Oh, that sounds so glamorous," Ms. Helen said, her eyes going wide with excitement. "Please tell us how to make loads of money."

"Yes," Ms. Nancy said. "Do tell us your secret, little Ella Wilson who used to sit in the back of the church chatting incessantly on the Sundays Addie was busy in the choir stand."

Ms. Nancy was also chairperson of the usher board, which meant it was her job to know everything that was going on in the sanctuary during service.

Ella cleared her throat. "Ah, Aunt Addie is right, sort of," she said. "I'm an art curator, so I do have experience with selecting items that I think will sell well. She mentioned earlier that you were planning an auction. I've run quite a few auctions that have brought in thousands of dollars for our gallery."

"But we're not selling art," Seth said. "We're selling Christmas trees." He didn't know why he'd spoken up again, except a Christmas tree auction couldn't really compare to one meant for priceless works of art. It was clear Ella was good at what she did.

The designer handbag and the take-charge tone she was now using were dead giveaways. She might be dressed casually and have a history here in Bellepoint, but there was no arguing that this version of Ella was different from the one he'd known long ago.

"Whatever you're selling, the strategy remains the same," Ella continued as she stared at him pointedly. "Put your best foot forward to meet your monetary goals." Before he could respond, she shifted her gaze to focus on Ms. Nancy. "The way to secure hefty donations is to provide something for everyone—that means expand your thinking to capture as many possible donors as you can."

For some reason, he'd started typing every word she said and when she paused, he glanced up at her again. He just couldn't believe it was her. That she was back here in Bellepoint after all this time. He hadn't seen Ella since they graduated from high school twelve years ago, and now, for the second time in a half hour's span, he was only a few feet away from her. Why that had him so unsettled now, Seth couldn't quite say, except that she was the last person he'd expected to see at this point in his life. "You're an avid coffee watcher and an expert on auctions. I never would've guessed." His tone held a tinge of humor, but the slow, unbothered gaze Ella offered was much cooler.

"I'm very serious about my coffee and was a curator at one of Philadelphia's top galleries for seven years before it recently closed." She sat with her back straight, arms folded on the table, a silver bracelet with three charms dangling on her right wrist.

"I see you two have been reacquainted," Ms. Addie said, giving Seth an assessing gaze.

He offered a smile and then sat up straighter in his seat as well. "Yes, ma'am. We ran into each other outside BB's just before the meeting."

Ms. Addie only nodded before looking back to Ella with a slow grin. "I think Ella would be a good addition to the committee. She's gonna be here until after Christmas anyway, right, baby?"

Ella nodded. "Right. I'll be heading back to the city after the holidays to continue my job search. But I don't want to intrude. I haven't been in this church for so long, and I know how tight-knit everyone is here. But I'd be happy to share my thoughts with Aunt Addie and she can convey them to the group." She reached for her purse as if she planned to get up and leave.

Seth wanted her to stay, or rather, he was still wondering why she was back in town. Not that it mattered what Ella had going on in her life. It was just that, because of her comment, he'd felt a tinge of intrigue, mixed with the uncomfortable feeling he'd had in high school sitting next to the smartest, prettiest, and quietest girl in the class. "Sure she would," he said without further thought. "Make a good addition to the committee, that is. Welcome home, Ella."

"I definitely agree," Ms. Helen added. "Ella's just what we need to make this year's event spectacular. And you were raised here in this church, just like your mama and your aunt were. I mean, your great-granddaddy used to be pastor here. Like Seth said, this will always be your home."

He hadn't exactly said that, but watching Ella's reaction to his words and now Ms. Helen's was interesting. The quick rise of her brows said she was surprised at their easy acceptance, maybe? It was the first hint he'd seen that contradicted the total boss-lady mode he'd been struck by since she approached him over the coffee.

Ms. Nancy wasn't about to let Seth or Ms. Helen have the last word. She cleared her throat loudly and pushed her glasses farther up on her nose before settling back in her chair. "Well, I guess since she's your niece and she does seem to have some experience in these things, we can give her a try. Tell us more about how we can attract additional donors, Ella."

Ella paused only briefly, sending a quiet look to her aunt, who nodded and smiled in return. "Well, I must admit I've never heard of a Christmas tree auction, and I'd definitely need to do a little more research to get a good idea of the scope of the event." The confidence came back in the square of her shoulders, the clear tone of her voice. "But what I know for certain is that Christmas is a very marketable theme, albeit for a short window of time. My gallery paid a lot of money each year to have the building professionally decorated for the holidays, so I know there's value in themed trees and decor. Especially from retailers who want the spirit in their place of business but don't have the time or inclination to do any of that labor themselves. Just off the top of my head, I'd say let's tap into that. And if your goal is to make this year's event bigger and better, I'd suggest doing something different. What else will sponsors get besides the glory of winning the bid for the tree?"

Seth followed her gaze around the room. The walls hadn't been painted in years and could use a refresh, but the beige color was still holding up. There was a long whiteboard on one wall that had already been draped with green and red garland. Two gold bells were at each end of the board, the scripture from last week's Sunday school lesson still scribbled in black dry-erase marker. On a small table in the corner there was a box marked "Christmas decorations" that he was certain Bea Cullen, their Sunday school director, would have unpacked and hung around this space before the end of this Sunday's service.

"Retailers—large-scale retailers like department store chains, malls, et cetera—love to have their establishments decked out for the holidays," Ella continued. "It brings in customers even if they aren't selling seasonal items. And they're certainly paying for design companies to come in and take care of everything for them. But what if we offered them an already curated design ready for assembly the next year? Something like Christmas in a box."

"How do you put Christmas in a box?" Seth asked. He'd been listening intently to her every word, typing them so he could reference them later. But he had to pause. "There's so much more to Christmas than just the decorations on a tree. Don't get me wrong—the tree is an integral symbol of Christmas—but there's so much more to the holiday."

Once again, their gazes locked. "But this auction is about trees," Ella replied.

"Trees that mean something to people at this time of year. Relegating that to items packed in a box and shoved into a closet until the next year is a bit trivial, don't you think?"

Elegantly arched brows rose as she watched him intently. What was it about her that made him want to continue conversations with her, regardless of her obvious dislike of him?

"There's nothing trivial about an artistically designed tree. In fact, there are fully decorated trees that have sold for hundreds of dollars. How many trees do you plan to feature?" she asked.

"Twenty," Ms. Helen chimed in. "We doubled it from last year because we had a waiting list."

"Okay, twenty trees. Imagine pulling in five hundred to a thousand dollars for each tree," she replied. "Correct me if I'm wrong, but the way this works is, you get donors to sponsor a tree. They decorate that tree and put it on display"—she paused, shrugging—"here in the church? Or do you rent a different space? Wherever you put the trees on display for people to see and make bids. But what happens to the tree after that?"

"After they take pictures for the local papers and for Brooke, who's our resident tech wizard who puts it up on all the social media sites, a few days after the new year we take it all down. Ralph Grant and his nephew come over and pick up the trees to be disposed of out at their tree farm. And we give the decorations back to the sponsors," Ms. Addie said.

Ms. Helen nodded her agreement.

"What if this year, we focus on high-end themed trees, and instead of sending the decorations back to the sponsors, we box them up and give them to the winner of the bid? That way, they have those same decorations they can use on their own tree next year. By using high-end ornaments, we're offering those man-ufacturers free advertising. In return, they'll want to show the world how charitable they are, so they'll talk about the auction. We bump up the advertising to include email blasts and lots of social media coverage. Opening the bids online and touting the names of the high-end sponsors and manufacturers will catch the eye of bidders with even deeper pockets, like retailers who'll want to have those decorations for their tree next year. This can be the church's most profitable auction yet."

"High-end?" Seth asked. "You mean fancy-schmancy trees that are color coordinated and filled with things like silk ribbons and expensive crystals?" He couldn't help the ire building at the thought. Christmas was about tradition and family—about home and heart. It wasn't about dollar signs and gimmicks.

She frowned a bit and shrugged. "What's wrong with that? If someone's willing to bid five hundred or more dollars for it, what difference does it make what's on the tree?"

"It makes a lot of difference," Seth shot back. "Christmas should be traditional. Trees should reflect the spirt of the holiday with things like stars on top, family-heirloom ornaments and bulbs, popcorn garland. There should be some sentiment behind each tree and the entire feel of this auction. We're not just trying to raise money to support programs that the church offers; we're also giving hope and showing how the Christmas spirit brings people together to do good for one another. Commercializing it further and putting the focus on big corporations is a mistake."

He knew he was going a little overboard with his tone, but he could feel his temples throbbing at Ella's suggestions. Seth couldn't help it; Rhonda had been on this committee for the first two years. Amid the bustle of all the things his wife had done in preparation for Christmas, this auction had quickly become her biggest priority because it gave her the opportunity to do two things she loved most—give back to the town and share the holiday spirit that lived inside her 365 days of the year. This was the first time since Rhonda's death that he was sitting on the committee in her place. He wasn't going to let her vision for the event be so easily dismissed by Ella's temporary presence and her big-city ideas.

"It's a Christmas tree—that's the tradition," Ella insisted. "I was also under the impression that this was a fundraiser, meaning your goal is to raise as much money as you possibly can. I'm suggesting a way to do this with high-end custom trees in a box."

Before Seth could respond, Ms. Nancy spoke loudly. "Well, this has turned into a spirited debate. And I believe the two of you have excellent points. Don't you agree, Addie?"

Hoping that if he stopped staring at Ella, the weird war of emotions surging through him would cease, Seth glanced at the two older women. They exchanged a quizzical gaze and then Ms. Addie looked at Ella before turning to him.

"I agree," Ms. Addie echoed Ms. Nancy. "Excellent points indeed."

"And with such excellent points coming from two people who obviously know a lot about different aspects of this event, I believe it's best if the two of you work closely on bringing this all together in the next few weeks." Ms. Nancy set her pen down on her pad and gave Seth and Ella a curt nod. "Yes, that's the plan. Seth and Ella will iron out the overall theme for the event and secure vendors. Helen has access to the church mailing list and we can certainly get new flyers printed up as soon as you let us know the specifics. I think this was a very productive meeting."

"Very productive," Helen said. "I'm so excited! I can't wait to see what ideas you two come up with for the theme."

"Yes," Ms. Addie said with a nod. "I'm certain with the two of you taking the lead, this year's event will be like nothing we've ever had before."

If he thought his flip-flop reaction to Ella was confusing, the looks being exchanged between the three senior members of this committee left him even more puzzled. The fact was, he didn't have time for any of this right now. He had to get back to the pet shop to pick up Teddy, then get them both dinner.

He'd deal with the new development that he'd once again be working alongside Ella Wilson, the girl he'd had a crush on all those years ago, who had grown into the woman with big-city ideas that could threaten his late wife's dream, later.

One minute she'd been having a nice visit with Ms. Phyllis, and the next she was being drafted to help plan a Christmas tree auction that needed to raise $30,000. At least that was the amount Aunt Addie casually mentioned during their lunch earlier that day.

It had been almost ten years since Ella had been in this church. Today when she walked in, she felt a familiar warmth encircle her, almost like an embrace from a long-lost family member. The sensation had added to the ease she felt spending the afternoon in the house where she'd grown up. After she told Aunt Addie about losing her job, they hadn't spoken about it again. Instead, her aunt launched into a catch-up session, giving Ella the scoop on everything that had been happening in Bellepoint—the Christmas tree auction included.

Still, Ella hadn't expected to be pulled into the committee meeting, or to be leaving that meeting with a leadership role in this year's event. Well, a co-leadership role. She frowned at the thought of her partner.

What were the odds that Seth Hamil, of all people, would be on this committee? Apparently those odds were very high, especially in a town the size of Bellepoint. Last time she checked, there'd been somewhere around 3,200 permanent residents in this town. That, of course, didn't include the influx of students who lived on the campus of Mt. Bellepoint University during the school year. In other words, Bellepoint was a very small world and Seth Hamil was apparently a big part of it. Or at least he was the part that Ella couldn't seem to stay away from.

Her initial reaction to him had been knee-jerk. She could

admit that, just as she could understand why Seth had seemed perplexed by the possibility of her holding a grudge after twelve years. And over something so trivial as a hole in her book bag. But what Seth hadn't known back then was that her sketch pad had also fallen out of her bag that day. The sketch pad that held three drawings she'd made of him. Even now her cheeks warmed at the memory of the ridiculous crush she had on a guy who never looked at her as anything other than the girl he sometimes served at his family's restaurant.

With a huff, she zipped her coat and headed toward the doors. Aunt Addie was going to meet her outside so they could go back to her house for dinner.

"Hey, listen, I know we were sort of at odds back there. But I want you to know that I'm not doubting your abilities in any way."

She was halfway down the hall, nearing the stairs so she could exit the church, when she felt Seth's touch on her arm. Ms. Helen had held him back in the meeting room talking about something Ella had no interest in, and she thought she'd make a clean getaway. Unfortunately, she was wrong and she turned just in time to see Seth drop his arm and stare at her.

"Let me guess: you're willing to admit I have experience in auctions and you'll even accept my help to make the auction successful, but only if I stick to your old, antiquated ideas." She hated how bitter she sounded. It wasn't intentional. The weird instinct to push back against whatever he said had surfaced with the memory of how horribly embarrassing that incident in high school really could've been. No way Seth ever would have understood why she preferred drawing pictures of him instead of just telling him she liked him. Only teenage Ella had understood that fear of rejection and the never-ending loneliness. And the more she tried to move on and forget about it when they were in school, the more James poked at her for one thing or another—she walked too slow, or she always looked like she was daydreaming; she wasn't friendly enough, didn't try to fit in with the rest of them enough. She'd despised James as much as she'd liked Seth. But when Seth did his best to ignore her after the incident, she told herself she should dislike him too.

Of course, none of that mattered now. Just like she told Seth when they stood outside the coffee shop, that was in the past. Grown-up Ella had conquered her fear of rejection by focusing on every goal she'd set for herself and smashing every one of them. As far as the loneliness, work was enough, and when it wasn't, she'd allowed herself to date and fall in love. And when that proved disastrous, she'd decided to go back to the plan that had given her success. It was as simple as that.

He sighed and looked as flustered as she felt.

"Look, we both want this event to turn out well for the church, so I'm willing to hear your ideas about themes if you're willing to listen to mine about traditions," he said and pushed his hands into the front pockets of his jeans.

"You're right," she conceded with a shake of her head and forced herself to push aside all the negative energy that had appeared on the heels of her high school memories. "We can discuss the theme in more detail. I'll listen to your ideas and then propose some of my own. And we'll come to some sort of compromise."

"Deal," he said and extended a hand to her.

Ella accepted it and made a mental note to chill out for the duration of her time in Bellepoint. She had enough to worry about without adding drama from her past. "I really need to get outside to meet my aunt."

"And I need to go pick up my dog before he thinks he's moving in with my sister."

He fell into step beside her as Ella headed for the stairs again. "You have a dog? Aunt Addie never allowed me to get one."

"Yep! Teddy's a big teddy bear, pun intended." He chuckled and Ella shook her head, recalling that Seth had always been the funny guy in class. "I mean, he actually looks like a teddy bear, which is how he got his name. His fur's this rich, milk-chocolate brown and it's all curly. Oh, and he loves to cuddle."

They were at the bottom of the stairs now and Ella added, "Just like a teddy bear."

He glanced over at her and his grin seemed to grow wider. "You're catching on."

She shook her head but couldn't hide her own smile. "It would seem so," she said offhandedly while looking at the dark cherrywood railings and the high-beamed ceiling of the front foyer of the church. This building had been in Bellepoint for a couple hundred years. Through the double doors to her right was the sanctuary. The same red carpet on the floor where she stood now would extend into that part of the space. Without going in there, she knew there were two sets of mahogany pews with worn red cushions on the seats. The aisle stretched about eighty feet down toward the altar and the pulpit, where a large wooden cross hung behind the podium and choir seats. Stained glass windows circled the entire building on the upper floors and this floor. The basement, where she recalled there was a kitchen and fellowship hall, had regular paned windows and had always smelled of fried chicken and sweet tea.

"You okay?"

She turned at Seth's voice, not realizing she'd walked away

from him and was now just standing and taking in everything around her.

"Yeah," she said with a shake of her head. "I'm good. Just got caught up in some memories, that's all." She took a deep breath and told herself it was okay to remember the place where she'd grown up. As for the feeling that some long-closed-off space inside her was just awakening—she decided to ignore that. "So yeah, we can set a time to meet up this weekend, or maybe Monday. I'm sure I'll be in church with Aunt Addie on Sunday and we'll have a big Sunday dinner afterward."

"No worries. I understand. I've got school during the day, but we can meet at my parents' restaurant around four on Monday. That way you can spend some time with your aunt this weekend before we have to get started with all the planning and stuff." He frowned and tilted his head. "You remember my parents' place, right? Beaumont's. It's over on University Lane."

She did remember Beaumont's. It was the first restaurant she'd ever been to that served a variety of grilled cheese sandwiches—the ham and cheddar was the best she'd ever tasted. And there was a booth close to the back, next to a window, that she liked to sit at and draw while she people-watched—or rather, Seth-watched. It had always been a lot easier for her to watch people rather than interact with them, especially the kids her age who never really seemed to get her.

"Yes, I remember it," she replied with a nod. "I'll be there Monday at four."

"Okay," he said.

The plan seemed to be settled, but neither of them had moved. Ella took the first step toward the exit, pushing on one of the heavy, red-painted wood doors and stepping outside. Seth came out behind her and they walked down the front steps in silence. When they were about to go their separate ways, he said, "It's great seeing you again, Ella."

"Yeah, it's good to see you too, Seth." Ella turned and walked in the direction of her car, which was parked around the corner, and when she got to it, she saw Aunt Addie was already waiting. Hurriedly, she climbed inside, and when her aunt was all buckled up, she pulled off.

It wasn't until she was once again in front of Aunt Addie's house that she breathed a sigh of relief. "Seth Hamil," she whispered after her aunt climbed out of the car.

He'd never figured out that she had a crush on him all those years ago, or that his reaction to the book bag incident had broken her heart. She was grateful for that fact. But now he was all grown up and so was she, and they were working together.

Aunt Addie had once told her, *"Fate has a way of stepping in and taking over."*

Ella got out of the car and locked the doors behind her. This wasn't fate's doing and she wanted to scream with frustration because she knew what was really afoot. *The jinx!*

But she definitely didn't have time for this. Not this year when her career might be falling apart. She was here to visit with her aunt for the holidays and find herself a job by the first of the year. That was it. Well, no, now she had this auction to plan. But okay, she could do all of those things without spending one moment of her time worrying over the fact that she would be working closely with Seth Hamil, her first love.

CHAPTER 4

C offee and bacon. Those were the scents that woke Ella from the most restful night of sleep she'd had in almost a month. Rolling over onto her back, she opened her eyes to stare up at the ceiling. It was painted lavender, just like the rest of the room—a selection she'd made when she was twelve and had finally decided to make this space her own. Aunt Addie was all for the idea, telling her she had the final say in the new design.

White lace curtains were at both windows, which faced the front of the house. The wide espresso beadboard dresser with a matching mirror was directly across from the bed, a shaggy dark purple rug covering the floor between them. Identical nightstands were on each side of the bed, and a desk with a spindleback chair was positioned against the wall between the windows. How many days had she spent sitting at that desk, doodling in her sketchbook and intermittently staring out the windows? Too many to count.

On the walls were pictures of unicorns, rainbows, and skates. She'd had a fixation with her skates and had once drawn a picture of them with the sparkly multicolored laces that Aunt Addie wasn't able to find at the store. Her aunt had insisted her sketches were brilliant and constantly provided frames for Ella to hang her work around her room.

"A reminder of the talent brewing inside you," she'd told Ella.

Seeing her drawings every day had inspired Ella to open up more in art class with Ms. Phyllis and to take hold of her teacher's words of encouragement to study art at the college level. A slow smile spread when she noticed the picture above her closet door. It was of a little girl playing with a puppy in front of a house that was identical to this one. That had been her way of asking Aunt Addie for a dog. Her aunt's response was yet another frame to hang the picture and a stuffed dog that Ella had spied sitting in the chair that was now pushed under the desk.

Last night was her second night sleeping in the double bed of her childhood, and while she supposed she should've felt a certain way about being an adult in this very kid-like atmosphere, she didn't. There was a level of comfort in this place she hadn't anticipated, and as she lay here bright and early on Sunday morning, she welcomed it with open arms.

"Breakfast!"

At her aunt's announcement, she glanced over at the clock to see it was a few minutes before eight. Sunday school was at nine forty-five and morning service would begin at eleven. Ella pushed off the white eyelet duvet and sat up on the side of the bed. She was expected in the kitchen within the next ten minutes, or her aunt would come upstairs and get her. Fondly recalling the ritual, she made her way out of the room and into the bathroom. She was downstairs in seven minutes, giving her aunt a quick hug from behind as she plated the bacon.

"Mornin', Aunt Addie," she said and went straight to the cabinet to take down a mug.

Spying one of her aunt's favorite mugs on the counter wasn't a surprise. Aunt Addie was a two-mugs-of-coffee drinker at a bare minimum. Ella could match that, and quickly moved to get started on her first mug of the day.

"Oh, I love this creamer," she said with a grin and picked it up from beside the coffee maker. "Frosted sugar cookie is delicious. I hate that they only sell it at this time of year."

"You mean at Christmastime," Aunt Addie said. In one hand she held the plate of bacon, and with the other she picked up a plate of eggs and walked them both to the table.

"I'd definitely buy it all year long," Ella continued and made her way to the table to take a seat across from her aunt.

Aunt Addie chuckled. "Got that sweet tooth from your mama."

"Eggs scrambled hard with cheese. Mmm." Just staring at the food had her stomach rumbling. "You remembered all my favorites."

There'd never been anything that her aunt forgot. Whatever Ella needed, her aunt had always provided, and Ella would never forget that. Nor would she take it for granted. She hadn't been here a full weekend yet, and already she was feeling guilty for not at least preparing one meal for her aunt. She wasn't a child anymore—for the time that she was here, she could certainly pull her own weight.

"What's for dinner tonight?" she asked after they said grace and began putting food on their plates. "I can head over to the market to pick up something after church. How 'bout barbecue spare ribs? Oh, and macaroni and cheese? I've been practicing and I think I've got your recipe down to a science now."

Aunt Addie chuckled. "I bet you do. That was always one of your favorite side dishes. But you know I like to get started early. I've already seasoned the chicken and I'll put it in the oven as soon as we get in this afternoon. But you can cut and season the potatoes for roasting while I put the green beans on later."

"Ooh, that sounds good too. Love your baked chicken and potatoes." There weren't too many of her aunt's dishes that she didn't love. And just like she had with her mother, Ella had been in the kitchen on many occasions watching and learning how to cook them. The thought of finally standing with her aunt preparing a meal made her feel good.

"You just love to eat." Aunt Addie took a sip from her mug. "Always did have a healthy appetite. Glad you haven't lost that."

Ella had just taken a bite of bacon when she heard the unmistakable tone. It was that I've-got-something-on-my-mind tone that Ella knew would be followed by some sort of lesson for her to learn. That was bound to put a damper on her I'm-happy-to-be-home mood.

"We can start going through the rest of those boxes after dinner, if you want." Decorating the house should've been a great change of subject. But Addie Gibbs could play that game just as well.

"You and Seth seemed to butt heads the other night."

And there it was. To be honest, Ella was surprised Aunt Addie had taken this long to bring up the meeting. They came home Friday night and ordered a pizza, which had been delivered by a college student whom Aunt Addie introduced as Jason, the grandson of one of her oldest friends Ella didn't remember. Unlike Ella, Aunt Addie had a plethora of friends who'd been here in

Bellepoint all their lives as well. Connections that Ella had never seemed to make on her own.

They'd eaten and watched *The Philadelphia Story*, one of Aunt Addie's favorites that she always insisted was a Christmas movie. Ella had seen the movie dozens of times while living with her aunt, and the DVD they watched was an anniversary edition that Ella sent her aunt two birthdays ago. But it wasn't a Christmas movie, not by Ella's estimation. Then again, holiday movies weren't really Ella's thing.

On Saturday, Aunt Addie had been traveling with the missionary ministry, visiting the sick and shut-in members of the church, so Ella had taken the time alone to do some more job hunting. Now, it seemed, the conversation that had been waiting precariously in the wings was about to take place.

"We were in chemistry class together senior year," she said by way of explanation.

"Oh, chemistry." Aunt Addie nodded before adding, "Huh."

Ella knew what that "huh" meant and she immediately began shaking her head. "No. There's no 'huh,' Aunt Addie. He was an annoying boy in high school and he was trying to be the same on Friday. But it's okay—I'm the outsider since I wasn't born here and then I left. I get it. Maybe you shouldn't have insisted I be on this committee. I mean, I don't live here anymore."

"Nonsense. This is your home and our family's been in that church for as long as that church has been standing. Don't you let me hear you callin' yourself an outsider again."

With that quick chastisement, Ella forked some cheesy eggs into her mouth.

"And Seth's not a boy anymore," her aunt added. "He's a very good teacher, a devoted son, and a widower."

"Oh." That last part was unexpected. "He was married?" She'd never thought about Seth being married before. Maybe because after graduation she'd vowed never to think about Seth again. Yet yesterday she'd found her thoughts drifting back to the light mustache he now wore, the crisp line-up of his close-cropped black hair, and his honey-brown complexion. He'd seemed taller than he was in high school, his frame more of an athletic build than she recalled, but the way he always stared at her as if there were words he wanted to speak, but for whatever reason didn't, was the same.

Aunt Addie nodded. "Yep. Got married about a year or so after he graduated from college. His wife came here as a student and she stayed once they fell in love. They were a nice-looking couple."

She could imagine. She should've assumed that Seth would find some semblance of happiness—for as long as it lasted. Everyone in Bellepoint seemed to find that. Everyone except her.

"That's nice. But a shame to hear about his wife's passing," she replied and kept eating to avoid discussing him further. "Well, yesterday I also had a chance to research more about auctions and themed Christmas trees, so I'll be ready for my meeting with him tomorrow."

"Oh, you'll be ready?" Aunt Addie arched a brow. "Well, I guess it's good to be ready."

Narrowing her gaze at her aunt, Ella decided she didn't want to play this game. By offering cryptic responses, her aunt wanted Ella to ask more questions, request more information about Seth, his wife, how the woman passed away, and whatever else. But Ella wasn't falling for that. She didn't need to know those types of details about Seth, or any other man for that matter. Since she'd been jilted before ever making it to the altar, she'd been on a self-imposed hiatus from men and all the sticky trappings of relationships. The same way she'd had to put the notion of Christmas miracles in a box to protect her peace, she'd tossed romantic relationships in that same space and closed herself to all possibilities.

"I think the church can raise more than its goal if we plan this right. Plus, I'm really thinking that opening this auction online is the way to go. They've got to reach beyond the walls of Bellepoint. Dig into some deeper pockets." She'd written copious notes on her ideas yesterday while she was at the house alone.

"I'll be out tomorrow afternoon, so I won't be here to cook dinner. You should probably just eat at Beaumont's since you're going to be there for the meeting," her aunt said.

Ella nodded. "Or I'll just come home and fix something. I can fend for myself, Aunt Addie. You don't have to feel like you're taking care of me." To the contrary, Ella really wanted to do more for her aunt while she was here, which was why she'd offered to cook tonight.

"Old habits," her aunt replied with a shrug. "Get yourself a grilled ham and cheese from Beaumont's and those wedge fries you always liked. And sit there for a while—you'd be surprised what will come back to you in that time."

"I don't need anything to come back to me, Aunt Addie." She sighed when she realized that may have sounded a little harsh. "I mean, I didn't come back to Bellepoint to find something I lost. I came back to visit with you while I look for a job. I'm not staying here," she said, because she had a feeling her aunt might have been thinking along those lines.

There was something about how casually her aunt had taken

the news that the gallery was closing. And the ease with which she brought Ella into that committee meeting on Friday. Well, okay, she'd actually dragged her into the room, but even that had almost felt planned. But Ella shook the suspicions away. She had to finish eating and get upstairs to go through her bags and see if she'd brought something to wear to church. She was certain she had—being prepared was one of her strong points.

Being ready to face the congregation on a Sunday morning in Bellepoint was not, but a couple of hours later, that's exactly what Ella did.

Just as she'd thought on Friday night, the sanctuary looked exactly the same. Except this morning it was decked out in all the holiday regalia. White twinkle lights wrapped around the beams overhead and covered the many wreaths that hung throughout the space. Red velvet ribbons were tied into neat bows and placed at the end of each pew, while thick swags of garland lined the doorways and hearty potted poinsettias flanked the two stairs leading up to the pulpit.

Forgoing Sunday school, she'd gone straight to the sanctuary and sat there until it was time for service to begin. This was the first time Ella had been in a church in a very long time. The feeling of peace and resolution settled over her even as pinches of guilt irritated her mind and soul. She'd been brought up in this place, raised to be guided by her spiritual purpose as well as the talents she was blessed with, and the ways she could use those talents to be of service to her godly sisters and brothers. Her heart thudded wildly as she could swear she heard her mother's voice echoing through the space. Before Mama passed, they'd lived in the city and had gone to church there, and her mother sang almost every Sunday morning. The hymns were her favorite, but there'd been many occasions when Mama with her angelic soprano voice was given a solo to bless the congregation with. Lyrics that taught of faith and hope and the Holy Spirit washed over Ella now as she closed her eyes to the memory.

But seconds later she realized it wasn't only a memory. Someone was playing the keyboard and singing. A deep, smooth voice sang the familiar words of "Amazing Grace," and she opened her eyes to look toward the front of the sanctuary.

Seth, dressed in a dark suit, white shirt, and gray tie, sat in the musician's corner, his fingers moving over the keyboard positioned on a stand next to the organ that had been in that space forever. It appeared to be a modern splash compared to the traditional look, and she couldn't turn away. Aunt Addie had said he was a teacher and a loving son. Ella knew the latter, or at least that he'd been very dedicated to his family's restaurant, as she recalled seeing him working there on many occasions when they were young. That may not have been an option, considering Beaumont's had always been a family-run establishment, but Seth had never seemed to mind being there. Ella refused to consider that his presence there had spurred her love of that infamous grilled ham and cheddar cheese sandwich.

"I don't know why he didn't take a page from your book and get out of Bellepoint when he had the chance. He could've gone on to be a famous gospel singer." A woman's voice jolted Ella from her thoughts.

She looked up to see a familiar face standing beside the pew. Ella was up before she could stop herself. "Max!"

"Hey, Ella!" Max said and opened her arms to receive Ella's hug.

"It's so nice to see you." And it was. Ella hadn't realized

how much she missed seeing Seth's younger sister's easy smile and laughing eyes.

"It's great to see you too," Max continued as the hug broke. "It's been forever. I think you've gotten even prettier than I remember."

Ella shook her head. "You've grown into a lovely young woman." Max had been a little tomboyish when they were young, following around behind Seth as much as she could until Seth's teen years, when their mother, Ms. Gail, started keeping Max away from Seth and his older friends.

Max was shorter than Ella, even in the four-inch nude-colored heels she wore today. Her dark hair was styled straight to hang past her shoulders with wispy bangs falling over her forehead.

"Sundays are the only days I get to dress to impress around here," Max said, doing a quick turn to show off the pleated sage-green skirt she wore with an ivory blouse.

They both grinned when she stopped, and Max looked at Ella once more. "I heard you were back in town and I couldn't believe it. How long has it been since you've visited?"

"It's been a while," Ella said, hating the truth of how long she'd actually been away. It had been almost ten years since she'd spent any considerable amount of time in Bellepoint. She hadn't even managed to make it back in time to show Aunt Addie her engagement ring after telling her about Ben over the phone. And just like that, it was over and done with anyway.

"But you're here now for the rest of the month, right? Working on the Christmas tree auction with Seth." Max glanced toward the front of the sanctuary where her brother had stopped playing the keyboard but was now talking to an older gentleman.

"Yeah, I kinda got swept into that," she said.

Max waved a hand. "Girl, you know how that is. If you're sitting around here too long, somebody's bound to give you an assignment."

It had been a while since that had happened to Ella. A while since she'd been pulled onto a committee or into a project that she hadn't planned to be a part of. But there was truth to Max's words. Being in the church almost always led to being on some ministry or committee, performing some task that would ultimately glorify the kingdom. Weird how all those words and situations came tumbling back into her mind.

"Well, I'd better get to my seat. Ms. Nancy, aka the Usher General, will be in here soon shuffling everyone to their places so service can start on time." Max looked around as if she actually expected Ms. Nancy to appear at any moment.

Ella looked around, too, and had to grin at the thought. "You're right," she said and then eased back inside her pew.

"But we'll have to get together for some coffee to catch up. I'm at my shop all day, but we can meet up one evening."

"I'm meeting with Seth tomorrow at your parents' place, so maybe I'll see you there," Ella said.

"Oh, that's great. Seth's always there for dinner. Thankfully, my folks hire a lot of the college students looking for part-time work to help out now, so we don't have to be there every moment we're not at our full-time jobs. But I can swing by when I'm done at the shop."

"Okay, I'll wait for you there."

With their meetup set, Ella settled back down on the pew, and once the service began, she let herself be swept away by the hymns and the powerful sermon. When she left the sanctuary hours later, her spirit had been lifted in a way she hadn't anticipated, and she couldn't wait to get back to the house to help her aunt cook and begin decorating.

Going up on his toes and extending his arms, Seth tried for a three-pointer and missed.

"Man, you havin' a bad day on the courts," Jordan Petis said. "That's not like you." Then he shook his head and chuckled. "But wait, yeah, it's exactly like your non-ball-playin' self."

They'd been friends for twelve years now, since they'd met two weeks into their freshman year at MBU. Junior year they'd both pledged Theta Psi Mu, the Pi Pi Chapter, and had been fraternity brothers from that day forth. Jordan was an inch taller than Seth, his complexion a deep sepia hue, and his head bald. Those traits, in addition to his name, led his best friend to believe he was equally as great at hoops as the famed Michael Jordan. Despite having missed his own last four shots, Seth begged to differ with Jordan's assumption.

"Stop stalling and take your next shot," Seth said, jogging over to the other side of the court. "You spend more time talking on the courts than actually playin'."

Jordan shot the ball and grinned when it sank inside the hoop. "That's because it's so easy to beat you."

Seth shook his head. "A little distracted, that's all," he said and walked over to the bleachers of the university gym to pick up his water bottle.

Jordan followed, clutching the ball he'd retrieved in his hands. "Work or family?" he asked as he sat on the bottom bleacher and put the ball on the floor.

Taking a gulp from the water bottle gave Seth a few moments to think about his response. On the one hand, there wasn't much he kept from Jordan. His friend was the first to know when Seth was considering proposing to Rhonda, and he was the first to know when he and Rhonda had started talking about having children. Rhonda had been a diabetic since her teenage years, and on the night two years ago when they'd received the news that she had also developed kidney disease, Seth had called Jordan to lay down his worries in order to remain strong for his wife.

But today seemed different. The woman he'd seen just a few hours ago at church had been on his mind heavily and he couldn't figure out why.

"The auction's coming up," he said when he realized Jordan was still waiting for a response. "Had a meeting about it Friday night."

"The tree auction," Jordan said. "The one Rhonda used to plan."

Seth nodded and so did Jordan.

"How was that?"

With a shrug, Seth tried to downplay just how much he'd been thinking about Ella since that day. He hadn't thought about her in years. That incident in school with her book bag was the furthest thing from his mind until she'd been standing just a few feet away from him, looking at him with those same russet-brown eyes that had mesmerized the gangly teenager he was back then.

This morning he'd seen those same eyes staring at him from her seat in the back of the sanctuary. When she stood and walked around the church to put her offering in the plate, he'd spotted her again. She wore a floral-print skirt that came just a little past her knees, a gray turtleneck, and suede pumps. Her twists had been pulled up into a high bun, and medium-size hoop earrings dangled from her ears. Why he recalled every detail about her wardrobe, Seth couldn't say. He was too busy trying to sort out the urge he had to go to her to start another conversation. About what? The committee? The weather? The fact that he hadn't been able to stop thinking about her? He was certain he was overreacting.

"Got another meeting about the specifics of the auction tomorrow." And he was looking forward to it a little more than he thought he should be.

"So what do you have to do? Just get some people to donate trees and then auction them off? That doesn't sound like too much work. I mean, don't you just go back to the same folks who donated last year?" Jordan leaned back, resting his arms on the bleacher seat behind him.

"Yeah, that should be it." But Seth had a feeling it was going to be so much more than that. He took another drink and then sighed. "Ella Wilson's back in town."

"Who's Ella Wilson?"

He glanced over to his friend and realized he wouldn't know who she was. Ella had been long gone by the time freshman year at MBU began. "She left Bellepoint a few weeks after we graduated from high school. Had a full scholarship and used it to go to Temple." In the city, instead of staying in the town where she'd grown up.

Where they'd both grown up, at least for a portion of their childhoods. He landed in Bellepoint when he was seven, after his father had been injured in the line of duty. Bellepoint had been his mother's hometown, so this was where they decided to settle and where his parents had taken over the restaurant that used to be run by his grandfather. Ella had come to town after her mother's death, a couple of months before the start of their fifth-grade year.

"Oh. Okay," Jordan replied, exaggerating both words. "Am I supposed to know how that relates to the tree auction?"

"Ella's on the committee," he said. "We have to work together on the preliminary plans. I'm meeting with her tomorrow after school."

"Oh." Then there was a pause and another drawn-out "Ohh-hhhh."

Seth shook his head. "Don't even go there. It's not like that."

Jordan feigned confusion, tossing his hands up in the air and shrugging when Seth glared at him. "I'm just following the conversation."

"No. You're jumping to conclusions."

"You're the one who said she was back in town and you had to work with her. All I said was 'oh.'"

He hadn't said it that simply, and Seth knew the implications of that one word. Which was why he wanted to be perfectly clear right from the start. "She hates me."

"What? Why would she hate a great baller like you?" Jordan asked, humor lacing his tone.

"You're not funny," Seth countered.

"Yeah, I am," Jordan replied. "But seriously, what'd you do to this Ella to make her hate you?"

"It's a silly story," he said and then realized that by saying that, he was diminishing the way Ella had probably felt when James ran around the building with her leotard on display. But a part of him had always wondered if there was more to that incident than he'd known at the time. Not that it mattered now. He sighed again. "I inadvertently burned a hole in her book bag, and when her stuff fell out, I didn't stop one of my goofy classmates from embarrassing her."

At this moment, as he had on Friday night when he watched Ella walk to her car, he wished he'd stopped James right at that moment instead of waiting months, when James's new hobby of tormenting Ella finally started to get on Seth's nerves. In fact, he wished he'd apologized profusely to Ella and asked her out for ice cream the way he'd imagined doing so many times back then.

"So it's a teenage thing? Well, you're both grown-ups now. And what better way to get over the past than to plan a fun Christmas activity like the tree auction?"

Jordan felt way more optimistic about this committee assignment than Seth did. But he didn't speak on it again. Instead, he stood and grabbed the ball from the floor, heading back out onto the court to continue giving the game to his best friend. And hopefully to get his mind off the one woman in the world who couldn't stand to be around him.

CHAPTER 5

Beaumont's was Seth's second home. It was located on University Lane, a two-block radius with shops, bookstores, and eateries that catered specifically to the college students who frequented the town. MBU's campus was just up the road, some of its gable-topped buildings and the snowcapped Mt. Bellepoint mountains visible from the street.

Monday was a chilly day with a frigid breeze that called for him to wear his heavy brown leather jacket and a brown skully. Even still, he shivered as he walked through the restaurant's front door. Overhead, the jangle of bells sounded, signaling that a customer had entered the establishment. Heat instantly warmed his cheeks as the low murmur of conversations mixed with the local radio station playing Christmas carols from the speakers around the space.

After the restaurant had closed Saturday night, Seth, his parents, Max, and Camille—one of the shift managers—had assembled to decorate the place for Christmas. Beaumont's was big on celebrating every holiday, so decorating wasn't anything new. But Christmas was the most important one, and it showed by the two Christmas trees—a traditional, colorfully decorated one near the hostess stand and a second one toward the back of the room by the small stage area. That one was decorated in his mother's favorite gold and green. The white tablecloths that normally covered each round table and booth-top had been replaced with alternating green and red cloths, and mason jars filled with sprigs of pine, cones, and holly and painstakingly tied with coordinating ribbons sat in the center of each table. He pressed his fingertips together, recalling the sting from the hot glue Max had insisted they use when she'd showed them how to assemble the centerpieces.

"You're a little earlier than usual for dinner," his mother said as she passed him. She dropped a stack of menus into the slot at the side of the hostess stand, and when she was close enough, Seth leaned in to kiss her on the cheek.

"Or I could just be stopping by to see my lovely mother," he said and removed his hat before stuffing it into the side pocket of his jacket.

She reached up to tweak his nose and grinned. "Well, I love seeing my charming son, so that's just fine by me."

Gail Hamil was the epitome of grace and beauty, with a short stature, warm smile, and boisterous laughter that came fast and frequently as she chatted with the students who hung around the restaurant. Every year she took them all under her wing, checking on them regarding their studies, as well as their physical and mental health. She worried over them as if they were her own, earning the title "Mama Gail," by which she'd come to be known throughout the town.

"And I've got a meeting in about ten minutes," he said, coming clean because not being truthful with his mother had never been an option.

"Oh, a dinner meeting? That's usually called a date."

79

"No." He shook his head. "It is most definitely not a date."

The rise of his mother's elegantly arched brow confirmed he'd protested too much, and Seth groaned at the knowledge.

"I'm just going to grab a booth over on the side where it's quieter. When Ella comes in, can you send her over?"

Again, his mother's interest looked piqued. She casually crossed her arms over the red sweater she wore, which looked especially festive with her ivory slacks and dangly snowflake earrings. "Ella? As in Ms. Addie's niece who's back in town for the holidays?"

He wasn't even going to ask how she knew who he was talking about. Bellepoint might be a college town, taking in thousands of students each school year, but it was still a relatively small town. The locals knew everything about each other, and they certainly knew when someone new came or returned to town.

"Yes, ma'am, that's who it is. And if you know that much, you also know we're working on the Christmas tree auction. We've got to get things moving so we'll be ready in time."

"She was such a pleasant girl as a youngster, and Ms. Addie's missed her since she's been gone. So I'm glad she's here for a few weeks." His mother reached up to brush something off his shoulder. "Now, you go on over there and have a seat. I'll bring her over when she arrives and then send someone to take your order. You can't just sit here and talk—you know the rules."

He grinned because he did know the rules. Beaumont's was a great place to gather and chat, even to sing karaoke and whatever other social ideas Max and Camille came up with to keep the place relevant, but the one thing that had to happen when anyone came in to stay for a while was that they had to eat. It helped that everything on the menu was budget friendly and tasty.

"Cool. Thanks, Mama." Seth left his mother at the front of the restaurant to continue doing what she did best—talking to people.

He found a booth in the back by a window that looked out onto the street to passersby on their way to do whatever it was they needed to get done in the late afternoon. It wasn't a view he hadn't seen before, so that's not what set off the spark of recollection as he sat down. Neither was this a booth he'd never sat in or cleaned out before, but as he flattened his palms on the table, the memory that had been trying to form came into focus.

Young Ella with her hair in a mushroom style used to sit at this table with her sketch pad open, colored pencils spread out around her. It had been a long time, but in this moment as he stared across the booth to the empty bench where she'd be sitting once she arrived, he could recall her being here some afternoons after school or on Saturdays when she didn't have anything to do at the church. She was always alone, except for when Max would drop by and chat for a while, or he'd come by to deliver what she ordered.

"Huh," he said quietly to himself and gave a little nod. Ella wasn't just back in town; she was about to be back in Beaumont's—a place Seth had rightfully called his own all his life. Shaking off the weird feeling he had, knowing Ella would soon be in this place that held a very personal meaning for him, Seth resigned himself to focusing on the present. Because the past couldn't be changed and the future wasn't his to worry over.

He'd carried his tablet in its case and now set it on the table before easing out of his coat and putting it on the bench beside him. Over the weekend, he'd taken some notes on things that he recalled were important to Rhonda about the auction. He wanted to make sure he didn't forget any of those points when he talked to Ella today. They'd both promised Ms. Nancy and the rest of the committee that they would work together to make this the best auction yet, but he had no intention of negotiating any of the important parts. Rhonda wouldn't have wanted him to.

The jangle of the bells at the door sounded a few more times—so many that he'd stopped looking up from his tablet each time, thinking that Ella had finally arrived. He let himself fall into the warmth of the place, the comfort of the sounds of dishes clinking in the distance, music and conversation. How many afternoons had he spent sitting at one of these tables getting his homework done before he had to go into the kitchen and help take and deliver orders? So many that he almost felt that same need to finish with the meeting and go back there and help now.

It had been a while since they'd needed him to serve, but he could still drop fries and plate a soup and sandwich the way he did years ago. The thought had a smile ghosting his lips as he continued to read over his notes. He'd even printed some pictures from previous auctions that he planned to give to Ella for reference. He had a feeling that while she may have been good at selling pricey artwork, she was less experienced in raising funds for a small-town church by auctioning off Christmas trees.

Besides that, he was still wondering why Ella was back in Bellepoint in the first place. He couldn't recall the last time he'd seen her and figured that was because she hadn't been here in a while. Not that he'd been looking for her over the years, but in the past two days he'd been thinking a lot about her and what she'd been up to since they graduated.

"Here she is!"

His mother's words pulled Seth from his thoughts and he looked up to see her and Ella standing beside the table.

"Sorry I'm a little late," Ella said. "I had an important call come through just as I was leaving the house and I had to stop to take it."

Whether or not she elaborated on the nature of the call, he couldn't say, because he found it very difficult to listen to her. Instead, he was pulled once again into the warm color of her eyes, the sound of her voice—even if he wasn't totally comprehending her words—and the faintest hint of a dimple in her left cheek.

He subtly shook his head and found his voice. "Oh, hey, no problem at all. I was just going over some notes." Then, before he forgot all the manners his mother taught him, Seth stood and moved his hand in the direction of the bench across from him. "Have a seat. Thanks for bringing her over, Mama," he said, and even though he meant the words as a gentle dismissal, Gail didn't do anything she wasn't good and ready to do.

"It's so nice to see the two of you here, sitting together," his mother said. She folded her arms over her chest and tilted her head. "My, how time has just flown by. Seems like it was just yesterday that Ella would come in here and sit doodling in her sketchbook while she ate. And you were moving around here so fast, trying to get finished with whatever duties you had to take care of before you skipped out to basketball practice or the music store."

His mother shook her head as she recalled, the long, dark brown curls of her hair shifting over her shoulders. Neither she nor Ella had any idea that the reason he used to hurry out of the restaurant most days Ella was here was because he couldn't stand being around her when he didn't have the nerve to just ask her out. Ella always had this forlorn look in her eyes, and he got nervous thinking of what might've put it there. Sure, he knew she'd lost her mother, but just like with the book bag incident, he'd wondered if there was more to the story. He'd wondered about so much where Ella was concerned and wished now that he'd had the guts to just talk to her back then.

"And now we have to plan an auction," Seth said, pulling his thoughts back to the present and praying his mother would please take the hint this time. "Could you get someone to bring us drinks? Ah, coffee? Do you want coffee, Ella? Dark roast, heavy cream, caramel, and two sugars?" He felt like a complete goof for remembering exactly what she had in her coffee three days ago.

Ella slid onto the bench and removed her black coat. She was setting it aside as she glanced at him and then to his mother. "Actually, I've had a grilled ham and cheddar cheese with wedge fries and a glass of water on my mind all day."

His mother chuckled. "Just like old times. Coming right up."

"Uh, I guess I'll have the same," Seth said.

"Food'll be out in a few minutes. Y'all go ahead and get started with your meeting. We're thinking about getting another tree in here, so I'm excited to see what's up for grabs this year."

"But you already have two," Ella said, looking around. "How many is too many?"

It was too late for Seth to answer that question for her. Gail was already shaking her head. "There's no such thing as too many, baby. It's Christmas! All the festiveness is a requirement.

Haven't you ever heard 'the more the merrier'?" His mother's hearty laughter followed her words, and Seth couldn't help but chuckle in response.

Ella, on the other hand, offered a cordial smile that held until his mother walked away. Then it faltered and her quizzical look fell on him.

"Really? Two trees aren't too many?" Her words were spoken lightly but seriously, and Seth sighed.

"Yeah, my mom's really into Christmas. There are three trees at the house, and that doesn't include the bushes in the front yard that she decorates with bulbs, lights, and garland too."

It was Ella's turn to shake her head as she pulled her tablet out of the huge purse she carried. "I just can't get into all that stuff. It's so much work."

"Wait, so you don't decorate for Christmas?"

"No," she answered as if that was a known fact. "I don't have the time or the inclination to buy a bunch of stuff, keep it stored, pull it out, put it up, then take it down and repeat the process over and over again every year." She waved a hand while she waited for her tablet to boot up. "It's a waste of time."

"I think it's fun," he said. At least he'd always thought it was fun growing up, and then when he met Rhonda and she loved Christmas just as much as—if not more than—his mother, he'd counted himself doubly blessed.

She shrugged. "Okay, so I had a chance to look into some similar auctions. Well, not Christmas tree auctions specifically but holiday-themed ones. And again, I think the way to go is to step things up, offer something that'll continue giving long after this year's event. I'm sure there are plenty of people like you, your mom, and my aunt Addie who love to pull those decorations out year after year. So we create the Christmas tree in a box that'll be shipped to the highest bidder once the tree is taken down."

When she finished speaking, she turned her tablet so that he could see the screen. There was a box in the top right corner, paper-bag brown with red writing and a big red bow. Directly across from the box were ropes of beaded silver and gold garland. In the lower two boxes were more tree decorations—ornaments and bulbs in the same silver and gold pattern.

"Of course, we could design the boxes to fit the theme of each tree to create a more cohesive look," she continued. "Or we could just go with a specific branded tone that we could carry throughout all promotions for the event this year and the following years."

"Theme?" he managed to ask in between her presentation. "You sound like my mother. Aren't trees just decorated?"

She blinked as if she truly didn't understand his question. "Where's the creativity in that?"

"Where's the tradition in planning some eccentric theme for a Christmas tree? I mean, I get the silver and gold you have here. There's a song for that after all." He glanced down at the screen once more. "But outside of that and the array of collected ornaments and bulbs, I don't see why there has to be anything else."

"Wait," she said and then huffed as she sat back in the seat. "Are you saying that all the trees looked alike last year? What makes them worth bidding on if they're all the same?"

"No one tree is the exact same. And there are always different ornaments and decorations on them, but the way you're saying 'theme' and 'branding,' I get the impression you're talking about something much more sophisticated than we're used to doing."

"My thoughts exactly." She reached for the tablet and swiped her finger across the screen. More trees popped up. "Variety. Color pops. The unique and extravagant. That's what's going to bring in the money!"

For some reason his jaw tightened as he searched for the words to calmly convey what he was starting to feel. This wasn't what the auction was about. "I don't think you understand," he began but was interrupted by Jason, who'd arrived with their food.

"Hey, Seth," Jason said. "Hi, ma'am."

"Hey, Jason," Seth replied and helped by taking his plate of food and glass of water from the tray while Jason served Ella.

"You can just call me Ella," she said in a tone that was way more cheerful than the one she'd been using with Seth.

Today she wore dark blue corduroy pants and a denim button-down top. Her long twists were left free to hang down her back and pearl earrings were at her ears. He was almost positive her face was makeup free as her skin was the same unblemished, rich mocha hue as it was when they were younger.

"Nice meeting you, Ella," Jason said.

"Oh, we unofficially met the other night when you delivered pizza to my aunt Addie's house," she said and reached for a napkin.

Jason nodded. "Yeah, that's right. Hope you enjoyed it."

"It was delicious, just as I'm sure this will be."

"Cool. Let me know if you need anything else," Jason said before meeting Seth's outstretched fist with a pound.

Seconds later, Ella leaned across the table and whispered, "Did you hear him call me ma'am? Do I look like a ma'am?"

The clear look of horror on her face broke through the

tension he'd been feeling just before their food arrived, and Seth grinned. "Well, if memory serves correctly, you and I are the same age, so that makes you thirty-one."

She leaned back, shaking her head. "You're seven months older than me. You turned thirty-one in September and my birthday's not until April."

"You remember my birthday?"

The question left a hush between them and their gazes held for a long moment while it seemed they both were struggling to find the next words to say.

"These pickles were always the best," she said finally and picked up a spear from the side of her plate. "They're even better than the ones at the general store. You know, the ones that were in that big barrel at the front?"

He watched her take a bite and chew slowly. "Yeah, I remember. One day Barry Reid poured a whole jar of hot peppers into that barrel and ran out of the store like he was being chased by a bear."

Her eyes widened. "Seriously?"

Seth took a bite of a wedge fry and chewed while chuckling. "Yup. I didn't want to get blamed for his nonsense, so I took off running too. Didn't stop until I was home in my room with the door locked." When she started to laugh, he continued, "What? I figured as long as the door was locked, Sheriff Glenn couldn't get inside to take me down to the station for questioning."

At that, she couldn't stop laughing, the naturally happy sound filling the space around them. He'd always liked her smile but recalled it hadn't been on display often. Unlike most of the girls in town, Ella wasn't into cheerleading or any of the other stuff girls liked to do. Most of the time she was hanging out at the restaurant, walking alone in the schoolyard, or sitting on the swing at the park or on a bench at the church. She wasn't normally alone at the church since there were always people around, but he couldn't remember her smiling much there either.

"You needed better friends," she said, interrupting his thoughts. "The ones you picked were always up to no good."

He knew she was speaking of James again and he sighed. "I really am sorry about James. I should've stopped him."

She shook her head and reached for her sandwich. "It was a long time ago. I was embarrassed and hurt. But I'm all grown up now, so I'm over it."

He knew she meant to deliver those words with conviction, but they sounded hollow to him and he couldn't figure out why. "Sometimes it can be a lot easier to say we're over something than to actually be over it."

She didn't respond but continued to chew, and he bit into his sandwich as well. For a few minutes they ate in silence, him going back to his thoughts of how he was going to tell her he hated her ideas for the auction, and her, well, he didn't know what she was thinking. All he knew was that she looked relaxed now, and oddly enough, that made him feel better.

In the next moment, the music stopped playing and a loud bell was being rung. Clapping began and some cheering started in one of the corners of the restaurant.

"Y'all know what time it is!" Camille announced from the stage. "It's Mega Eats Monday!"

Across from him, Ella frowned as she finished a sip from her glass of water. "What in the world is Mega Eats Monday?" she asked.

Seth used his napkin to wipe his mouth. "It's the weekly

eating contest Camille and Max started after watching way too many of those competitions on the food channels."

"So you're saying somebody's about to attempt to eat a ridiculously large cheeseburger for a chance to win a T-shirt?"

He grinned and shook his head. "Nah, this week it's my mama's famous sweet potato pie, and the prize is not only a T-shirt but a one-hundred-dollar gift card to be used at the restaurant. It's really geared toward the college students. My parents' way of giving them a chance at free food."

"That's thoughtful," she said and was about to pick up her sandwich when Max appeared.

"Hey, we need two more participants, so you two are it!" His sister grabbed his arm and Ella's and began pulling at them.

"Oh no! I'm just here to have a meeting and enjoy my grilled ham and cheese," Ella immediately rebutted.

"Come on, please! We need the table to look full but only two students signed up this week. We're going live on Instagram in five minutes," Max said.

Seth shook his head and stood. "You might as well just come on and do it," he told Ella. "You don't really have to try to eat it all. Like I said, the contest is for the students."

"We get over thirty thousand tuned in each week for this. Come on, don't let this be our first week without a full cast." Max had begun pulling them along again and Ella looked at him with pleading eyes.

He chuckled. "It won't be that bad. I promise."

CHAPTER 6

Seth Hamil was a promise breaker.

Not only was Max holding her phone camera on them, streaming everything live to the restaurant's Instagram page, but someone wearing a hunter-green-and-white *BP Gazette* jacket was snapping pictures every few seconds. At the other end of the table, which had been positioned on the stage for every patron at the restaurant to see, was a handful of people holding up their cell phones to record the contest as well.

Ella felt like a spotlight was shining directly on her. It shouldn't have been that way because she was hardly alone on the stage. But even with Seth sitting to her left and two more contestants on the other side of him, the urge to put her best foot forward pressed against her ribs like a lead weight.

"See, it's already cut into slices," Seth whispered as he leaned over close to her. "Just eat what you can. The others will be trying to devour theirs in the fifteen-minute timeframe."

Ella stared down at the pie Mama Gail had just set down in front of her. The sweet cinnamon and brown sugar scent filled her nostrils and she smiled. "Aunt Addie used to order all her holiday pies from your mother. She said she was fine with baking cookies from that frozen roll, but cakes and pies weren't her strong suit."

"We sell more pies and cakes during Christmas than the two other bakeries in town. That's why they always put the baked goods into the contests in December," Seth said.

"All right now!" Camille spoke into the microphone. She had a pretty smile—a diamond piercing winked from her nose and her short natural curls were dyed midnight blue at the tips. "We're ready to get started. Y'all know the rules—whoever eats the most in fifteen minutes wins!"

Ella glanced down at the pie again. What was she doing? She'd come here for a meeting and now she was about to be broadcast to who knew how many people, stuffing her face with pie. Was this what all her studying and hard work had come down to? The call she'd taken on the way to the restaurant was from the headhunter she'd enlisted to help find her a new job. So far, her résumé hadn't garnered any interest. She doubted adding sweet-potato-pie-eating champion to her list of attributes would help.

"Five, four . . ." Camille began counting down and Ella cleared her mind.

She was here now, in this seat, doing this thing she hadn't come here to do. What she wasn't about to do was fail. Not again. She rolled her shoulders and prepared to eat as much of this pie as she could.

The crowd cheered as Camille sounded the bell to begin, and Ella picked up the first slice of pie. It was delicious, just like she remembered. The creamy and spiced sweet potato mixture coupled with the flaky homemade piecrust was a slice of hometown heaven that she hadn't realized she'd missed so much. The first slice went down quickly and easily and she eagerly went in for the second. But she made the mistake of glancing over at Seth to see that he was already going for his third piece. Competitiveness needled her and she took bigger bites, vaguely tasting the pie this time. When she reached for the third slice, her stomach began to revolt.

A camera flashed and people continued to chant. It seemed like so many more people than had previously been there. They were mostly rooting for one of the two students at the other end of the table, which made sense because none of them knew her. And she didn't know any of them. So why did it matter if she won in front of them or not? It didn't, or rather it shouldn't. But Ella needed a win. She needed something to counter the stupid jinx that she was certain followed her around every Christmas.

"You okay?" Seth asked.

"Fine," she snapped seconds before the bell rang again, stopping the contest.

Disappointment was her first reaction, but relief quickly followed as she put the last piece of pie back on the plate.

More cheering came as the guy at the end of the table jumped up, hands in the air, while he claimed victory. Looking down the table, she saw that he'd finished one whole pie and half of another one in just fifteen minutes. She groaned.

"These kids have way bigger stomachs than mine," Seth said as he stood. "But you did good."

She shook her head because the way he said "those kids" reminded her of Jason calling her ma'am just a little while ago. Seth followed her back to the booth they'd shared before they were drafted into the eating contest and sat across from her once more.

"You know it was just for fun, right? You don't have to be salty because you didn't win."

She wasn't salty.

Taking a deep breath instead of saying that out loud was probably the smarter move. "Nobody enters a contest intending to lose."

"They do when they know what the contest is really about. You know, the college students?"

Was it his tone or just the sound of his voice that was irritating her right now? "I don't know that it's such a good life lesson to have these young adults believing that everyone is going to take pity on them. What happened to working hard for what you want?"

"They are working hard at their studies. Some of them aren't here on full scholarships. And what little they have left over from their financial aid each semester doesn't last very long. They have to eat and my parents want to do whatever they can to facilitate that need."

She sighed. "Great. Now, on top of losing, you make me feel like a Scrooge for thinking we should play fair and honestly, regardless of their age."

He tilted his head, wagging a finger at her as a slow grin began to spread. "Aha, you do know something else about Christmas other than how much money can be made this time of year."

Why did he do that? Each time she got wound up about something, he tried to defuse her ire with some casual remark, which he obviously thought was funny. Well, she wasn't easily humored, and besides, this was a business meeting.

"We should get back to the auction planning," she said, trying to ignore how badly her stomach was hurting at the moment.

"Whatever you say, ma'am," he said and moved his plate out of the way to bring his tablet in front of him. "Do you want something else to drink? Hot chocolate or another glass of water?"

"No." She shook her head. "I'd just like to get this done and go home. I can type up a memo giving Ms. Helen all the details for the Christmas-in-a-box idea. Sponsor sign-ups need to begin right away, with a cutoff date of the fifteenth. That'll leave three and a half days for tree delivery and setup." Something else occurred to her and she frowned. "That's a really small window of time. What if the online advertising brings in a sponsor from California? Would that give them enough time to get their theme together and have everything shipped to us?"

"You know this has always been a local event," he said, and she looked over at him as if just remembering he was there.

Getting swept away by work was easy for Ella. It was what had saved her on so many occasions—most recently, the end of her engagement. Work was her safe haven. It was the one constant she'd had in her life besides her aunt. And now that was gone. Perhaps that was why she was taking the closing of the gallery so hard.

"The original goal was to help local children, to provide them with a healthy meal before school each morning. So we asked local businesses to help and they all thought it was a great cause and a fun event. This auction is about sentiment and community. It's about taking care of our own." His tone was serious again, a tinge of sharpness in his last words as if to drive home his point.

Ella had a point to make too. "If you do the same things, you get the same results."

He sat up straighter, his gaze locking with hers. "Is that why you're back, Ella? Because you were tired of doing the same things in the city?" When she didn't immediately reply, he continued. "You returned to your small hometown and now you think your sophisticated ideas are better than our traditional ways?"

She was getting a headache. Too much was happening, too

many thoughts and emotions. She felt like she was floundering, in addition to being sick from all the pie. "Look," she said with a huff. "I didn't ask to be on this committee. I was just fine sitting in that house visiting with my aunt."

"You said the gallery where you worked closed. Is that the only reason you're back in Bellepoint?"

"That's none of your business," she snapped and then clamped her lips shut.

The Johnny Mathis version of "It's Beginning to Look a Lot Like Christmas" had begun to blare through the speakers. A glance out the window showed night had fallen, the strings of colorful lights on the lampposts illuminating the streets. It was a pretty sight and a lively song, yet all Ella wanted to do was scream.

"What do you want to do, Seth?" she asked, unable to hide the exasperation in her tone. "Do you want me off the committee? You want to get twenty trees all decorated with the same multicolored ornaments and see how much money you'll get for them? Tell me your plan to raise this money for the church, because so far all you've done is shoot down everything I say."

He sighed. "You're right. I apologize."

She hadn't expected an apology, nor did she really believe she needed one. If she'd been in his position, she'd probably be pushing back against some new person dropping in on the committee and tossing out ideas too. But wasn't that what they'd asked her to do?

"I'm not averse to everything you've said. I just want to make sure we preserve some of the traditional tones of Christmas. The heart of this event is giving and caring for others. I don't want to lose that in all the sparkly decorations and themed boxes."

"That's fair," she said and reached for her tablet again. "What if we keep the donated trees to the local businesses, but open the bids online? This way the local businesses will get the advertising that could hopefully play out for them throughout the year."

He nodded. "I like that."

"As for the themes, if we're keeping it local, maybe reach out a little farther than the shops on Main Street. Perhaps MBU would like to donate a tree and decorate it in the college colors? Maybe the hospital? Oh, how about the candy factory? Is that still open?"

"Yeah." He grinned. "You remember the candy factory?"

There was no reason for his smile or the way his tone seemed just a hint lighter to have her relaxing, even if slightly. This was like any other work meeting she'd ever had, nothing more.

"Of course I remember. It was our holiday field trip every year in middle school. We didn't graduate to the Grant Christmas Tree Farm until high school. I guess they thought we were mature enough to roam around the acres of trees unsupervised by then."

Now he laughed. "Which we weren't. Remember Jenny and her crew got lost and we were late getting back to the school because they had to send out a search party for them?"

The memory had her chuckling too. Not because the girls had been lost—that had been serious at the time. But when Jenny and her three friends were found with their faces covered in chocolate and marshmallow because they weren't actually lost but had decided to build a fire and roast some s'mores instead of looking at the trees and participating in the guided activities that had been planned, the cheers for their independence had rung loud and clear from the students on the bus.

"I remember that day very well. Aunt Addie was lined up at the school with the other parents when we got back. She fussed all the way home about kids thinking everything was a joke. I couldn't figure out why I was getting the lecture when I hadn't even been involved."

"No, you weren't involved. You didn't hang with Jenny and her crew. Or anyone else for that matter."

She shrugged. "I didn't need a crew to hang with."

"Everybody needs a friend," he said solemnly.

"What? Is that, like, your everybody-should-love-Christmas mantra?" It was a snippy question and the moment of nostalgia quickly passed.

"I'll make a deal with you." He closed his tablet and rested his elbows on the table.

"Why?"

"Just hear me out," he continued. "I'll agree to you adding your splashy boxes and other touches to the auction, but you agree to let me show you why Christmas is about more than just decorations and other stuff that you don't have time for."

He was being ridiculous. There was no need for him to show her anything. All they had to do was work on this auction. Then she'd head back to the city and be out of his hair until whenever she decided to come back to Bellepoint. "Look, I know you're a teacher and all that, but you don't have to make this a lesson for me. I can help out on the committee and then get back to my life once it's over."

"But while you're here," he said, taking one of the sprigs of holly from the centerpiece on the table, "why not be filled with the Christmas spirit?"

He tucked the holly into an opening on the side of her tablet case, and she couldn't help but grin at how silly and, at the same time, whimsical it looked. "Whatever you say, *sir*," she said, mimicking his tone from when he'd sarcastically called her ma'am a few moments ago. "Let's just get this auction started. I'll type up the memo and email it to you for your approval, then I'll send it to Ms. Helen."

Nodding, he replied, "Cool. And you can come by the church Thursday night to hear the youth choir practice for the concert."

She frowned. "How's that supposed to get me into the Christmas spirit?"

"It's not. I'd just like your company. Besides, the kids will be excited to meet the new IG sensation who barely ate three slices of pie during the contest."

There was a pause, and then he laughed out loud. Ella wanted to continue frowning, but a smile broke free. "You're not funny, Seth Hamil. Not one little bit."

Ella found herself sitting inside a church for the third time in less than a week. And not once had she asked the question that had plagued her for so many years.

Why?

Why had her mother been taken from her?

To someone on the outside looking in, it may have been a silly question, but as she sat in the first pew in the sanctuary listening to the talented group of teenagers sing "O Come, All Ye Faithful," she felt a familiar bone-crushing pain. It started in her chest and spread until her only recourse was to get up and run out of the sanctuary.

For a few seconds she paced, shaking her hands at her sides as she willed the tears stinging her eyes to stay put. No way was she going to break down in this church at this moment. There was no breaking down allowed, at least not out in public. Well, not in Bellepoint at all. After the funeral, she hadn't cried in front of her aunt or anyone else again. What difference were those tears going to make? They couldn't bring her mother back. But in the quiet darkness of her bedroom, her cheeks had been streaked with that hurt on more occasions than Ella cared to admit.

It was foolish that after all this time she could still become overwhelmed with grief. That the anger that bubbled just beneath the surface every second of every day could simply punch through at any moment. Finally, exhausted by the swift turn of emotion, she dropped down into one of the guest chairs that lined the wall. Leaning forward, she rested her elbows on her knees and cradled her face in her hands.

This right here was why she hadn't come back to Bellepoint in so long. This constant barrage of memories only reminded her of all the time she'd been forced to live without her mother. Her body shook with the intensity of that thought.

She was just stressed. That's what she'd been telling herself the past few days. Each morning she awoke and moved throughout Aunt Addie's house—helping to put up decorations, finally cooking her aunt dinner, organizing the doll collection her aunt had kept for her and contemplating donating them. Not to mention the job search. She spent hours each day poring over job sites. She'd even started to look outside of Philadelphia, something she'd never considered doing before. But there was no way she could go into the new year without a job prospect. She'd never let the jinx keep her down for long, and she wasn't going to start now.

"You know, if they were singing off-key, you could've just told me."

She sat up at the sound of Seth's voice and realized rehearsal must have ended while she was having her little breakdown. The hint of laughter that was always present in his tone eased over her like a much-needed balm. And yet she sighed heavily when their gazes met.

"They sang wonderfully. That young guy who you reminded to take off his baseball hat has a phenomenal voice." He'd sung the first verse of "O Come, All Ye Faithful" and Ella could've sworn she was back in the house with her mother, lying on the couch while the Nat King Cole Christmas album played.

"Demarco." Seth moved slowly until he could sink down into the chair beside her. "He's sixteen going on thirty-five and thinks he's ready to be the next Marvin Gaye."

"Oh wow, you're taking it back. You couldn't come up with anyone in our generation to compare him to?" she asked.

He sat back, letting his hands fall to his lap. "I like the classics. I mean, there are a few current artists that are worth a listen, but Demarco has a lot of soul in him. When he's ready to focus on the music instead of all the money he thinks is gonna come the moment some record exec hears him, he'll really be able to find his full talent."

"Is that why you didn't leave Bellepoint and try to get a record deal? You wanted to focus on the music?" When he only stared at her in response, she shrugged. "I had coffee and a fabulous cinnamon raisin bagel with Max yesterday morning."

He nodded. "And my sister told you the story of how she wishes I would've gone on to become a famous recording artist."

"She just wishes you would've followed your dream."

101

"Who said my dream was to become a famous singer?" He paused. "I've always loved music. I could sing a little and the church choir honed that skill. That's it."

"It's my turn to apologize," she said. "I didn't mean to bring up something that would irritate you."

With another sigh, she stood and rubbed her palms down her thighs. She wore jeans today, a lavender sweater, flats, and her puffy coat, which she'd left in the sanctuary with her purse. "I think I'm gonna just go. I'm in a weird mood and I don't want to take it out on you."

He stood, too, touching a hand to her shoulder. "You didn't irritate me, and if your mood has anything to do with the song the kids were singing or how it made you feel, I'm here to listen. Or we can just go for a walk and talk about something totally different."

"I don't want to talk about it," she said quicker than she wanted to. "I'm just gonna grab my coat and purse."

Putting some space between them suddenly became imperative. The way he'd come out and sat with her, his easy tone as he said he'd listen, was all too uncomfortable. Perhaps because deep inside she wondered if that was what she actually needed, while on the surface, that shield she'd taught herself to keep in place had almost faltered.

"You never liked singing in the choir."

She didn't startle at the sound of his voice because she'd known that he would follow her back into the sanctuary. For one, his coat was in here, too, and he had to turn off the lights before they left.

"No," she replied as she pushed her arms into her coat. "I preferred ushering because I could sit in the back."

"And nobody could stare at you." He came up beside her and

just stood there while she zipped her coat and looked straight ahead.

"When I first came here, everybody stared at me. In the classroom. At the park. In church. It was annoying."

"Because you thought they were waiting for you to break down."

She turned quickly to stare at him. "How did you know?"

The corner of his mouth lifted. "Because that's the same way they looked at me after my wife died."

He walked over to the music storage box and grabbed his leather jacket. She watched him put it on, then check to make sure the keyboard and the organ were both turned off.

"She got really sick pretty fast. That was a blessing and a curse, I guess," he said.

"Yeah, Mama did too."

They started to walk up the aisle together.

"It's weird how one minute things are going just fine, and the next the whole world shifts and leaves you feeling like you're dangling off the edge," he continued.

She sighed. "Whew, you just said a whole word."

"And the next thing you know, you're handling your grief and warding off the pity from everyone around you. And you know they mean well, but it's still exhausting."

"Preach!" She clapped her hands and gave a weary smile.

They took a couple more steps before she said, "I read about your wife on the church website. Everything she did for the youth and her dedication to the church and the town—she sounds like a wonderful woman."

He opened the sanctuary door and let her exit first. "She was," he said and followed her out into the foyer once again. "We had good years together. That's what you remember, Ella. All the good times."

"The sadness seems more persistent," she blurted out without thinking.

"I know." He nodded.

They stepped out into the evening air together, and Seth turned back to lock the front doors of the church. Then he continued down the steps with her.

"Let's try this," he said and linked his arm through hers.

For a second, they both stared down at that connection, but then he started walking and she didn't want to be dragged along, so she fell into step beside him.

"While I promised to teach you about the joy of Christmas, I also recognize that this and other holidays can be a touchy subject for different people for lots of reasons. So for the next few weeks, I'll be here for you to lean on when it gets too hard, and you can do the same for me."

Nothing had ever seemed too hard for Seth. He was a natural athlete, a gifted musician, had always been good-looking, and came from a perfect family. But she knew losing someone he loved had to have been the ultimate punch to the gut, so she nodded and said, "That sounds like a good plan."

"Really?"

She didn't miss his surprised tone and she grinned. "Yeah, really. But I don't want to hear any whining if I call you in the middle of the night when I'm having a tough time sleeping."

"You can call me whenever you want, Ella."

His words were spoken softly as they continued to walk down the street, but Ella heard them. And later that night when she was alone in her room, she thought about them and about Seth.

CHAPTER 7

T he sound of her laughter was as cheerful as the Jackson 5's "Up on the Housetop" lyrics blaring throughout Beaumont's on Friday night. Seth sipped from the mug filled with snickerdoodle hot chocolate and leaned back against the counter across the room. He grinned at both the rich taste of the drink flavored with cinnamon, nutmeg, and vanilla and the way Ella had squeezed a tube of icing over a gingerbread cupcake and a mountain of the sweet confection had oozed out.

Two long tables had been set up in front of the stage area by the time he'd arrived this evening. It was, thankfully, after the speed dating event that Max had oddly forgotten to remind him about this week. He'd remembered anyway and had taken Teddy on a very long walk after school, then sat in his home office grading the pop quiz he'd given his class yesterday until his stomach began to growl. When he checked his watch to see that it was well after six, he figured the speed dating had begun, and by the time he made it to the restaurant, it would be over. He was elated how accurate his timing was when he walked in, yet surprised to see Ella there.

She wore black pants this evening, with an oversized burgundy sweater and natural-colored boots that came midway up her calf. The top half of her twists were pulled up into a bun, while the back cascaded down to hang almost to her waist. He'd never paid a lot of attention to a woman's hair before but could admit to himself that he liked this style on Ella, loved the way it seemed so versatile with her Sunday-go-to-church flair and her casual playing-with-royal-icing look.

"You want dessert, Seth?" Jason asked from the other side of the counter.

Seth glanced back at the young man wearing a navy-blue T-shirt with "Beaumont's" in white script over the left chest pocket. "Already got it," he replied and lifted his mug in a mock toast.

Jason chuckled. "Yeah, that's a pretty sweet drink you've got there."

Seth took another sip. It was sweet and delicious, although still not as wonderful as the Crock-Pot hot chocolate they sold down at BB's—something he'd never utter to his mother. But this was certainly a close second. Even if sometimes it made him yearn for a plate of snickerdoodle cookies fresh out of the oven.

Cheers sounded from across the room and his gaze once again found Ella. How long had she commanded most of his attention? From about three seconds after he'd finished the bowl of beef stew he had for dinner. He knew she was there, helping to set up the supplies for the gingerbread decorating event, but recognized it would've seemed strange if he didn't take his evening meal sitting at the counter as he usually did. Now, however, with a delicious beverage in hand, he found watching her to be a much better pastime than hurrying back home to finish grading those quizzes.

"Thinking about rushing the table to see how many cup-cakes and cookies you can grab before your mother stops you?"

Jordan came up and clapped a hand to Seth's shoulder. He hadn't seen his friend arrive but grinned in his direction. "I'm not feeling particularly bold tonight," he said. "You know my mama's quick."

Jordan joined in the laughter. "Yeah, I know. I've gotten plenty of hand slaps for reaching for some food item she wasn't ready for me to take just yet. Even when her back was turned."

Seth could only shake his head. "Eyes in the back of her head. She says every mother has them."

"My mama and grandmama used to say the same thing," Jordan added.

Ella finished the cupcake. She'd cleaned it up quite a bit so that it didn't look like one of Bellepoint's snowcapped mountaintops anymore, but it now had a reasonable dollop of icing that she'd added multicolored sprinkles to. She held it up triumphantly to receive a round of applause from Max and the half dozen other patrons who'd gathered around the tables to participate. His mother came to the tables periodically, refilling supplies and giving encouraging words about the decorating. This wasn't a competition like Monday's pie eating but a simple holiday activity that fostered laughter and festiveness among all who'd dropped by.

"So how long have you been standing here debating whether to go over and say something to her?"

"What?" Seth looked over at Jordan.

His friend wagged his brows before nodding toward the table with the gingerbread fun. "You gonna go over and say something to her or just keep staring at her like a lovesick pup?"

Seth took another sip from his mug, still enjoying the choco-latey treat. "Man, you know it's not even like that," he said, hold-ing the mug in one hand and pushing his other hand into his front pants pocket. "They're just making a huge mess. I'm trying to hurry up and finish this drink so I can skip outta here before my mama comes over and drafts me for the cleanup crew."

Jordan stood with his arms crossed over his chest. He nod-ded and stared over at the table, just as Seth had resumed doing. "Nah, you're used to hanging around for whatever Mama Gail needs, without her having to ask."

"You're right," he conceded, but the other nonsense Jordan had just spouted, Seth wasn't hearing at all. "I am thinking about grabbing one of those cupcakes to go, though. I do love a gingerbread cupcake."

"Especially one with too much icing and a ton of sprinkles," Jordan added.

"We're working on a committee together," Seth said without looking at Jordan this time. He knew exactly what his friend was thinking and needed to shoot that down immediately. Of all the people in his life, Jordan knew best that Seth wasn't in the mar-ket for romance and didn't plan to be anytime soon. "Matter of fact," he continued, "have you seen the graphics on the town's social media pages? Brooke did a fabulous job incorporating all the ideas Ella gave her. Luckily, I was at school when they met to go over all the creative stuff. But I've got a good feeling about the auction this year. A really good feeling." The last words were spo-ken a little softer than his previous comment, his chest warming with the thought of the auction being successful.

The program at the church would be expanded, and prayer-fully, they'd have extra to make the improvements to the playground. That would be a huge blessing, one the community was counting on and one he knew would've made Rhonda happy.

"That's what's up," Jordan said. "And it helps that you and your old crush are getting along."

His head snapped in Jordan's direction. "I never said I had a crush on Ella."

Jordan's grin was slow this time. "Who said I was talking about Ella?"

Seth frowned. "We both know that's who you're referring to, and you are way off the mark."

"Am I?" Jordan let his arms fall to his sides. "Weren't you totally off your already bad basketball game the other day because you'd just learned she was back in town? Going on and on about something you should've stopped from happening in the past. For a minute, I thought you were gonna go find that guy who embarrassed her and straighten him out once and for all."

Jordan didn't know Seth had done something of the sort back in high school, not to mention James had left town to join the US Marines shortly after graduation. The last time he returned to Bellepoint was about four or five years ago when he brought his wife and baby daughter home to meet his parents.

"Can't erase the past," Seth said solemnly.

If he could, Rhonda would still be here.

Just when he'd told himself to push that thought aside and finish his drink so he could leave, his gaze found Ella's and held.

She'd stepped away from the gingerbread table and now held her phone to her ear. She pressed a finger to her other ear and broke eye contact with him as she walked toward the back of the restaurant in what he suspected was an attempt to escape the volume of the carols. That wasn't likely to happen altogether, but he was more concerned about the sober look that was now on her face. Seeing her this past week had proven one thing—he liked that grown-up Ella smiled more than teenage Ella ever had.

When he caught Jordan staring at him again, he shrugged and took a last gulp of his hot chocolate before turning and placing the mug on the counter. "When's the last time you went out on a date?" Seth asked, even though he tried to steer clear of his friend's dating status. If he didn't talk about anyone else's love life, they wouldn't worry about his. That had been his thought on the matter, but it rarely ever worked.

"One, I've had plenty of dates this year," Jordan replied. "And two, I'm not the one who was staring hard at a woman instead of just going over and saying whatever I had to say."

"I don't have anything to say to El—"

Seth didn't get her name out completely before she was walking up to him, a frown marring her face.

"We got a problem," she said without preamble.

"What is it?"

"Gypson's Department Store just filed for bankruptcy." She stuffed her phone into the back pocket of her jeans and shook her head.

"I don't get it," Jordan chimed in before Seth could respond. "There's no Gypson's here in Bellepoint, so how's that a problem?"

Seth had almost forgotten Jordan was still standing next to him. In fact, in the seconds since Ella had appeared, he was only vaguely aware of anything else going on around them.

"Ella Wilson, meet my frat brother Jordan Petis," he said by way of introduction as the two of them shared nods of greeting. Then he replied to Jordan, "Gypson's is the parent company.

They bought out the old Simpson warehouse a couple years back and expanded it to three larger buildings total."

"Oh yeah, that's right," Jordan said. He still had one arm folded over his chest but was now rubbing a hand over his bearded chin. "I lost the bid to design the new space, but the daughter still runs the place. She drives that nice black Range Rover too."

Ella sighed. "Linell Simpson. She manages the warehouse, and she contacted Ms. Helen yesterday morning to say they would sponsor the trees. You remember I texted you about that?"

Seth nodded because he did remember. Checking his phone while the students were taking their quiz and seeing Ella's name appear on the screen had given his spirits an unexpected boost. Of course, the message had been about the auction, delivering the fantastic news that they'd met their twenty-tree quota. Now, just twenty-four hours later, that excitement had dwindled.

"Apparently the board members just voted and an urgent email was sent to all the Gypson stores and holdings. As a result of the bankruptcy, they won't be able to take on any new extra-ordinary expenses," she continued.

"Purchasing and decorating twelve trees isn't an extraordi-nary expense. Especially not to a department store chain the size of Gypson's," Seth said.

"Exactly. They're a national chain," Jordan added. "You mean to tell me they're in such a financial jam that they can't make good on their commitment?"

"A small-town tree auction wouldn't be of concern to the big corporate picture," Ella stated.

Her quick response and curt tone reminded Seth that she was a big-city businesswoman. Although neither of them were lawyers and quite possibly didn't know all of the legal ins and outs of filing for bankruptcy. Of the three of them having this conversation, Ella probably had the best idea of exactly how corporations thought. Seth had taken a few finance classes during college because he hadn't wanted to know only music for the rest of his life. Besides that, he'd always been available as a backup in the running of Beaumont's. His parents weren't going to be able to manage the place forever, and he was determined that the restaurant would remain in the family.

"So that leaves us short twelve trees and the deadline expired at six this evening. We're not going to get any more sponsorship offers." She rubbed her temples. "Flyers are out all around town and on social media. Email blasts have been sent this week and are scheduled to go out four more times before the auction. Bidding is set to begin on the nineteenth at noon."

Exasperation laced every word she spoke, and when she finally eased her fingers from her temples, Seth found himself struggling not to take her hand in his. To step closer to her and put an arm around her shoulder—anything to ease her worry. Not sure either of those was a good option, considering they were in a crowded restaurant and Jordan's mind was already running with unfounded romantic notions where Seth and Ella were concerned, he decided on another tactic.

"Okay, we'll figure this out," he said. "We need twelve trees. Let's go over the list of sponsors we already have, then first thing tomorrow morning we can hop in my truck and start visiting all the businesses that haven't already signed up. We'll make a face-to-face appeal to them. I'm sure we'll be able to recoup the loss by the end of the day."

"People are more reluctant to tell you no to your face. Especially when you're asking for such a good cause like feeding the children," Jordan said. "I know this is normally a local event, but I can make some calls, too, reach out to our other chapters in the city and surrounding area."

Seth nodded. "Good looking out. Desperate times call for desperate measures," he said. "At this point we're gonna do whatever is necessary to make this event a success."

"Hey, what's going on?" Max asked when she joined them. She was wiping her hands on a napkin and looking from one of them to the other, waiting for a response.

"Hey, Max," Jordan said.

Max had come to a stop directly in front of Seth with Ella to her left. She looked over her shoulder briefly and replied, "Oh, hey, Jordan." Her attention quickly reverted back to Seth and Ella. "What happened? How can I help?"

Seth disliked the lines of worry that had immediately stretched across Max's forehead. Though his sister was the youngest of the family, she carried the concerns and problems of their family on her shoulders as if they were all her own. And as if she didn't have issues of her own to deal with.

"It's just a little glitch," he told her. "We're working it out."

"Yes, we are," Ella said. She was nodding now, a tiny smile slowly forming. "I've got an idea. I'll be right back."

Before any of them could reply, Ella had walked away. She stopped by the gingerbread tables and grabbed her coat from one of the chairs before going outside.

"She's got an idea to do what? Freeze? It started snowing about twenty minutes ago," Max said.

Seth frowned and reached for his jacket that he'd hung on the back of one of the counter stools.

"Whoa, not so fast." Max put a hand on his arm to stop him. "Somebody still needs to tell me what's going on." She was as persistent as she was concerned, but Seth didn't have time to stand here and give her a recap.

"Yeah, Jordan's gonna fill you in. I'll be right back." He left the two of them staring at each other while "I Saw Mommy Kissing Santa Claus," another Jackson 5 tune, filled the room.

"You'd be doing me a huge favor, Claire, and getting your name into circulation in an untapped arena." Ella folded her arms across her chest and walked along the sidewalk in front of the restaurant.

It was cold and fat snowflakes dropped at a hurried pace, making the street look like a scene from a snow globe. The carols playing inside Beaumont's could be heard out here, and they were the perfect backdrop for the decorated storefronts and enough Christmas lights to illuminate the entire town. It should've been a perfect scene—a picturesque sample of what the Christmas season was supposed to be.

Instead, here she was trying to deal with another jab thrown at her this season.

"I know it's short notice, but if you agree, I'll provide the tree for you. It'll be amazing." On the other end of the line she heard only Claire's silence, which was never a good sign. "Your name will be on the box—a Claire Castille original Christmas tree. You could take off into a direction you never even imagined. A Caribbean Christmas in a box! Your publicist will love all the possible directions you could go with this—paintings of the trees, those paintings scanned to become Christmas cards, note cards, wrapping paper."

"I'll do it!"

Ella stopped walking, her feet freezing in the boots that were really cute Italian leather, but no match for a Bellepoint snowstorm. "For real?"

"Yes!" Claire said, excitement clear in the rise of her voice. "How many did you say you needed?"

"Twelve," Ella replied, a nervous and relieved chuckle escaping. "But I'm not asking you to do all twelve, Claire. I know you're busy and—"

"No, not me. But I've got friends who haven't been able to get gallery deals. What if they did a tree to get their names out there too? I mean, this is a good cause, so don't think we're all just lookin' out for ourselves. But like you said, it's also a great opportunity."

"I absolutely love you right now, Claire." Her heart pounded with the quick punch of unexpected joy, and all Ella could do was shake her head. "If I were back in the city, I'd drive over to your place and hug you."

Claire chuckled. "If you were back in the city, you wouldn't be in this Christmas tree mess. But I get it—I love you too! Now, let me get off this phone and make some calls. I'll hit you back in a little bit."

"Okay, great. And thanks again, Claire. Thanks so much for saving my reputation." She disconnected the call and murmured, "And for saving me from the jinx."

"Didn't have you pegged for the superstitious type."

Ella spun around to see Seth leaning against a mailbox that had been wrapped in gold and red paper like a present.

115

"I'm not," she said and stuffed the phone into her pocket. "Just something that came out. Anyway, I've got great news!"

"Yeah, I figured that's what was happening."

He looked way too calm and casual dressed in khakis, steel-toe boots, and a black bomber jacket, hood up just like hers. It was so obvious he belonged here. He'd known to wear the right type of boots tonight. But not only that. Seth and his frat brother had immediately jumped into troubleshooting mode while she'd been ready to spiral into the vortex of the dreaded Christmas jinx once more.

It wasn't that she wouldn't have gotten around to coming up with a solution to their problem—she had eventually—but Seth never missed a beat. His demeanor never changed, and he'd simply eased into crisis mode with the same mild temperament he had when dealing with everything else. It had to be a crime for anyone to be that laid-back. And if it wasn't, she needed to know what he was flavoring his water with so she could do the same.

"One of my former artists, Claire Castille. She's an amazing oil-painting artist bringing a fresh and unique Afro-Caribbean vibe to her portraits." She shook her head when it felt like she was rambling. "She's going to sponsor a tree. I have no doubt it's gonna be colorful and full of island flair. I can't wait to see it. Also, she's going to ask some of her friends to sponsor trees, so we may be well on our way to getting the twelve trees."

He pushed off from the mailbox and crossed the short distance to where she stood. The snow had already begun sticking to the sidewalk. A truck drove by, making tracks in the street.

"Great work under pressure," he said when he stopped just a

few steps away from her. "But you didn't have to feel like it was just your reputation on the line. We're all in this together."

She sighed, her breath sending a cool cloud of steam up in front of her. "So you heard that part too, huh? You do know that eavesdropping is rude."

His shrug was way too nonchalant and alluring at the same time. She resisted the urge to return the quick grin he flashed. "I had to come out here to make sure you didn't turn into an icicle trying to fix this problem by yourself."

"It's just snow," she replied. "It snows in Philly."

"Not like it snows here and you know it. But anyway, like I said, you aren't in this alone."

"I didn't say I was."

"But when we were in there discussing how we could fix this, you decided to come out here and do your own thing. We're on a committee together, so whatever happens, whatever needs to be done, should be done together. I know that's probably not how you're used to working, but that's how we do it here."

"Well, that was snippy," she replied and stuffed her hands into her pockets. She had gloves but they were in her car. "But you're not entirely wrong. I know we're a committee and I didn't walk away intending to handle the issue myself. The music was too loud for me to hear clearly. Jordan gave me the idea of reaching out to some people I know to ask for their help. I wasn't sure how that was going to go, so being alone when I took the next blow was more appealing."

"The next blow? You're referring to being jinxed."

She sighed. "I didn't say that. Look, can we just pause whatever this is for a second? We had an issue, your friend came up

117

with an idea, and we're all implementing it. End of story." Stopping to take a deep breath, she held his gaze. "Now, I actually am about to turn into that icicle you predicted, so I'm just gonna head home."

He stopped her when she started to walk past him, but when she glanced up at him, he immediately dropped his hand from her arm.

"I apologize if I was—what's the word you used? 'Snippy.'" He frowned and she almost chuckled because he obviously didn't like her word selection. "We're all trying to make this the best auction possible. So let's help out the people we're asking to be sponsors at the last minute. Let's go out to Grant's farm tomorrow and see if we can get him to donate the twelve trees."

"Sure, that's a good idea." She could've said no. They could've just called Ralph Grant and asked that question, but Ella knew what Seth was trying to do. "We can go out there together to continue fixing this problem."

"Great. Now let me take you home before you freeze to death." He turned around and was about to start walking beside her, but she held up a hand to stop him.

"It's okay. I drove tonight. Even though I didn't suspect snow, it was cold when I was out earlier today so I knew I didn't want to have to walk home after the gingerbread event." She smiled. "But thanks. I appreciate you wanting to see me home. It's really chivalrous of you. Teenage Seth could learn a lot from grown-up Seth."

He chuckled. "Oh, okay, you got jokes now."

She couldn't help it—she laughed too. "That was impossible to resist."

"I'll let you have that one, but I'll also share that grown-up

Ella has a pretty terrific smile; too bad teenage Ella never showed hers."

That wasn't supposed to make her feel all warm and fuzzy inside. After all, they were standing in the middle of a snowstorm. She pushed her hands into her pockets again and prayed the voluminous hood of her coat prevented him from seeing her blush.

"So, um, tomorrow," she said and cleared her throat. "What time?"

"I'll pick you up at eleven—that way we'll be just in time for the grilled sausages and hot cider they serve for lunch."

That sounded oddly like a date. Nervous laughter bubbled up and she couldn't hold it in. She was not going on a date with Seth. They were simply going to ask for some Christmas trees. And have lunch. But the latter was more of a convenience, not an arrangement to spend more time together. Right?

"Eleven it is," she said with a nod and then, because she felt this night had given her enough ups and downs, she took a step away from him. "Good night, Seth."

He lifted a hand and waved. "Good night, Ella."

CHAPTER 8

Gingerbread people held hands and danced around the Christmas tree singing "Let It Snow! Let It Snow! Let It Snow!" and Ella rolled over onto her back, humming the tune.

It was the Nancy Wilson version, one of Mama's favorites, and even though she'd awakened from the dream, she lay still with her eyes closed, letting the afterthoughts circle in her mind. She was nine years old and had just lost another tooth, leaving a gap in her bottom row. Although she wasn't the only child in her third-grade class to have lost a tooth or two, that wouldn't stop her classmates from making fun of her. It was too late to add the tooth to her list of things for Santa to bring her that year because she'd mailed that list weeks before and in just four more days, Santa would be making his deliveries.

Mama had attempted to cheer her up by reminding her that she didn't have to return to school until January 2, and Ella had followed along with that train of thought, suggesting that perhaps her new tooth would make an appearance by then. With her beautiful, warm smile, Mama had set a plate of fresh-baked gingerbread people, along with a cup of hot chocolate overflowing with marshmallows as big as snowballs, in front of Ella. Her little legs had swung happily from the kitchen chair as she ate until her tummy hurt.

Cracking her eyes open to the rays of bright sunlight peeking through the blinds of her bedroom window, Ella wondered how those gingerbread people had made their way to the Christmas tree to dance a happy jig. A slow grin spread across her lips as she stretched her arms above her head. A big yawn followed, and then she sat up.

"Can dreams come true?" eight-year-old Ella had asked.

"Most definitely," Mama had replied and kissed Ella's forehead. *"Always have faith that whatever you wish for in dreams or in real life will come true."*

At that memory, Ella's happy mood faltered and she dropped her hands into her lap.

Have faith.

Something else she'd been taught and reminded of throughout her childhood years. First from her mother and then again from Aunt Addie.

"Now faith is the substance of things hoped for, the evidence of things not seen."

It had been quite some time since Ella had hoped for anything. More years than she could recall since that scripture had played in her mind.

She'd never hoped to get over losing her mother. That wasn't a loss she thought anyone would ever get past. And there were no *dreams* of getting out of Bellepoint—that had been a nonnegotiable decision she made almost as soon as she arrived on Aunt Addie's doorstep with suitcases in hand. Bellepoint had been her mother's and Aunt Addie's childhood home. Ella's had been in Philly where she lived in that three-bedroom row house, rode her bike on the cracked sidewalk in the summer, and built a one-eyed snowman—because she hadn't been able to find another black button to match the first one—on the small patch of grass they called a front yard. There was never any doubt that she would leave Bellepoint when she graduated from high school and make her home someplace else.

College had been much of the same—a decision she'd made and worked hard to achieve. No wishing and no praying for it to come to fruition. Those things had no place in her life, and she'd made it to thirty years old just fine without them.

With that thought came a familiar resolution, the sensation that had gotten her through each day of her life. She scrubbed her hands over her face and pushed the covers away from her legs before turning to sit on the side of the bed. The desk was on that side of the room and on top of it was a stack of old sketch pads. Across from the sketch pads, pushed to the back left side of the desk next to a heart-based lamp, was a mug that read "Make each day your masterpiece." The mug was filled with her sketch pencils.

Ella eased off the bed, her bare feet moving across the carpeted floor until she stood at the desk. Her fingers moved slowly over the tips of those pencils, memories pouring into her like a flood. She'd drawn Mt. Bellepoint, paying special attention to each detail of the mountain's peaks, the rippling waters of the lake below. The flowers in Mrs. Pettigrew's garden with all their bursts of color, a "rainbow maze" as she used to call it. Inspiration bubbled in the pit of her stomach and before she could think better of it, she was pulling out the chair to sit at the desk. Pongo, the stuffed dalmatian that Aunt Addie had given her, was still occupying that space, and she grinned as she lifted him out and set him on the edge of the desk.

Sitting in the chair as an adult felt oddly comfortable and she instantly reached for one of the sketch pads. In the next instant, it was open and a pencil was in her hand. Bottom lip tucked between her teeth, she let go of every thought—all the worries, fears, and hesitations. Inspiration seeped into her mind, trickled down to her shoulders, and landed in her fingertips as she moved the pencil over paper.

Ella had no idea how long she sat there, but she didn't bother to move until a nervous chuckle bubbled free. Feeling as if she'd run a marathon on a brisk winter's morning, she sat back in the chair and exhaled. Her gaze fell to the sketch pad and what she'd drawn. Laughter erupted at the gingerbread people marching along the countertop at Beaumont's. Their destination? A grilled ham and cheddar sandwich, with a slice of sweet potato pie on the side.

Now she really did laugh at the memory of the pie-eating contest that she'd never had a chance of winning and the sandwich she hadn't known she'd missed so much. What wasn't captured in the picture was Seth's easygoing smile. Or the way he rubbed his thumb across his chin when he was contemplating something. Or those perfectly shaped full eyebrows that any woman would pay an aesthetician generously to create for her.

No, she hadn't drawn Seth. And why should she? She wasn't a teenager anymore.

That thought had her closing her sketch pad slowly and dropping the pencil back inside the mug. Last night Seth had commented on teenage Ella never smiling. He had no idea that was because teenage Seth never had a clue how much she liked him.

He liked grown-up Ella's smile. She was certain that was because grown-up Ella knew better than to waste her time falling for another guy. Two guy-related heartbreaks in her lifetime were enough to add to the pile of the other pain and sorrow she'd experienced. The broken engagement to Ben had sealed that deal.

This time last year, she thought every aspect of her life was finally in sync. After she and Ben had dated for eight months, he proposed at a Labor Day cookout they attended at his grandparents' house. Although a public proposal had always been on her list of things she never wanted to experience because the expectation of a positive ending to the scenario placed an unfair amount of pressure on the recipient, she was elated. The ring was blindingly gorgeous and a future of happiness had been on the horizon. She'd believed wholeheartedly in that moment that all would be well, and so after she told Aunt Addie about the proposal and the ring, she began planning her wedding. A few months later, still in a state of bliss, Ella had stood in Ben's living room helping him put up his Christmas decorations. Like her mother, he preferred a star to adorn the top of the tree and he wanted Ella to do the honors.

The moment she held that star in her hand, she thought it was a sign from Mama that it'd been too long since she'd believed and that it was time to make another wish. She closed her eyes, rubbing her thumbs over the frosted gold-and-white star, and let the wish whisper through her mind: *I wish for a big, lavish summer wedding in the park.* There'd been a tingle at the base of her neck the moment her eyes opened again. She dismissed it and hung the star.

One week after the new year, Ben received the job offer and

decided that he no longer wanted to get married. The Christmas jinx had once again proven its point.

"Fool me once, shame on you," Ella muttered. "Fool me twice, shame on me." Shaking her head as she left her room, she headed to the bathroom and whispered, "Never again."

Forty-five minutes later she walked down the stairs, this time wearing tan-colored snow boots, dark blue jeans, and a blue, gray, and white plaid shirt. It seemed to be appropriate tree shopping attire. And besides, this wasn't a date. She had to remind herself of that after catching herself spending the last fifteen minutes fussing with her hair. It didn't matter how she looked—not that she'd ever go out of the house looking a whole mess, but she wasn't trying to impress anyone today. Least of all Seth.

A clanking sound followed by raucous laughter stopped her at the foot of the stairs, and instead of walking back to the kitchen for a cup of coffee, she continued forward to open the front door. She expected to see the snow-lined street, bushes sprinkled with white, and perhaps a few children who were happy it was Saturday and were out having a snowball fight. Not her aunt, holding the base of a ladder, colorful twinkle lights draped around her scarf-covered neck, and a man standing at the top of that ladder.

"Aunt Addie? What's going on?" Ella stepped out onto the porch.

"Oh, good morning, sleepyhead," her aunt said in a cheerful voice.

In addition to the deep purple scarf, her aunt had on a light gray coat, black slacks, and black boots similar to the ones Ella now wore. Aunt Addie sported a wide grin as she lifted a hand to clear from her face the wisps of hair fluttering beneath the purple wool hat she wore. "I didn't know when to expect you to come down for breakfast, but coffee's been brewed. I'll be in just as soon as we finish out here."

"As soon as 'we' finish?" Ella had come to a stop beside her aunt on the porch, and when Aunt Addie tilted her head to look up, Ella did the same.

"Mornin'!" The man with the deep umber complexion and low-cut, winter-white beard smiled down at her.

Ella found a small smile and waved. "Mornin'."

"This is my friend Oscar," Aunt Addie told her when Ella's gaze returned to the woman still grinning broadly to her right. "He came over to hang the lights around the porch like I wanted. You know, after you and I declared we weren't getting up on no ladder."

"I wouldn't want either of you up on this ladder," Oscar yelled down. "It's a little shaky, Addie. You could use a new one. Besides that, I wouldn't want you to fall."

There was no mistaking the tone of apprehension in Oscar's voice, just as Ella couldn't deny the earnest look he tossed down to her aunt that stretched well beyond just ordinary concern. Okay, so her auntie had a man. Ella resisted the urge to chuckle or give her aunt a high five. In fact, she thought this was more than a little cute. Aunt Addie's husband, Johnny, had passed away a few years before Ella came to live here, and in all the time that Ella had been in Bellepoint, she never saw her aunt with another man. "You go, Aunt Addie," she murmured to herself.

"He's such a gentleman," her aunt whispered as she leaned in close to Ella. "Ooh, those boots look nice on you. When I went into your room to open the blinds the other day, I saw all the shoes and boots you'd unpacked and lined across the wall by the closet. There weren't any snow boots and I figured that by Christmas you'd definitely need them."

Ella looked down at the boots that had still been in the box sitting on her bed when she came home last night. "Thanks for ordering them for me. They're definitely going to come in handy today since I have to go out to Grant's farm to get twelve Christmas trees."

Aunt Addie waved away Ella's gratitude, as she often did. "I've gotten the hang of online ordering," her aunt said. "I can place an order before noon one day and it shows up by eight the next day, or sometimes another day later. It's the easiest thing."

Ella figured her aunt was most likely paying extra for the convenience of such quick delivery, especially since Bellepoint was two hours from the nearest city. She'd have to ask her to pull up the account she was ordering from later so she could check out just what the store was charging her in delivery fees. But in the meantime, her gaze went back up the ladder to Mr. Oscar, who'd just reached down for her aunt to hand him the next set of lights.

"I've got a few minutes before Seth picks me up," she said. "Let me go in and get my coat and then I'll come and help you."

"Oh, Seth's coming to get you?" Aunt Addie asked. "You two are going to the Christmas tree farm together?"

Mr. Oscar had returned his attention to hanging the lights while Aunt Addie stared at Ella with a raised brow.

"Yes. We ran into a snag last night with some of the sponsored trees and were forced to come up with a plan B. This morning we need to ask Mr. Grant if he'd be willing to donate the additional trees so our new sponsors will only have to decorate them."

Aunt Addie nodded. "Oh, I see."

And so did Ella, but she didn't like the thoughts she could see playing out on her aunt's face. "No, you don't," Ella said lightly. "We're just going to get these trees. It's work for the committee you put me on, remember?"

"Oh yes, I remember very well," her aunt said. "I remember exactly what it's like to tell yourself something is much simpler than it is."

The quiet look exchanged between Aunt Addie and Mr. Oscar was borderline uncomfortable, and Ella instantly felt like a third wheel. If her aunt was experiencing a new love with this man, hip, hip, hooray for her. But Ella was certain there wasn't anything of the sort kicking off between her and Seth. That ship had long since sailed and left Ella behind.

"Fine," she said. "I'll just go in and get my coat and wait for Seth."

Mr. Oscar moved slowly down the ladder. "Hold on a minute, Ella," he said. "I'd like to invite you and your aunt out to the ranch tomorrow night. It's my family's annual holiday housewarming."

"I didn't know you were doing that this year, Oscar," Aunt Addie said. Her tone had softened and Ella sensed there was some history behind this gathering Oscar was speaking of.

Mr. Oscar nodded. "I know, and I felt mighty bad about that. But things with the ranch were looking a little sketchy in the last couple of years and I wasn't feeling too much in the spirit of things." The older man nodded as if he'd made peace with that time and decided to move on.

"My grandmother started the tradition of inviting the townsfolk out to the ranch to see all the Christmas decorations. She loved to cook, so there was always a huge spread of delicious food and cakes." He shrugged. "Now, I don't go too heavy on the cooking, but you know my nephew Jason has been working at Beaumont's. Well, Gail and Don came out to the ranch a few weeks ago proposing to do all the cooking for the event if I just took care of the decorations."

"You didn't do all that decorating yourself, did you, Oscar?" Aunt Addie asked, then looked to Ella. "Oscar's family owns the Mountaintop Dude Ranch just on the outskirts of town. They've been out there giving horse-riding lessons, hosting rodeos in the summer, and taking in guests for as long as I can remember."

Mr. Oscar smiled proudly. "I worked that ranch all my childhood. Left for the Marines for about twenty years, then came back when my daddy was dying. Been trying to keep the place afloat since then."

"And you're doing a good job. Especially if you're ready to open it back up to the town for the housewarming." Aunt Addie shook her head. "I sure remember all the good times I had out there. All the pretty lights and the nice homey feeling of the holidays."

"Seth came out a few days after his parents left and he brought some of his frat brothers with him. They got out all the old decorations and set things to right again." Mr. Oscar nodded. "Yeah, the younger generation sure has showed out to help in these past years. I can't thank Jason enough for rerouting his school plans to move here with me. Getting right lonely out there by myself."

With that, Mr. Oscar's gaze once again found Aunt Addie's and held. Ella felt torn between sighing with happiness for her aunt and making a hasty retreat for fear she might be front and center to some PDA she definitely did not want to see.

The crunch of tires over snow caught her attention and she

looked out to the street to see Seth pull up in a big white pickup truck. The truck was nice enough—it was a newer model and built for rugged terrain travel. It didn't quite fit Seth's personality in her estimation, but that wasn't what really struck her. She startled at the loud bark that sounded as soon as Seth put the truck in Park. And her heart leapt at the sight of the tall dog covered in chocolate-brown curls in the back.

She was elated.

Seth watched as Ella stood on the tips of her toes at the back of the truck so she could reach Teddy's head. With both hands, she scratched behind the shameless dog's ears while Teddy groaned with pleasure.

"He's adorable!" she crooned and made some other sound that Teddy appreciated so much, he lifted his front paws and tried to get out of the truck and closer to Ella.

"He can't stay!" Ms. Addie yelled from the porch, and Seth turned to see her shaking her head.

After parking the truck, he got out to greet Ms. Addie and Mr. Oscar, who was standing amid strings of lights and a rickety old ladder. Ella broke away from Teddy long enough to run into the house and back outside just as quickly, and he bid his good mornings and informed Mr. Oscar that a light was out on one of the strands. Now Ms. Addie and Mr. Oscar smiled and waved as if they were sending their kids off to the prom.

Seth didn't know how to respond to Ms. Addie's comment, so he simply waved at them in return before moving closer to get a handle on his dog.

"Okay, okay, sit down, you goof! She's coming with us." He touched a hand to Teddy's back to ease the dog down into a sitting position. "If you don't get in the truck, he's gonna jump out and have you running up and down this street playing with him."

All his words were obviously being ignored by his dog and Ella as she continued to ruffle her fingers through Teddy's thick coat, and Teddy attempted to lick her hand and keep the sitting position Seth had asked of him. Something shifted deep inside him at the sight, and his lips spread into a grin. These two were hitting it off much better than he'd anticipated. He remembered Ella mentioning that she wanted a dog when she lived here with her aunt, but he wasn't sure where she stood with dogs these days. Did she still love them? Hate their mess? Was she horribly allergic? As he'd driven over here this morning, all those thoughts raced through his mind.

Sure, they were also accompanied by the memory of seeing her so happy when she finished with her phone call last night. There was something about her standing beneath the glowing lamppost and the sparkling Christmas lights while big, fat snowflakes had fallen from the sky that was almost surreal. It was like nothing he'd ever imagined before. As he stood at the mailbox, he was struck silent while watching her pace and talk on the phone, sounding professional and passionate all at once.

The sound of her voice, the hitch that broke her words when her ire rose, the lace of humor that appeared when she was excited—all were like music to his ears. And for a man who'd dedicated his life to melodies and lyrics, that was saying something profound. Something he didn't want to explore.

Clearing his throat to bring his thoughts back to the present, he said, "At this rate, all the trees will be gone by the time we get out to the farm, and then what are we going to do about the auction?"

That question was successful in snapping her out of her Teddy-trance and she looked over at him. "There're acres of land and thousands of trees out at Grant's," she said. "But I'm certain I've only ever met one Teddy."

"Oh no, what have I done?" He mock-groaned because he couldn't really express how good it felt to see and hear her reacting to his dog in this way. "He's an attention hog and you're falling right into his trap."

She'd already shifted her attention back to Teddy. "He's gorgeous and friendly and I think I might be in love."

That last word had his breath catching. She was referring to his dog, not him. It took several times for those words to float around in his head before Seth got a handle on the weird reaction.

"Well, can you put all that affection into the cab of this truck so we can get going? I don't want to miss lunch."

She stepped away from the back of the truck, giving him a smirk before fully grinning. "I guess if we have to make your stomach a priority, then we should get going."

"Hey, I'm gonna be driving all the way out to the farm, hauling trees into the back of this truck, and then bringing them back to the church. I need sustenance for all that manual labor."

She'd already started walking around to the passenger side and he followed, opening the door for her before she could reach for the handle.

"Your chariot, milady," he said with a mock bow and a quick chuckle.

"You can't call Teddy goofy when you're acting like this," she said before climbing into the seat.

But she was smiling when she looked at him again. A smile that had her dark eyes alight with humor and Seth's chest filling with joy.

Ella was right—Grant Christmas Tree Farm featured acres and acres of land, and a good majority of that land was filled with rows of Christmas trees. From Fraser fir to balsam and white pine to all the variations of the spruce, over a dozen types of trees were ready for cut and purchase. And while there'd been plenty of years Seth recalled coming out here to hunt for the perfect tree, the highlight of his trips always was venturing into the large red barn that had been converted into a Christmas market.

Once he parked the truck and they'd both climbed out, she insisted on taking Teddy's leash, and the dog who liked to give Seth a five-to-seven-minute runaround every day stood obediently while Ella hooked it onto his collar. Traitor. That's exactly what his dog was—a stone-cold traitor. Now Teddy walked beside Ella, looking up at her with his big brown eyes, expecting an absent pat on the head or a tasty treat to be offered at any moment. Since Ella was the one walking with him, Seth had stuffed a few of Teddy's treats into her coat pocket in case she needed them for reinforcements. Of course, Teddy had watched him do this and was now casting hopeful gazes at her coat pocket every few steps they took toward the large barn.

"This place looks like a Christmas explosion," Ella said when they walked through open barn doors.

"It's *the* go-to spot for all your Christmas needs," he told her. "That's what the website says, and I stand by that claim."

"Who even needs all this stuff?"

"You're kidding, right?" he asked and then shook his head when she gave him a definitely-not-kidding glare. "C'mon over here to the wreath and roping section."

She followed without qualm, but he knew she really just wanted to get those trees and be gone. Bringing Teddy along may have been his best idea because as long as she was with the dog, she didn't seem as anxious to get the work done and get back to whatever else she had going on.

"Smell that," he said and then sucked in a huge breath, closing his eyes to the fragrant pine that filled his nostrils.

"It's pretty strong—it'd be hard to miss," she said, then glanced down at Teddy, who was also sniffing about.

"It's the scent of Christmas." He moved closer to a set of crates piled high with pine ropes. "No matter where I am, whenever I smell pine I think of Christmas. I know people often associate the holiday with the sounds—Christmas carols, bells, and stuff like that. But I always link it with the scents."

"So you don't like the carols? Because that's pretty strange coming from the music teacher, slash musician, slash choir director."

He didn't miss the sarcasm, but he chose to latch onto the lift of her brows and the light that had remained in her eyes throughout their ride here. Those were the things that let him know there was hope for wrangling her into some semblance of Christmas spirit. After all, he had told her he would teach her a thing or two about the true feelings of the holiday. He knew she'd agreed only to get them moving with the auction plans, but Seth wholeheartedly planned to move forward with his teaching. It was, as she'd just pointed out, one of his jobs.

"I love Christmas carols, especially the hymns and the jazz renditions—"

"Really?" she asked with a quizzical stare. "You like the jazz Christmas carols?"

"Yeah, why's that so hard to believe? Do I look like I only enjoy certain types of music?"

She shook her head. "No, that's not what I meant." She pushed back a few twists that had fallen from the loose bun she'd pulled them back into today. "My mother loved jazz music. She listened to it all the time, but especially the Christmas carols. She loved it so much she even named me after—"

"Ella Fitzgerald," he said, wondering why he'd never connected those dots before. Most likely because all he'd ever known about Ella's mother was that she had a beautiful voice and had sung first soprano in the choir with his mother when they were teenagers. The older choir members from the church often spoke of her. When Ella moved to Bellepoint, he recalled his mother mentioning how much she resembled her mother in looks and how her mother had left town when she married, not too long after they graduated from high school. He'd always wondered if following in her mother's footsteps hadn't been what led Ella out of town so soon after their graduation as well.

"Yeah." She nodded. "She had all these albums, crates of them that she kept in our third bedroom along with some other stuff."

They were walking along the farthest wall of the barn now, where rows of plain and decorated wreaths, long stretches of pine garland, and buckets of pine cones were stored. At the other end of this section were two long tables with benches where the wreath-decorating lessons took place.

"Who were her favorites? I mean, other than the obvious."

She answered with a small smile at first, that light in her eyes being replaced by a slightly haunted look. He knew that look well and resisted the urge to reach out and take her hand. It wasn't like he hadn't touched her before, but more and more, each time he brushed a hand over her shoulder or took her elbow to lead the way, he found himself wanting to let that touch linger. To stand closer to her more often. It was odd and possibly unwelcome on her end, so he was trying really hard to stop.

"Oh," she replied with a sigh. "There were so many, but the ones I recall singing along to most were Nancy Wilson, Nat King Cole, Lena Horne, and Dinah Washington. I think she must've played them more and that's why I always think of them first whenever the topic of jazz comes up."

"You said she had the albums, not the remastered CDs?"

She nodded. "She had most of her favorites on CD too, but she said she'd been collecting albums since she was a young girl and didn't want to part with them. She even had a vintage record player that she would play them on. I used to laugh because they sounded so crackly at times."

Knowing that sound well, Seth gave a funny moan. "Ah man, that is the best sound. That authenticity, the slight echo that always makes it seem as if you were right in the studio with them as they recorded. I've got a Cab Calloway vinyl that took a month's worth of paychecks to purchase, but whew, the sound."

"Don't tell me you've got a vintage record player too?" Her eyes narrowed a bit as she quirked her lips and glanced at him.

He shrugged. "Then I'll tell you that I have three of them. But only one that I use. The other two are just displays, even though they're functional as well."

She laughed. "You do know there's a thing called a CD player now? And artists even release their music on streaming services."

"Technology might be the new way of the world, but it's not the best way. Especially not in music."

"Whatever you say," she replied and kept walking.

When she paused to touch a wreath that had been decorated with fresh pine cones and holly berries, he found himself following the movement of her hand. She wore white gloves that matched her coat, and they seemed awfully bright against the green and red of the wreath. Her fingers trembled slightly as she touched it and her gaze remained focused. He wondered what she was thinking. Was it about the music they'd been discussing? Or the memory of her mother loving that music? Pushing the conversation in the direction of her memories could be tricky, as sometimes people only wanted to hold the memories of a lost loved one in their heart and mind. It could be safer that way—he knew from experience. But sharing those memories could also help keep that person alive in the only way they could be in this world.

"What was your mother's favorite Ella Fitzgerald song?" he asked.

She waited a beat, but he assumed it wasn't to try to think of the song. No, he was certain she knew what that was the second he'd asked the question. What she needed time for was to find the courage to share what he knew felt like a very intimate thing between her and her mother. Ella had been an only child, so he knew the years she'd had with her mother had been without any competition from a sibling. She would've cherished every second of their time together and been broken the moment her other half had been taken from her. He stuffed his hands in his pockets because he was about to touch them to her shoulders, to whisper that he knew exactly what she was feeling, but he refrained.

"It was a Christmas one," she said, her voice so soft in the big, busy market that he'd had to step closer to hear her. "Mama loved Christmastime the most. There were two albums—one that was all gospel carols and then another that she'd explained to me was secular music." A small smile ghosted her lips and she gazed at him before returning her attention to the wreaths.

The next one she touched had even more pine cones pressed into the circle but was also accompanied by painted wooden stars. Her fingers paused over one of the stars.

"The one album had a white cover with some type of animal—it looked like a giraffe, but it had a horn and I always thought it was the silliest thing to be on a Christmas album cover."

Seth felt a momentary tightness in his chest as he pictured exactly the album cover she was referring to. "*Ella Wishes You a Swinging Christmas*," he said.

"Yeah." She looked back at him again. "That's the one. Mama loved 'Have Yourself a Merry Little Christmas.' She always played that one first when she pulled the holiday stuff out on the day after Thanksgiving."

"That's when my mother starts decorating too."

She shook her head. "I'm telling you, that's the most pointless process to go through."

"I don't know, I think it's kind of therapeutic."

She huffed.

"Wait, just hear me out. We go through all year experiencing the ups and downs of life. Then here comes a time of year when you can just focus on the magic of the season. On the important things like hope, love, peace. It's the only time of year when the majority of the world is of one accord."

"Not me," she said softly. "I'm not in the majority."

"Why do you dislike Christmas so much?"

She paused, then pulled her hand away from the wreath. That hand went into her pocket as she stared down at the floor, or possibly Teddy, who was sitting beside her now.

"Not getting wrapped up in all this decorating and singing and stuff isn't a crime," she said.

"No. It's not."

"And there's no law saying I have to believe all the silly notions and myths that go with this one day of the year."

Seth did touch her this time. He'd taken both his hands out of his pockets and closed the small space between them, resting a hand lightly on her shoulder until she turned around to look at him. "But there's something about this time of year that I know you believe in. I watched you in church on Sunday singing along with the choir, reading the scripture. You believe in Jesus' birth."

"Of course I do," she said and shook her head. "But that's not what all this is." She pulled her hand from her pocket and waved her arm around to gesture at everything in the barn.

"You're right, to an extent." He let his hand glide down her arm until he could take her gloved hand. "All this is the tangible examples of the hope that Jesus' birth brought to the world. These decorations are a visible reminder for people that love, peace, and hope are obtainable."

She shook her head. "I don't need the tangible," she replied. "It doesn't last."

Then she eased her hand from his grip and walked away.

CHAPTER 9

They'd selected eight of the twelve trees so far and Ella was happily out of breath as she bounded around another corner trying to keep up with Teddy, who'd been doing a great job selecting some of the trees. For this to be her first time ever handling a dog, she thought she was doing pretty well. Especially once they made it out of the Christmas market, because that's when Teddy thought it was time to run free.

After a brief conversation with Moses Grant, who'd conveyed his uncle Ralph's apologies for being under the weather today, Ella and Seth had his firm commitment to donating the needed trees. And Seth had immediately launched into his explanation of each type of tree and which were the best ones to get for the auction. Almost two hours later, Seth was still giving her tree-shopping lessons.

"I still say it would've been much easier to purchase artificial trees. That way they could be included in the box that'll be delivered to the winners," she said when she released the slack on Teddy's leash so he could wander at least five trees down from where she and Seth now stood.

Seth dropped his hand from the branch he was examining. He touched every single tree they considered. Touched it, surveyed it, talked about it. If she didn't know better, she'd think he worked at the tree farm and not at the local middle school.

"Remember, I told you Christmas trees are an agricultural commodity. By choosing real trees each year, the sponsors are supporting the farm that Ralph and his family have maintained all these years." He wandered over to the next tree, leaning in to sniff it.

Ella resisted the urge to say what she knew she'd also said a time or two today—*all* the trees smelled like pine.

"Besides that, real trees absorb carbon dioxide and other environmental gases. They emit oxygen and preserve green spaces. And after the holidays, they can be recycled or composted. They're a valuable renewable resource."

"You sound like an infomercial," she said and moved behind him.

He glanced back over his shoulder. "I'll take that as a compliment."

She didn't bother to tell him that this light banter between them was so much easier than the heaviness of the conversation they'd shared inside the market. Ella didn't know how they'd gotten on the topic of her mother and how Christmas really made her feel. One minute they were surrounded by wreaths, and the next she was going on about her mother's love of jazz and Christmas. The pain had moved in like a dull ache then, settling in the center of her chest as a reminder. But there was also a light surrounding the memories that had come to her mind as she shared with Seth. It hadn't been that way before as she'd recalled her mother's love of music and thought about some of the other albums that would often play in her house. Mostly, Ella's memories had reserved themselves for her dreams, coming to her in the dark of night, haunting her, she'd always thought. Today, they were the topic of a conversation she'd never anticipated having with anyone.

"This one." The words just tumbled out as she stood in front of a tree, staring at it while her thoughts sifted through her mind.

Yanking off her glove like she'd seen Seth do the moment they started down the endless aisles of trees, she reached out to touch a branch. "It has more of a blue-green, silvery color. And it feels softer." She pressed the needles.

"How does it smell?" He stepped up beside her, but he didn't touch the tree. Instead, he watched her in that curious and assessing way he always seemed to have.

She wondered what he thought when he looked at her like that. Was she a puzzle he was trying to figure out? A person he pitied because she didn't love Christmas? A woman who he'd never known had a crush on him?

Pulling away from that last thought, she did as he said and leaned in closer to sniff the tree. "Oh! It smells kind of citrusy."

He smiled as if he knew she'd have that reaction. "It's a white fir, also called a concolor fir. It releases a citrus aroma when the needles are crushed. Nice, huh?"

"Yes, it is." There was no use denying it—she did like this one a lot.

"This one isn't as popular as the white spruce, which we've got a few of because it's great for holding ornaments. But last year when Moses joined us for a basketball game and we were out at lunch later, he talked about how it was gaining popularity, so they planned to plant more."

"That's right," she said with a nod. "You were into sports too. That and music seemed to dominate your life when we were young. I mean, when you weren't hanging around your rowdy friends." She'd had to follow up with that even though she'd gotten past the James-and-her-leotard thing. But she didn't mean to let him know just how much she recalled about him all those years ago.

He shrugged. "My parents always encouraged us to use our talents and God-given gifts."

"Yeah," she said, nodding. "Mama used to say that too." And so had her aunt and Ms. Phyllis on many occasions. Ella always thought that's what led her to the gallery and the career she was trying so desperately to save. But after this morning's impromptu sketching session, she wondered if that was actually true.

Her thoughts were interrupted by a round of barking that had her jolting. It startled her so much—or she'd been so deep in thought that she forgot there was a dog nearby—that she dropped one hand from the tree and the leash from her other hand. Teddy took off running and Seth sighed before calling after him.

"Oh no!" She ran after Seth.

Teddy dodged between the trees in ways that neither she nor Seth could. He seemed focused, like he was chasing something, but then again, as he ran them in a complete circle, maybe not so much. Eventually, she started to laugh at the thought that they might never catch this dog. He'd been so good on the leash all this time, even though Seth insisted the dog liked to have free rein. Now she was seeing that and thinking he'd picked the perfect place to exercise that control. There were trees and snow-lined paths as far as the eye could see. There were also other people out here shopping for trees, but the ones closest to them were laughing and had joined in the great Teddy chase.

When the dog surprised her by bolting out from between

the trees directly in front of her, Ella lunged forward to grab his leash. But he saw her effort and decided he wasn't quite through playing, so he ran in the opposite direction. She missed her chance but was determined to get him this time, so she ran a little faster. Most of last night's snowfall had been walked down to a manageable trek by now but it still crunched under her booted feet, making an all-out running speed almost impossible.

The dog was close and the leash dangling behind him was even closer—all she had to do was gain a little more speed. That's what she was thinking as she continued moving, focusing only on the leash. Until something—or rather someone—slammed into her, sending her falling backward to the ground.

Grunts and laughter surrounded her as she lay on the ground and looked up to see Seth's always-grinning eyes staring down at her. There was the faintest splash of light brown freckles across the bridge of his nose, and she wondered why she'd never noticed them before. Truth be told, she'd never been this close to him before.

"Sorry," he mumbled, his gaze locked on hers.

"No need to apologize," she replied.

Neither of them said another word, nor did they move, which was beyond odd since they were lying on the snowy ground in the middle of a Christmas tree farm. And his dog was still running wild.

Heavy panting sounded just as she had that thought, and Teddy's warm breath greeted her when she turned her face slightly to the side.

"He's back," Seth said with a grin as he reached for Teddy's leash and carefully got to his knees before standing.

He immediately extended his other hand to Ella and she accepted the help up. Seth held on to Teddy's leash this time, but the dog still had enough leeway to dance around the two of them happily, almost as if bringing them this close had been the pooch's intention all along. She didn't know how she felt about that idea. Or what to do with the warmth that had spread throughout her chest as she and Seth were locked in that very intense gaze. And when Teddy yipped again, plopping down to sit right next to where she and Seth stood, she pushed the thought out of her mind.

"Goofy dog," she said and then reached down to pet his head.

While her mother had loved the jazz Christmas tunes, Aunt Addie preferred the more soulful hits and never failed to blast *A Motown Christmas* every day of the season. On Sunday afternoon, as they got ready to prepare the potato salad and Christmas punch that Mr. Oscar had insisted Aunt Addie bring to the holiday housewarming, Stevie Wonder's rendition of "Someday at Christmas" blared through the speakers of the old stereo in the living room.

It had started to snow earlier in the afternoon as they left the church, and when Ella came downstairs a few moments ago, she'd peeked through the front windows to see that it was still falling steadily. Not as heavily as it had a couple of nights ago but at a pretty trickle of white that only added to the atmosphere. She turned to stand in the living room and look around for a few moments. During their decorating days, Aunt Addie had happily hung both their stockings on the mantel, rubbing her hand over the crooked letters of Ella's name. Whoever thought of glue and glitter as the perfect mix was sadly mistaken.

The Christmas tree stood proudly in the corner. It was an artificial one because Aunt Addie said it was easier for her to maintain here alone. It was barely dark outside, but her aunt had already plugged in the lights so that they blinked and cast color throughout the space. Ella moved toward the dining room, noting that her aunt had changed the white tablecloth on the dark cherrywood table that had been in this room since the day young Ella arrived. It was a sparkly red one now, and in its center was a crystal bowl full of red, gold, and frosted-white bulbs. On each side of that bowl were her aunt's favorite candleholders, which now held red taper candles. On Christmas evening, Aunt Addie would light those candles as they sat down to dinner.

"Ella Bee, you comin' in to help me?"

Christmas had even made its way into the kitchen as red ribbons holding small artificial wreaths hung from the top of each window. The only real pine in the house came from the long lengths of roping they'd hung along the tops of the cabinets and draped around the back door. The tea towels that her aunt loved to keep hanging from the oven door handle and the drawer handles had been switched to red-and-black plaid ones with different Christmas-themed slogans on them—"Merry and bright," "'Tis the season to be jolly," and "Christmas cookie calories don't count!"

And it was warm in the house. It always seemed warmer inside around Christmastime. Grown-up Ella knew that was because it was snowing outside and therefore the heat was on, but nostalgic Ella held that close as a holiday memory.

Seth had said yesterday that he associated certain scents with Christmas. For Ella, it was feelings—the warmth of the house, the quickened pattern of her heart at the sight of the fully decorated Christmas tree, the bubble of laughter at her messily decorated stocking. She'd forgotten about those things.

"I'm here. What do you need me to do?" She spoke as she went directly to the sink and turned on the water, squeezed out some soap from the snowflake-shaped dispenser, and washed her hands.

"Finish chopping the celery and onions while I get this punch together." Her aunt stood at the counter in front of a huge plastic bowl that she now poured a can of pineapple juice into.

"The potatoes are cooling, so by the time you finish chopping, I'll be ready to start mixing the salad," Aunt Addie continued.

"I thought Mr. Oscar said Mama Gail was doing all the cooking," Ella said as she wiped her hands on a tea towel and moved over to the table where her aunt had placed the celery and onions that needed to be cut.

Ella had learned her organization skills from Aunt Addie, and she pulled out a chair and sat at the table after seeing that the cutting board, knife, and bowl to put the veggies in were already out. The celery had also already been washed and the onions peeled. She was certain her aunt didn't really need her help preparing these two things—she'd most definitely been preparing for parties and get-togethers all the time Ella had been in Philly—but she was glad to be here right now doing so.

"He did, but before he left here yesterday, he asked if I'd make these two things. And you know I don't mind. I've been making some of my specialties and taking them to functions all around town since I was a teenager."

Ella began with the onions because she hated the smell and wanted to get them out of the way first. When she was at home and had to cut onions, she always wore plastic gloves. A fresh lemon and hot water did wonders to remove the stench from her hands once she was finished, but she'd discovered that the extra layer of protection was even better. She didn't dare ask for gloves today. Aunt Addie was an old-school cook—she'd laugh her right out of this kitchen if Ella told her she needed gloves to chop onions. The thought had a smile ghosting Ella's mouth as she got started.

"Mama used to tell me about you both being in the kitchen with Grandma. She said y'all used to cook for all the church functions," Ella said.

"We sure did." Aunt Addie chuckled. "Nell could bake. She used to make the best 7UP pound cake on the East Coast. That's what my daddy used to say, since at that time he was the only one of us that had ever traveled outside of Bellepoint."

"Why didn't you ever leave?" Ella had always wondered that. Her mother told her about how excited she'd been to leave town with her new husband to start their new life together. But Aunt Addie had stayed.

"It's my home," her aunt replied. "Your grandparents left me this house when they passed, and me and my Johnny, we sold our little place by the lake and moved in here. It made sense because I felt closer to my parents and to Nell here in this house where we grew up."

"I don't think Mama missed it here." At least her mother never talked about wanting to move back to Bellepoint, not even after Ella's father passed away.

"No, she didn't. Not like I would've anyway. Nell had another path to walk."

The path that walked her right to her death.

Ella clenched her teeth with that thought, her hands freezing momentarily over the onion. After a slow breath, she got back to work.

"I've got a job interview tomorrow," she blurted out. She saw the email yesterday when she returned from the tree farm with Seth, but she'd just confirmed with a call this morning and hadn't gotten the chance to tell her aunt before now.

"Oh really? So you're heading back to Philly tomorrow?"

Ella didn't miss the sound of disappointment in her aunt's voice, and it caused an unwelcome pang of guilt to surface. "No, this gallery is actually in Pittsburgh, but the curator is on vacation in Florida for the holidays. I spoke to her assistant earlier and they want to fill the position by the first of the year, so that's why we're going to do a Zoom interview tomorrow."

"Working on vacation." Aunt Addie tsked. "People got to learn how to slow down."

"Time waits for no one, Aunt Addie."

"Yeah, but life's not a race, Ella. It's a journey to be experienced and savored. You can't savor anything if you're spending every second of every day working your fingers—or in your case, your brain—to the bone. When do you have time to get out and experience things?"

"Well, I've experienced plenty of heartache, thanks to the Christmas jinx, I can tell you that." But no, that wasn't what she wanted to tell her aunt. Too late: the words were out into the atmosphere and she knew her aunt was latching onto them quick.

"You still believing in that foolishness?"

She looked up to see her aunt walk the two empty cans of pineapple juice and the empty two-liter bottle of ginger ale to the recycle bin she kept near the back door. On her way back, Aunt Addie stopped at the table to sit across from Ella.

"There's no such thing as a jinx, baby. Things just happen— good and bad. That's how the world works."

"Why?" Ella asked, feeling like she was that eleven-year-old orphan all over again. "Why did my mother have to die?"

"Should it have been another little girl's mother?" Aunt Addie waited expectantly.

Ella didn't respond.

"The Lord never puts more on us than we can bear, Ella," Aunt Addie said. "And He put you right in my arms the minute I got the call that my baby sister was gone. I rushed to the city and ran straight to you, holding you while we both cried."

That was the truth. Her aunt's had been the first and only hug Ella accepted. She didn't want to be touched by any of the nurses at the hospital, their neighbor Mr. Randolph, or anyone else who showed up in the hours after her mother's death. But when Aunt Addie arrived, Ella had all but fallen into her arms. She held tight to the only other person she'd loved as much as her mother and prayed every prayer she knew that the Lord wouldn't take her away too.

Ella set the knife down because emotion had her hands trembling. "Mama said wishes came true, so I wished. But my wish didn't come true that year. Instead, my mother was taken away." Taking a deep breath, she let it out slowly. "And when I thought it was time to try again, I wished again."

"And that fool of a man left you." Aunt Addie shook her head and reached out to take Ella's hand. "Nobody ever said life would be easy. That doesn't mean you shouldn't still live it to its fullest. We don't get to pick the time and the place that our prayers, or wishes, are answered. And sometimes, Ella, sometimes the answer to our prayers is no. We don't like to accept that, but it's the truth.

Yes, no, or wait. Those are the three answers the Lord gives. It's our faith that carries us through whichever answer we receive."

Ella shook her head. "I don't have it. Not anymore."

"Then you've gotta find it again. Everything happens for a reason, and maybe you've been circled back to Bellepoint for that reason. Maybe there are some answers for you to find here."

Discomfort came in the flush of her cheeks and the twisting of her stomach. She eased her hand away from her aunt's and went back to cutting the onions. "I came back because you asked."

"I've been asking for years," her aunt said with a wave of her hand as she got up and went back to making her punch.

"Well, I had a job all those years and now I don't. So there wasn't any real reason to say no this time."

"You seemed right happy to see that dog yesterday." A change of subject that Ella wasn't sure she should feel good about. "I haven't seen you smile like that in ages."

"If you'd let me have a dog when I lived here, I probably would've smiled all the time." The thought lessened the pressure she'd started to feel in her temples.

"And I would've been cleaning up after that dog every second that you weren't in this house. No thank you." Aunt Addie moved to the refrigerator to grab the bag of oranges and fresh cranberries she'd asked Ella to bring back from the Christmas market.

"Teddy's a sweetie pie," Ella said. She neglected to mention that the sweetie pie had her running around the farm like she was an out-of-retirement track star yesterday.

"So is his owner," Aunt Addie said as she pulled a knife from the block and started slicing the oranges. "You know this is Seth's first year working on the committee. Funny that it should also be the first year you come back to town."

"Coincidence," Ella said and hoped that was the end of this conversation.

"No such thing. Fate is what it is."

Fate. Prayers. Wishes. Faith.

Her aunt had a word for everything. A saying for every situation. A supposed solution for every one of Ella's problems. Well, Ella didn't have any of those things. She also didn't have a job or any idea of what her life would look like after Christmas.

"If you stop sitting over there focusing on all the things you don't have or can't control, your mind might just open up to new possibilities. New beginnings. This is the time for it, you know. Rejuvenation. It's a gift from God. Honor Him and that gift by standing still in this moment. Think about the life you've been living in a thoughtful and meaningful way. Then be intentional about the next steps you take."

"Yes, ma'am," she replied in the hope that this conversation would indeed finally end with her seeming acquiescence.

Her aunt began singing the next song that played—"Jingle Bells" by Smokey Robinson and the Miracles. Aunt Addie loved herself some Smokey Robinson. Ella started to sing along too, allowing herself to get lost in the tunes and the relaxation of cooking. But hours later, when they'd delivered the food and drink to the kitchen at the Mountaintop Dude Ranch, her thoughts had circled right back to one of her aunt's words—*fate*.

"Hey, Ella," Seth greeted as she stood by the window looking out to the evening sky and contemplating her talk with her aunt.

"Hey, Seth," she replied and thought about that word again.

Was she meant to be back in this place, at this time, with this man?

CHAPTER 10

The Mountaintop Dude Ranch consisted of a huge stone-and-log-front ranch-style house, five guest cabins, a stable, and a large pen for riding lessons and performances. From April through October, the place was abuzz with families and individuals who'd booked packages that included hiking, horseshoes, volleyball, horseback riding, hayrides, campfires, and fishing. During the winter months—namely November and December—the seventy-five-acre property was magically transformed to resemble a rustic Christmas wonderland.

"You did all this?" Ella asked Seth as they made their way from the living room in the main house to a spacious family room.

She and Aunt Addie had arrived early to see if Mr. Oscar and Jason needed any additional help, but Mama Gail; Seth's father, Don; and Max were already here. So were a few other women from the town and the ranch staff, so Ella didn't need to do anything other than explore the house and take in the decor.

"Not by myself," he replied. "Jordan and a few of our other frat brothers came out to help. A couple of them have girlfriends, so they were here too. We all wanted to help make this place as fabulous as it has been in previous years."

He smelled good tonight—like a mixture of dark spices and a hint of earth. The faded jeans and forest-green hoodie he wore yesterday had been exchanged for black slacks and a slim-fit gray sweater. A different pair of black boots were on his feet. They still had the hard rubber soles made for trekking through dicey terrain but simultaneously managed to give a business-casual appearance.

"I don't think I ever paid much attention to MBU or the fraternities or sororities coming out of the school. What other things do you and your brothers do here in town?"

With one hand in his front pants pocket, he continued moving until they were tucked into a corner of the room, away from the small groups of other people who'd begun to file into the space. "I'm in the alumni chapter now, and as part of our mission statement, we're dedicated to building leadership, community service, and brotherhood. We do a lot of work at the children's hospital just outside of Bellepoint, as well as host a few outreach activities at Theta Psi Mu Pi Pi Community Center over on Collegiate Boulevard. And then there's our annual gala that helps fund local scholarships."

"Wow." It was an instant reply that matched the shock she felt at listening to him. When she'd asked the question, she didn't imagine their organization doing so much. "I don't think I ever took fraternities that seriously."

"Let me guess: when you were in college you only heard about us regarding homecoming, the parties, or step performances." The comment was followed by a mild chuckle, but there'd been a hint of tension in his tone.

"I apologize if that was offensive," she said. "But honestly, I just went to class and studied. The most socializing I ever did was attend the art department's fundraising banquets, and that was because I wanted to network with all the top art people in the area."

"Focused and determined," he said as they stood next to a mantel draped in pine garland and white lights. "That part of you hasn't changed."

She shrugged, not certain how she should take that remark. "Don't fix what's not broken."

He nodded. "I guess you've got a point there."

"Well, look at our two committee members," Ms. Nancy said as she approached, wearing a brilliant emerald-green dress. "I hope you two aren't talking about the auction tonight. This housewarming is strictly for socializing and eating. Seth, I hear your parents have prepared a classic southern-inspired feast for tonight."

Seth met Ms. Nancy's comment with a warm smile and another nod. "Yes, ma'am. You know my dad's originally from Montgomery, so he's added a lot of his family's recipes to the menu at Beaumont's."

"Delicious recipes," Ms. Nancy added. "Howard and I have been thinking about this meal ever since Oscar announced he was bringing the housewarming back. It's such a pleasure to be back on the ranch at this time of year. The Baines family always did know how to host a warm and welcoming function. Now, you two be sure to get yourself plenty of food and punch and just have a good time tonight. I hear there will be moonlight hayrides." The wag of her brows and wink were an over-the-top exit that left Ella surprised and amused.

But when she glanced over to see Seth's reaction, she found him frowning.

"You wanna get some air?" she asked in the hope that it might change what looked like a sudden shift in his mood.

When he returned her gaze, those lines that had formed in his forehead faded a bit and he cleared his throat. "Sure. I'll get our coats and meet you at the front door."

A few minutes later, they were outside, a light wind blowing the falling snowflakes in every direction.

"They're calling for at least a foot of fresh snow by the morning," he said after they made their way to a path at the side of the house.

The wood-plank guardrails of the path were draped with more pine garland and white lights, which came in handy in the dark of night. Red bows were placed on both sides about every six feet or so. Ella had worn her snow boots too, along with high-waisted beige corduroy flare pants and a dark brown sweater. She zipped her white coat up to her chin and pulled the hood tight on her head.

"It's beautiful here when it snows," she said, looking around.

The mountains were a dark shadow behind the house that looked like a cutout in the indigo sky. The main house itself had white lights along its border and around each window and wood post of the wide front porch.

"Yeah." It was a clipped reply that matched his now contemplative mood.

Ella had no idea what brought on the change. Their conversation had been upbeat and informative—at least for her—before Ms. Nancy appeared. Now he seemed to be brooding about something. It was probably none of her business—after all, she and Seth were only committee members—but she decided not to give him the option of being alone just this second.

"Teddy's a great dog. Is he okay to leave at home alone? I mean, do you worry that he'll chew up everything in the house?" Aunt Addie had made numerous comments about dogs being messy and a chore to take care of, both when Ella was young and last night when Ella had happily gone on about her day at Grant's farm with Teddy.

"He's been my lifeline." It was a solemn statement and based on the way he hurried to follow up, Seth knew it. "Rhonda wanted children. Four, she told me on our second date to the movie theater on Frankford Street. 'Let's adopt a dog,' she'd said. 'It'll give us practice taking care of someone besides ourselves.' That comment came much later, after we were married."

Love laced every word he spoke. She knew that sound well. Not because she felt that way whenever she spoke of Ben—to the contrary, she was certain there was nothing but loathing any-time she mentioned that man and his rude and hurtful decision to drop her and move to another country. No, it was how she knew she sounded anytime she spoke about her mother. Sure, Seth's was a different type of love, but it was still similar and her heart ached as he continued.

"We found Teddy on this online adoption site. Rhonda was meticulous about research. She spent three months looking up reviews for coffee machines before finally purchasing the first one I'd suggested." He chuckled and turned at the break in the railing.

There was open space in front of them now and, without the lights guiding them, darkness straight ahead. But he seemed to know where they were going, so she simply kept in step beside him.

"A coffee machine is an invaluable possession. And the right one can be a lifesaver," she added, hoping her tone was light enough to ease his mood.

"BB's sells great coffee," he replied.

"Yeah, but there are mornings when you don't want to get up and get dressed just to get your first morning jolt of happiness. And there's nothing like waking up to the smell of fresh-brewing coffee. Back in Philly, I have mine set to automatically brew at six every morning. But here, Aunt Addie is an early bird and is down in the kitchen preparing breakfast and beginning to think about the evening meal while she sips her first cup of java." She shivered and smiled with the thought, stuffing her hands deeper into her pockets.

"Rhonda didn't care much for BB's. She liked to brew her own coffee and sweeten it at home because she swore baristas could never get it right."

"They don't," she said. "Remember? Your name was on both our cups of coffee."

He laughed heartily then, and Ella grinned at the sound. When had she started enjoying Seth's laughter so much?

They continued in companionable silence for a few more minutes, until coming to a stop at the back of the stable. This large building had been trimmed with white lights too, and more pine draping and red bows. It seemed festive, even though it smelled earthy.

"I always knew I'd get married," he said, leaning his back against the building.

She followed his lead and leaned back beside him.

"It's what my parents did." He shrugged. "What I figured I was supposed to do."

"But you also fell in love." That was a prerequisite for her.

Even though she wasn't thinking about traveling that path again anytime soon, she wasn't a person who'd ever marry for anything less than love.

"I did," he said. "Rhonda was so easy to fall in love with. She was generous and funny. And talented. She sang contralto, like Anita Baker and Sarah Vaughan. That's how we met—she joined the school choir in her sophomore year. I was a junior and I'd left some sheet music in one of my professor's rooms. I heard her singing before I even saw her."

"And you knew she was the one." The words tumbled free from Ella's lips because they seemed to fit the mood.

"That cliché, huh?" he asked, but his tone was light.

"No, not cliché. Romantic."

He turned his head to stare at her and she turned her head to stare right back.

"I never would've pegged you as a romantic," he said.

"I'm not." Usually. "That doesn't mean I don't know it when I see it."

"Have you ever been in love?"

"Yes," she replied honestly. There was no sense in denying it, even though it hadn't ended well.

"Did you break his heart, or did he break yours?"

She inhaled deeply and let out a loud sigh. "I like to think of it as a lesson," she said. "Not a heartbreak."

"Fair. And what lesson did you learn?"

"Never fall in love again."

Their gazes held for what seemed like eons, snow continuously falling around them. When a huge flake plopped down onto her nose, Seth reached out and used a gloved finger to swipe it away. Time seemed to stop at that moment. At least,

Ella's breath slowed to an almost imperceptible rhythm as she watched him move slowly until he was standing directly in front of her.

"That's a pretty ominous statement you just made," he whispered.

Why was he suddenly whispering? More importantly, why did the now-husky timbre of his voice have her forgetting how chilly it was out here?

"It's the truth. I plan never to fall in love again." She wanted to do something with her hands. Lift her arms and wrap them around his neck perhaps? Pull him down closer? It seemed like the romantic thing to do. And that was weird since there was nothing between her and Seth. Thankfully, her hands were safely tucked into her pockets.

"Love isn't usually planned." He swiped another snowflake, this one from her chin.

Letting his finger linger there, he tilted her chin up and leaned in so that their lips were now just a breath apart.

"Love isn't like romance," he continued. "Romance can be planned. It can be thought out and contemplated to fit the circumstances. Does she like flowers? What's her favorite romantic song? How about candlelight?"

She cleared her throat. "All valid questions, if you're trying to make someone fall in love with you."

He shook his head. "I don't think you can make someone fall in love with you. Love is a natural thing."

He traced that finger along the line of her jaw, then cupped his hand to the side of her face.

"When it happens, it's like breathing. Like needing the same air as the other person to survive. It seeps inside your soul and takes a strong, permanent hold. Capturing you before you've had a chance to decide if it's what you want or not."

"I don't," she whispered, her eyes fluttering closed because his hooded gaze was too intense.

"You sure?" he asked, pressing into her slightly. "Be sure, Ella. Be very sure."

"I . . ." She tried to speak the words, but they tumbled in her throat, sticking there as her mind grappled with what was going on—what was about to happen.

"Stop me if you're not sure," he continued, this time tilting his head as he moved his mouth closer to hers. "Stop this, Ella."

She sighed and closed her eyes. "I can't—"

His lips touched hers before the word was fully out in the air. A gentle pressure, a tender touch, which deepened seconds later. Her hands did come out of her pockets now, her arms going around his waist to hold him close. Silently telling him not to end the kiss, not to stop this moment.

A moment she had no idea how she was going to feel about in the morning.

***

"Ayanna's singing off-key, Mr. Hamil," Tia Stewart announced.

"I am not! That's you sounding all stuffy like you can't breathe out of your nose!"

"Not true—I can breathe just fine!" Tia Stewart stood from her seat with her declaration.

Seth had been watching these two since they walked into his class forty minutes ago. They had a hot and cold relationship. One minute they were the best of friends, and the next, they couldn't stand to be near each other. It was typical preteen behavior, he thought, and normally he'd provide a little redirection and class would move on. But today was not only Monday; it was also the Monday after the kiss.

Closing his eyes to the dread that had weighed heavily on his mind all night, he stopped playing the keyboard he'd set up in the front of the classroom and stood.

"I think we've had enough for today," he announced. "Tia, you can collect the music and file it in the back bins correctly." When that directive looked like it might set off another argument between the two girls, he continued, "And, Ayanna, I'd like you to make sure all the instruments are properly stored. The rest of you make sure you've copied your homework from the board. Tomorrow we'll pick up with rehearsal. The theater club is counting on us to sing the songs that will accompany their rendition of 'How the Grinch Stole Christmas.'"

This led to a round of mumbling among all the children. Homework wasn't their favorite topic, and while singing in the school chorus was a part of their overall grade, several of them weren't thrilled with that either. Music was a part of the general curriculum and every student needed to pass his class to be eligible for graduation to high school. Same went for theater. It was an elective, but students needed three electives—one each year of middle school—to advance. Seth often worked in conjunction with Melanie Lombardo, the theater director, to ensure they were providing projects that the students could be enthusiastic about working on. They thought doing a classic holiday cartoon would work well with their sixth-grade students. Now he was thinking: not so much.

"Ask him."

"No, you ask him."

"I'm not gonna ask him."

This back-and-forth came from two of the boys in his class—Devon Gibson and Malik Sharp. They'd both come bustling over to the keyboard where Seth stood.

Folding his arms over his chest in his stern teacher stance, Seth gazed at them. "Devon, you ask me whatever it is the two of you want to know."

The taller boy frowned and the shorter one grinned.

"And tomorrow, Malik will read the drill instructions at the beginning of class," he said, to the shorter boy's chagrin.

Devon grinned then, but only for a second as Seth stared at him expectantly.

"Um, so, ah, last week Tia and her friends were in the cafeteria talkin' about you having a girlfriend. And we"—he pointed at himself and then to Malik—"me and Malik, we was like 'Nah, Mr. Hamil's cool. He's not checkin' for none of the single women in town.' Right, Malik?"

Malik nodded. "That's right. We had your back."

These were eleven- and twelve-year-old boys, who not so long ago were likely still afraid of the dark. Why were they standing here talking to him—a grown man—about having a girlfriend? Let alone declaring that he didn't have one, at least not in Bellepoint.

"Okay," Seth said, even though he still wasn't certain where this was going. "Thanks, I guess."

"That's not all," Malik said, nudging Devon to continue.

"Well, this mornin' Ms. Crantz in the office and Ms. Monroe from math class were talkin' and they said you were walking around with that new lady that came to town. And, well, we just wanted to know if you're 'bout to get married or somethin'?"

Where in the world had that come from?

The bell rang before Seth could respond and he counted that as a blessing.

"C'mon, let's go," Malik said, and the two boys moved quickly to their desks to grab their books and make a hasty retreat out of the classroom.

Seth dragged a hand down his face and was just about to push the incident aside and assist the rest of his students with exiting the room when he heard a boisterous chuckle.

"Kids weren't asking those kinds of questions when I was in school."

Glancing toward the door, he saw his father inching past a couple of students to make his way closer to where Seth stood.

"You heard that?" Seth asked, still a little stunned by the very mature conversation his students had just brought to him.

"I did. They weren't really whispering, so I'm sure a few other students heard it too." His father came closer. "In fact, I know they did because they were as intent on finding out your answer as those boys were."

"Wow," Seth said with a shake of his head. The word made him think of Ella's response to his description of his frat activities last night.

In the last twenty-four hours it seemed everything reminded him of Ella. And as if that wasn't enough for him to deal with, his students were defending his love life, or lack thereof.

"I don't know what to say," Seth continued as he walked over to his desk and took a seat in the chair behind it. "How do they even know this stuff?"

His father sat on the edge of the desk. Don used to be an athletically built man with a hidden strength that had come from years of physical conditioning in the Marines. Now, he'd filled out a little more but wore the extra pounds well in khaki pants, a burgundy turtleneck, and a black leather jacket.

"Two things," his father said, holding up one finger. "Television and the internet." He had put up the second finger before chuckling. "I used to tell your mother those things were gonna be the demise of normal life, and I wasn't wrong."

This wasn't a new conversation between him and his father. Don was as old school as they came. From his strict but loving southern upbringing to the regimen of the armed forces, Don was a stickler for rules and more than a little on the unyielding side when it came to change.

"I don't know that the internet tells kids to mind their teacher's business." While he was still thrown off by the subject of their conversation, Seth was a proponent of children using their own minds and asking the questions they desired answers to. How else would they learn?

"It doesn't teach them good manners, that's for sure," his father replied.

Seth couldn't argue that point.

"Well, I don't know what they're talking about," he said and lifted a hand to wave at the last of his students leaving the classroom. "What brings you by the school today? You don't normally come around here unless there's a program or something going on."

"You're right," his father replied. "And when I asked one of the ladies down at the office about your schedule, they said you didn't have a class right after this one so I figured I timed my visit right. Your students were actually talking about what's brought me here."

Narrowing his gaze at his father, Seth propped an elbow up on the arm of his chair. "What do you mean?"

"Well, you know there's nothing in Bellepoint that your neighbors, and their neighbors, and their cousin's neighbors don't know about just two point three seconds after it happens."

It wasn't news to Seth that everybody knew everybody else's business in Bellepoint. It was a way of life around here. So far he'd managed to stay on the outskirts of the rumor mill, though.

"I couldn't get to you last night to talk about this, and that's a good thing because that meant your mother couldn't get to you either. We were pretty busy in the kitchen at the ranch."

"Everything turned out really well," Seth said. "Mr. Ridgley singing the wrong lyrics to every Christmas carol there is while he led the moonlight hayrides was the talk of the evening."

Of course, that was after Seth and Ella had returned to the house. And after that kiss.

His father laughed. "And when he came back, he kept right on singing. Said he didn't care—nobody was taking his holiday spirit away. Nancy wanted to pop him upside the head when he stood beside her and sang so loud she had to move into the other room."

Ella had thought that was hilarious and Seth watched her enjoying herself, wondering what she was thinking about, aside from the unplanned entertainment.

"Your mother just kept saying she was glad he's not in the choir so we don't have to be treated to his voice every week." His father shook his head. "Now, somebody should have told *him* he was singing off-key."

Seth grinned but then tilted his head. "So you've been standing outside my classroom door long enough to hear that exchange too? What's up, Dad? Is something wrong with Mama or Max?"

Sitting up in his chair, he was prepared to take whatever action was required, and he waited for his father to reply.

"No, no," his father said, holding up a hand to still his son. "Nothing like that. They're both just fine. Well, physically, that is. As for the other, well, they had a two-hour phone call very early this morning. I mean, like, before we had to get to the restaurant at six. Then at lunchtime, Max came over and talked to your mother some more. They're both in a mood and waiting very impatiently to see you tonight at the caroling."

For the first time in many years, Seth was considering skipping the annual caroling that started in front of the church and ended at Town Square, where some of the stands from Grant's Christmas market would be set up for shopping, eating, and more merriment.

"Uh-oh," he said. "What are they waiting for me for? I haven't done anything."

Don arched his brows. "You went for a long walk with Ella Wilson last night, and when the two of you returned, you couldn't wait to get away from each other. Your mama, sister, and just about every other woman in town's talkin' about it today. As for us guys, while we have better things to do, being pulled into the women's conversation is impossible to avoid. Case in point, your two students having your back when their classmates were saying you and Ella are an item."

"We're not an item." He needed to clear that up first. "We're working on a committee together. That's all."

167

He wasn't sure if it was his words or his tone that had his father easing back and giving him a quizzical glare.

"You're certainly allowed to court any woman you want, son," Don told him.

"Nobody courts anymore, Dad. It's called dating. And Ella and I aren't dating." They couldn't be. Not only was she heading back to Philly after Christmas, but he wasn't ready to start dating again.

And while his family and Jordan might feel differently about that, Seth was the only one whose vote counted in that area. Well, he and his wife, whom he was certain wouldn't take kindly to him being with another woman. How many times had he apologized last night for the slipup? How much guilt could one person withstand before breaking completely? Both were questions that had kept him up all night and had him wanting to avoid running into Ella today.

Ella. The woman who'd once been the girl he had the biggest crush on. If he could've kissed her twelve years ago, his life would've been absolutely perfect and perhaps drastically different than it was now. Today, the shared kiss didn't seem perfect, and he had only himself to blame for that.

"But you know that you could date her if you wanted to, right?"

"I thought you said I didn't need permission." It was a snappy retort and he regretted it. Still, frustration boiled in his gut at a situation he neither liked nor possessed the power to change. "Look, we know how things work in this town. People talk about something until it's time to talk about something else. Ella and I going for a walk last night was nothing. Everybody will realize that soon enough."

Don eased off the edge of the desk. "Okay, son. You're probably right. This will blow over and people will move on to the next tidbit of gossip. But I'm tellin' you right now, you'd better come up with a better response for your mother and sister, because they're waiting for me to bring you down to the restaurant once school is out so we can pack up all the Sterno racks and pots of soup we'll be serving tonight."

Yeah, he'd forgotten about that. Even if he wanted to bail on tonight's festivities, to stay shut away in his house, just him and Teddy and maybe a good book, he couldn't leave his family hanging. Beaumont's always had a booth at Town Square for the carolers to get warm drinks and food when they finished walking the designated route singing about the joy of Christmas. Tonight wasn't any different—at least it shouldn't be.

But Seth knew that wasn't true. Tonight wasn't going to be like any other night because Ella would be there. And seeing her again would only continue to cloud his mind and distract him from the promise he'd made almost two years ago. There couldn't be any more kisses with Ella, not when he'd promised Rhonda he'd love her and keep her memory alive forever.

CHAPTER 11

S o we're just going to ignore the obvious?" his mother asked when Seth stopped moving and stared across Town Square.

While the rhythm of Bellepoint was no doubt centered around MBU and all the students who received their academic and a pivotal part of their life's education there, Town Square was the heart of the town. The space was more of a circular area with cobblestone streets making their way around a center stretch of grass and an ornate, turquoise street clock in its center. A walking path cut through the grass, and on summer days, the perimeter was filled with seasonal flowers and shrubbery that rivaled the most majestic of gardens. At Christmas, Grant's provided the tree that was decorated and lit during a special ceremony within the first few days of December. Tonight, that tree stood loud and proud, casting the Square and the town government buildings that surrounded it in a cloak of holiday cheer.

It was after seven in the evening and the carolers ended their trek through town by standing next to the massive tree and singing their last two songs of the night. This year's blue spruce stood sixteen feet tall and had been decorated with what seemed like every available ornament, bulb, bow, string of lights, strand of beads, and whatever else was Christmas-related in the town. It was a beautiful and magnificent sight.

Tonight, the multicolored lights blinking from the tree, along with the carols that had begun to play through the speakers mounted on some of the lampposts, were only a backdrop to the woman who stood talking to other members of the town. Her long twists had been pulled up into a high ponytail and she wore a black coat, belted tightly at her waist. Red gloves were on her hands and a look of pure enjoyment covered her face. The punch of awareness left him breathless, even while his mother's comment rang in his ears.

"We've been over this, Mama. Please, just let it rest," he said in as even and respectful a tone as he could manage.

Just as his father had predicted, his mother and Max were waiting for him to arrive at the restaurant, and then they'd both pounced. Questions about what he and Ella had talked about on their walk last night, about their time at Grant's tree farm, and about what he may or may not have felt for her in the past consumed the first forty minutes of his time there. Eventually his father had intervened, insisting that they needed to get the truck packed and head to Town Square before the carolers made it back. Seth looked around to see where his father was now, feeling like he might need another mediator between him and his mother.

"I just want what's best for you, Seth. It's been more than a year and I don't like seeing you alone," she continued.

"I'm not alone. I've got Teddy and my job, the restaurant, the town, Jordan and my brothers." He paused and took a deep breath before releasing it. "I'm fine, Mama. Trust me."

To punctuate those last words and help ensure that this

time his declaration would finally sink into her mind, Seth leaned in and kissed his mother's cheek. "Now, we'd better get ready for the onslaught. You see how many people came in behind the carolers?"

That did it. Reminding his mother that it was time for them to be of service effectively snapped her out of that hovering, gotta-get-her-son-matched-with-someone mindset, and she nodded. "Yeah, it looks like at least thirty or so have been walking around caroling this year. They sounded marvelous."

Seth agreed. The group had sounded really good coming into Town Square singing "Go Tell It on the Mountain." He wished he'd gone along with them, but the moment he saw Ella, he realized he'd made the right decision by staying here. It was obvious that doing things with her outside of the committee was giving the townsfolk ideas that he didn't want to encourage.

"Addie still does a phenomenal job directing the adult choirs at the church and the annual caroling. She and her sister, Nell, were always very musically talented," his mother continued.

She had moved away from him, going to the table with the Sterno racks and Crock-Pots behind him to check on the three different hearty dishes they were serving tonight: chicken noodle soup, vegetable soup, and his mother's famous beef stew. There were trays of honey corn bread and brownies, with and without walnuts, for dessert. Seth checked to make sure the stainless-steel carafes of snickerdoodle and regular hot chocolate were filled. There was also hot water to go with the tea bags he'd placed on a tray beside stacks of napkins. It seemed like they were ready for the crowd.

What Seth hadn't been ready for was Ella to come walking up to their booth.

"Hi," she said cheerfully. "Missed you tonight. I thought for sure you'd be at the church, but I should've known you'd be helping out here."

Words caught in his throat as he wrapped his mind around the sound of her voice and the sight of her smile close-up. It was a good thing she wasn't alone.

"Ella said she didn't have the opportunity to share our good news with you yet, so we decided to come over and tell you now," Brooke said.

Brooke had been a classmate of Max's as well as a member of the high school volleyball team with his sister. She was one of Max's closest friends, and as such, Seth saw a lot of her as they were growing up. Now she worked at city hall and ran all the social media accounts for the church.

"What's the good news?" he asked, because it was a lot easier to focus on the committee and whatever Brooke had to tell him than it was to accept that those nagging feelings for Ella he'd been trying to hide from all day were bubbling to the surface anyway.

"After being open for just about six and a half hours, we've already received over two thousand bids!" Brooke announced and clapped her gloved hands.

Ella matched her excitement with a little squeal of glee. "Isn't that amazing?" she asked. "I read that last year's bids reached thirteen hundred, and not even a full day in, we've already exceeded that goal."

"Ms. Nancy is ecstatic," Brooke continued. "We've got a great head start toward our financial goal and we don't even have all the trees on display yet."

"That's fantastic news!" The burst of excitement was just

what Seth needed. "But wait, I didn't think we had all the trees decorated yet."

Ella shook her head. "We don't. The artists that agreed to sponsor couldn't all make it to Bellepoint, so we've got six undecorated. They're shipping their decorations, though, and we should have them by Wednesday. Then we'll have to get some volunteers to help put them together."

"Oh, that won't be a problem," his mother chimed in as she came up to stand behind Seth. "If there's one thing the people of Bellepoint are good at, it's coming together to help. You just walk around here tonight telling people where you need them and at what time, and we'll get it done."

"That's a good idea, Mama Gail," Brooke said. "We can make it a decorating party. Have cookies and treats, hot cocoa, coffee. It'll be perfect! I'm gonna go find Ms. Nancy to tell her."

Brooke was gone before anyone could speak again.

"Well, that was easy," Ella said. "If I were back in the city, I'd have to prepare a memo asking for volunteers and then share it via email. I'd be happy to get responses from even just one-third of the people I asked."

His mother shook her head. "That's not how it works here in Bellepoint," she said. "Now, what kind of soup can I get for you? You must be chilled after walking all those blocks."

"Not really," Ella said with a shake of her head. "I'd forgotten how much fun caroling is. I don't think I've done it since . . . since I was in high school. Wow."

She hadn't gone caroling since she left Bellepoint. The sting of regret that she left before he'd had the courage to tell her how he felt about her pricked Seth's skin.

"You want hot chocolate?" he asked. "Our snickerdoodle flavor is really good."

Her gaze found his and held. "Sure. And, um, I'll take a cup of chicken noodle, Mama Gail."

When his mother turned away to dish up her soup, Seth reached for a cup and began to fix her drink. She watched him while he moved, but she didn't say anything. He knew she wanted to, though. The tension between them was palpable and he knew he was going to have to do something about it. They still had some time to work together on the auction that seemed to be going so well. The last thing he wanted was to disturb that dynamic—the auction was too important.

"You've been here for a while, Seth. Why don't you and Ella go for a walk," his mother said as she appeared beside him again and reached over the counter of the booth to hand Ella her cup of soup.

"I'm not leaving you here alone," he said, and not because he was dreading having this talk with Ella. He knew they needed to clear the air, but some of that crowd they'd seen before, in addition to a number of the townsfolk who'd already been mingling about the Square, were starting to walk in their direction.

"She's not alone," Max said, coming up behind Ella. "I'm back! And Daddy's coming. We had to go all the way back home to find the extra box of hot-or-cold cups because there weren't any more at the restaurant."

"Hi, Max. Love your boots," Ella said as she grabbed a napkin and soup spoon from the counter.

Max looked down and then back up to Ella. "Hey, yeah, I picked these up on a trip to the outlet mall a few miles outside of town. I keep showing up at the town council meetings telling them we need to clear some land out there by the lake and get one of those big outlet malls right here in Bellepoint."

Their mother tsked. "That's never gonna happen. We don't need all that development here. Folks want to go shopping at those places, they can just get in their cars and drive to them the same way you did."

This was yet another conversation Seth didn't want to take part in. He'd had the discussion with his mother, sister, and Rhonda a time or two before and had hated when he had to go against his wife, who agreed with Max.

"Cool," he said. "I'll carry your drink, Ella. There're some seats down by the bank entrance—you can sit down and eat there."

Ella caught his gaze and nodded.

"Y'all have a good walk," Max said with way too much cheer in her tone.

Seth tossed her a chilly look as he exited the booth and fell into step beside Ella. But his sister only chuckled as she took his place beside their mother and prepared to help serve. His mother didn't say another word and Seth didn't bother to look back at her, but he knew what she was thinking. A small part of him felt sad for her and the rest of his family. They loved him and wanted what they thought was best for him. He couldn't begrudge them for that. But he did want them to back off—only he knew what was best for him right now.

Ella ate her soup as they walked, blowing on each spoonful before putting it into her mouth. "This is so good," she said after a few minutes. "I love chicken noodle soup."

Seth kept his gaze ahead, his mind circling around how he wanted to start the conversation.

"What's your favorite type of soup?" she asked.

He shrugged. "Chicken noodle is okay. It's what Mama always fed me when I was sick."

"Oh my goodness, my mother did too! I used to think this was the only type of soup there was." She laughed.

He wished he could turn off the pleasure that always bloomed inside him at that sound. If he could just stop feeling this way about her, everything would go back to the way it was and he could be at peace. Silence fell between them again as they walked a little farther before coming upon the two rows of bright turquoise benches along the sidewalk in front of the bank. The benches matched the old town clock, and the spot was one of the stops on the town's trolley route.

About ten years ago, the Bellepoint Chamber of Commerce came up with the idea of a trolley to give tours around the town. It was supposed to be similar to the ones someone had seen when they visited family in New Orleans and had taken a guided tour. Bellepoint was in no way as big as New Orleans, nor did it have as many historical or just plain lovely sights to be seen—still, the COC had presented their case to the town council and received enough votes to purchase an actual trolley and create a route for it to travel. They charged tourists a fee to see the town, and to Seth's surprise, it had been pretty profitable. Mostly because of the families coming with their children to visit MBU. It was an added bonus that students were allowed to board the trolley to travel around town free of charge.

Ella sat down on one of the benches, and Seth lowered himself beside her.

"Look," she said the moment they were both seated. "We kissed. And the last time I checked, the rules said we can't go back and undo the past. Even though there are so many things I'd like to undo."

Well, she'd obviously been thinking along the same lines he was, despite her cheerful demeanor and chicken noodle soup small talk. Seth sat back and stared ahead to the people still walking along the paths and in the middle of the cobblestoned street in the direction of the Christmas tree and all the booths in the Square. The Square had been blocked off for tonight's event so people were free to walk anywhere.

"You're right," he replied. "We kissed." And it was a wonderful kiss.

He'd thought about it for hours last night before the guilt had gotten the best of him. "I'm guessing you don't want me to apologize for it."

Her eyes widened in surprise. "Apologize for what? You told me to stop you if I didn't want it. I didn't stop you."

Because she'd wanted him to kiss her.

"I probably shouldn't have done it, though. I mean, that's not what you came back to Bellepoint for."

"You're right," she said. "And speaking of that, I had a great conversation with someone about a job this morning. It's at a gallery in Pittsburgh, so I'd have to move if I got the position."

"That's great. I'm sure you'll get the job." For some reason he couldn't make his words sound happier. "And that's exactly what I meant by saying I shouldn't have kissed you last night. You're not staying in Bellepoint and I—"

"And neither of us are looking for anything romantic," she said as if she thought she'd known the rest of his sentence. "It's okay, Seth. We don't have to make this any bigger than it was. We're both consenting adults and we shared a kiss." She shrugged. "That's it. End of story. We can move on to the next thing now."

Was that the end of the story, though? For a few seconds he stared at her, wondering if he should ask that question. If he should tell her that she should be looking for romance because she deserved it. She deserved a man who could appreciate her and treat her well, who could love her without any reservations. Without his past commitments holding him back.

"What's the next thing?" he asked.

Ella finished her soup and resisted the urge to scrape the bottom of the cup, because it was really good. She was convinced that shredded chicken breast, savory broth, and tiny chunks of carrots and celery were the key to great chicken noodle soup. The noodles she could take or leave, but there was no doubt this was amazing, and it almost succeeded in totally erasing the anxiety that had been building in her throughout the day.

Every second that she didn't see or hear from Seth, she worried. Had he hated the kiss? Did he regret it? And why, oh why did she even care either way? He was totally correct when he said she hadn't come to Bellepoint to find romance. That hadn't been on her radar at all. And yet last night had been, hands down, the most romantic moment of her life. Come on, kissing under the moonlight while snowflakes fell softly around them? Romance to the second power was what that was!

It was also a colossal mistake.

He obviously agreed.

So okay, fine, they were on the same page.

"Well, tomorrow we definitely need to go over to the church to make sure all the trees are in place. Ms. Nancy said Mr. Paulie, the sexton, has been watering them, but I want to check the layout of the space again." She dropped the empty soup cup and spoon into a trash can sitting on the other side of the bench and reached out to him.

For a second he looked a little confused, but then remembered he was holding her cup of hot chocolate. His lips moved into a small, short-lived smile as he handed it to her.

"Sorry."

"No problem," she said. "Thanks for carrying it for me." She took a sip and groaned when the warm, flavorful liquid slipped down her throat. "This is phenomenal! Is there anything your parents don't cook or make well?"

"I've never liked okra, so maybe that's the thing," he replied. "But nah, it's one of the top requested vegetables whenever they cater something at the church, so I'm guessing it's just me."

Ella took another sip and crossed one leg over the other. "Nope, I don't like okra either. My mother used to have some elaborate recipe for it, but it never grew on me."

"So we have something else in common."

She looked over at him again. "What's the other thing we have in common? Oh, we both love Teddy."

"I was referring to the album you told me about on Saturday. The Ella Fitzgerald one that's your favorite. It's my favorite by her too."

"Oh." He hadn't mentioned that when they were standing in the Christmas market, and she wondered why he was telling her that now.

"Three Christmases ago, Rhonda gave me a remastered CD.

I knew it wasn't going to sound the same as the album, but she'd recalled that I said I liked it and she bought one for me."

That's why he hadn't told her—because it was a reminder of his wife. A slither of something akin to jealousy eased down her spine, but she quickly pushed it away.

"She had great taste and I can tell you loved her very much." The fact that they both seemed stuck in this vortex of grief wasn't lost on Ella, and she wished there was something she could do to help them both. As it was, she could always fall back on what had saved her for so long—focus on the future, not the pain.

"I need to get Aunt Addie a gift," she said and then stood. "Maybe I can find something at one of the booths tonight. You wanna come with me?"

She held out the hand that was empty and waited while he stared at it and then up at her.

"Sure, because I love shopping." Sarcasm dripped from every word.

She chuckled and then stared down at the hand he'd put in hers. "Oh, come on, it'll be fun. At least it's not a massive shopping outlet like Max wants to bring to town."

He groaned. "Oh, please don't tell me you agree with her."

Ella shrugged. "Okay, I won't tell you."

A couple of hours later, Seth and Ella turned down Tenderleaf Lane. They'd walked from the Square after Beaumont's and others had begun to pack up their booths. When Seth offered to walk her home, a part of Ella urged her to say no. To insist that she could walk home on her own. It was a gorgeous, if a bit brisk, winter's night and she was still riding high on the music, the good food—she'd gotten a smoked sausage loaded with mustard and fried onions from another stand, along with more hot chocolate from Beaumont's—and the friendly people. Besides that, they'd gotten past the uncomfortable memory of their kiss and had managed to shop and enjoy each other's company for the remainder of the time. There was no logical reason she couldn't accept the very chivalrous offer of a walk home, and so she had.

"You enjoyed yourself tonight," he said as they passed the fire hydrant on the corner. Despite what she figured might be some type of hazard, someone had wrapped sparkling silver garland around the hydrant and she smiled upon seeing it.

"I did," she admitted. "So go ahead and say it."

"Say what?" He feigned innocence.

She rolled her eyes. "Say that you told me you were going to teach me about the good feelings of Christmas."

"Oh, I don't think I taught you as much as I stood back and let you discover it on your own."

He carried four of her bags, while she had another three in her hand, her wristlet dangling from her left arm. She'd gotten way more than one gift for her aunt, as well as a few things to send Josie and Claire.

"I can admit that I've been bombarded by memories being back here after all this time. Sitting in church on Sundays, singing the hymns, strolling along the streets instead of jumping in my car and rushing here and there." She swung her arms, the bags slapping against her legs. "It's been really nice."

"Caroling is one of my favorite nights of the season," he told her. "Seeing the Square all lit up, people bustling about and simply enjoying that moment. It's definitely a highlight of living in a small town."

"You really never thought about leaving Bellepoint?" That thought still amazed her, even though Aunt Addie shared the same sentiment.

"I never really had a reason to."

Those words fell over them and Ella didn't know what to say next. A ridiculous thought popped into her mind—would Seth consider moving back to the city with her? There were hundreds of schools in the city. He could teach there.

A giant Santa on the lawn of one of the houses gave a guttural "Ho ho ho" as they passed it and they both laughed. Ella shook her head and inwardly laughed away the silly thought of Seth in the city with her. Hadn't they already decided they weren't looking for romance?

As they walked up onto the front porch of her aunt's house, she peeped in the front window to see Aunt Addie and Mr. Oscar sitting in the living room. They were side by side on the couch, sipping from cups of coffee and watching an old black-and-white movie on television.

"*The Bishop's Wife*," Ella said with a shake of her head. "Aunt Addie loves her old holiday movies as much as she does the music. Whenever I see one of her favorites, I buy it and send it to her. I know I bought her *The Preacher's Wife* a couple years ago and told her it was an updated version of the movie she's watching now."

"That's a great version. My mother watches it every year and Rhonda was a big Whitney Houston fan, so I've seen it more than a few times." Seth stood beside her. "But there's something to be said about classics."

She looked over at him. "Yeah, I know how you feel about your old-school music." It made her smile to know things about Seth. Growing up, she knew the things that were obvious, like the fact that he played whichever sport his friends were playing at the time and that he was often at the music store. But she'd never felt like she knew about the parts he didn't show anybody else. Similar to the way, she guessed, nobody had ever really known those parts about her. Still, the not knowing hadn't stopped her from liking him too much.

Would it make a difference if she told him about her crush now? Or was that just water under the bridge at this point?

"Oh!" she said, taking a step back from the window as another thought crossed her mind. "We can't go in with all these bags. Aunt Addie will ask what's in them. She's terribly nosy about gifts." And so was Ella, which was why the only gifts under Aunt Addie's tree right now were the ones her aunt had purchased for her friends, church members, and people around town. Whatever she'd gotten for Ella, she knew to keep hidden in her bedroom somewhere.

"I've got to take them up to my room before she sees them," Ella continued.

Seth shook his head. "There're way too many bags, Ms. Shopping Diva. Give them to me and I'll run them up to your room while you go in and distract the movie watchers."

He hooked all the bags he'd been carrying on one arm and with his free hand reached for the ones she held. Ella gave them to him.

"Your room's at the front of the house, right? The big windows with the lacy curtains," he said and moved toward the front door.

"How'd you know that?"

"I made it a point to know a lot of things about you, Ella."

Once again, she didn't know what to say. Seth had paid that much attention to her when they were young? Enough to know which room in the house she'd grown up in was hers? For all that it may have seemed weird—perhaps borderline creepy— something deep inside warned her that it was so much more.

She opened the door and stepped inside the house, warmth greeting her instantly.

"Ella Bee, is that you?" Aunt Addie yelled from the living room.

"Yes, ma'am!" she answered and then turned to Seth. "Hurry up."

Ella went into the living room. "Hey, Mr. Oscar. I didn't notice you two leave the Square."

"Oh, we left about an hour ago. Your aunt was getting cold," Mr. Oscar said and pointed to the plaid fleece throw now covering Aunt Addie's lap.

Ella removed her coat and placed it on her aunt's recliner. "Yeah, it's chilly out tonight."

"Did you enjoy caroling?" Aunt Addie asked.

"I certainly did," she replied, perhaps a bit too quickly. "I mean, I hadn't done it in so long. Singing and being with all those people who were just there to have fun and celebrate the season as well—it felt . . . good." Her words startled her momentarily because, just like what she'd admitted to Seth a few minutes ago, they were true. She had started to remember how much fun Christmas was, despite how much turmoil it had often thrown her into.

"Good evening," Seth said as he walked into the living room.

185

"Oh, Seth," Aunt Addie said and then glanced over to Ella. "I didn't know you were here."

"Hope you don't mind, Ms. Addie. I, uh, had to wash my hands so I came right in and used your powder room down the hall," he replied.

Ella resisted the urge to give him a thumbs-up at the quick thinking. As old as she was, Ella knew her aunt wouldn't take too kindly to a man going up to Ella's room. She hadn't thought about that until this moment, but thankfully Seth had.

"I don't mind at all. Why don't you come on in and watch the movie with us? I've got some cookies in the kitchen and some more punch," Aunt Addie said.

"No thanks," he said with a shake of his head. "I want to get back to the Square to make sure my parents got everything all packed up."

"Oh, okay, well, Ella, walk Seth to the door," her aunt instructed, and Ella moved to do what she'd been told.

"Thank you," Ella said when she and Seth were once again on the porch.

He shook his head. "No thanks necessary. Even though now I'm feeling like we're teenagers again, sneaking around so we won't get popped upside the head for sneaking around."

She joined him in laughing.

"I bet your aunt was a stickler about your boyfriends staying where she could keep her eyes on them. I know my parents were like that with me and Max," he said.

Ella's laughter stopped but she tried to hold the smile. "I didn't have that many boyfriends."

"I know," he said after a moment's hesitation. "Wendell

Cherry in ninth grade and Dash Lipman in the first part of our junior year."

"Wow," she whispered. "You really did make a point to know things about me."

He nodded. "I did."

"Why?" She had to know, because whether it should or not, she was certain it meant something to her now.

He stuffed his hands into the pockets of his leather coat. "Because I liked you." He cleared his throat. "I really liked you, Ella. For so many years, all I could think about was you."

Her legs wobbled and she prayed she didn't fall on her face. The warmth growing in her cheeks would certainly increase if she embarrassed herself that way. As it was, trying to decipher what he'd just said and reconcile it with what she'd felt all those years ago was taking her breath away. "I . . . I don't understand," she said softly. "Why didn't you ever tell me?"

There was a rough chuckle and then he looked away before returning his gaze to hers again. "You have no idea how many times I've asked myself that question. Back then, and now since you've been back. I still don't have an answer."

"I was scared to tell you that I liked you," Ella said since they were apparently putting all their cards on the table tonight. "Scared you'd think I was just silly old boring Ella. And then, after that leotard incident, I was just mortified. I could barely look at you after that."

"I thought you hated me and that's why you requested a seat change in chemistry class," he said.

She shook her head. "No. I didn't hate you. When my bag fell, the leotard wasn't the only thing that embarrassed me. My sketch pad was also in there, and I'd, uh . . . I'd drawn a picture of you." Waving a hand, she tried to play it off, even though the memory of those sketches still made her heart pound a little. "It was just something I'd doodled one day at the restaurant but I didn't want you to see it. Didn't want you to laugh at me for being so silly."

"Never that, Ella," he said, his voice softer. "I never would've thought anything you did was silly." Then he sighed. "You left so fast after graduation. I missed you for a very long time."

She'd missed him too, and the town, but she'd never wanted to admit it.

"Well," she said with a nervous chuckle. "We're certainly a pair of goofballs. Guess we missed that chance big-time."

He didn't immediately respond, his gaze boring into hers until she clasped her hands together in front of her, unable to keep them still.

"Yeah," he said finally. "I guess we did."

She nodded her agreement.

"Well, um, good night," he said and began walking down the porch steps.

"Good night, Seth," she called after him, but he didn't turn back to look at her. And Ella didn't wait for him to do so. She went into the house, closed the door behind her, and ran to her room like she'd done so many times before when she was younger. When it had felt like her heart was breaking into a million pieces.

CHAPTER 12

"T was the night before Christmas, when all through the house, not a creature was stirring, not even a mouse,'" Seth read from the book he held.

"Ewwww, mice!" A little girl who couldn't have been more than six or seven years old scrunched her face and shook her head.

"There's nothing wrong with mice," the boy sitting next to her said. "I've got one in a cage at my house. His name's Nemo."

"Nemo was a fish, silly!" the little girl snapped back.

The circle of nine children all laughed and Seth shook his head. "Let's get back to the story, you guys."

Ella hung back behind the shelf she'd been just about to pass in the library. During her successful Zoom interview yesterday, Pamela Tramonte, the curator of the Steven Werner Gallery, had mentioned they were trying to secure the work of a reclusive Nigerian sculptor for a new exhibit. Acting on the feeling that she would get the position—or on faith, as Aunt Addie had said yesterday when she came running down the stairs to tell her how well the interview had gone—she'd wanted to research the region where the sculptor was from and the history of his specific type of art beyond what Google had already told her.

Bellepoint's library wasn't as large as the one that she frequented in the city, but she was happily surprised to find two really great books. Mrs. Nixon, the librarian who'd been sitting behind the front desk twelve years ago when Ella had last been here, was gracious and accommodating when she told Ella to take the books home with her. Ella's response had been to remind Mrs. Nixon that she wasn't back in Bellepoint for good. She planned to just take the books over to one of the round tables in the corner and sit and read for a while. Story time had stopped her.

Ella clutched the books to her chest and leaned against the shelf, peering around its edge to watch. Seth sat in a chair holding a big book in his hands. He wore gray slacks and a navy-blue-and-white checkered shirt. The children formed a semicircle around him and, after settling down from the mouse discussion, now gave him their full attention.

His voice was riveting, hitting all the right expressive notes as he continued with the story. He'd even altered his tone to sound different for the narrator part and when Santa spoke, something that made a few of the children giggle and warmed Ella's heart. How had she never seen this side of him? Sure, she'd known he was easygoing, always ready to smile and be helpful—except for that one time when she believed she'd needed his help the most. Even that brief memory of the leotard incident didn't dissuade her from what she was now thinking about Seth Hamil.

He loved children. It was apparent in the way he calmly stopped to answer their questions and the way he engaged them after that question with some of his own. And when they laughed, he laughed right along with them, showing them that adults could have a sense of humor too. The book was almost finished when one of the girls, whose hair was styled in two puffs tied with pretty pink bows, went to stand beside Seth. She leaned against him, looking down at the book to read along. The glance Seth gave her, the look of pure adoration and enjoyment on his face, melted Ella's heart.

Seth had told her that he and his wife had wanted children. They'd gotten Teddy to prepare them for the responsibility of taking care of another living creature. Ella hadn't thought about children or building a family in a long time. To be honest, even when she was planning her future with Ben, she still hadn't considered children. They were both very busy in their careers—as evidenced by Ben's haste to accept a job in another country— they had active social lives that spun from those careers, and they'd enjoyed being with each other in between. They'd never discussed if someday a child could be wedged between all of that.

Now, Ella wondered what it would feel like to share in the creation of another human being with someone she loved. To watch as the best parts of them were manifested in the child. To raise that child with the same values that her mother and her aunt had raised her with. To love that child as unconditionally as her mother had loved her.

"If I'd known you liked *'Twas the Night Before Christmas*, I would've read it to you years ago," Seth said.

The sound of his voice and the close proximity at which he now stood startled her, and she almost dropped her books. He reached out to catch them, taking them into his hands before she made a huge mess. She couldn't figure out what to do with her hands. That had been happening way too much when he was around. Since the night of the housewarming, to be exact. The night she finally decided to wrap her arms around him and hold on tight. For obvious reasons, she had no intention of doing that again.

"Uh, thanks," she said and smoothed her hands down the fronts of her thighs. She wore light-colored jeans today and a green sweater. When she first entered the library and began looking around, she'd unzipped her white coat so that it now hung open.

"Checking out some books, I see," he said and looked down at the two she'd selected.

"It's something for work. I mean, for the job I interviewed for yesterday."

"Oh, did they make you an offer?" he asked and flipped through one of the books.

"No," she replied and shook her head. "Just trying to get ahead of the game. Just in case."

He looked up from the book. "You'll get it," he said. "You're smart, tenacious, and good at what you do. I don't doubt you'll get an offer."

Had he said that too quickly? Like maybe he wanted her to get another job to speed up her departure from Bellepoint? That shouldn't have made her feel as bad as it did.

"What are you doing here during the day? Shouldn't you be at the school?"

"I don't have a last period class on Tuesdays, so I usually come over here and do story time with some of the elementary school students who don't have anyone to pick them up once school is over."

"Does the elementary school still release before the middle and high schools? In the city, it's the other way around—high schools start earlier and release earlier, then middle and then elementary last."

He was nodding as she spoke. "Yeah, Bellepoint has their own way of doing things, so elementary students get out earlier. Unfortunately, that means if they have older siblings, those siblings won't be home in time to keep an eye on them until their parents get home from work."

"Too young to be latchkey," she said. "I get it, but what about day care centers?"

"There're a few babysitters around, but they mostly take infants and toddlers. We don't have an official day care center, although last year Ms. Phyllis's granddaughter was thinking about opening one."

"I see," she said softly. Bellepoint wasn't like the city, where there were hundreds of childcare centers, both private and home care. Some businesses even had on-site childcare facilities for their employees who might need the service. "That's a shame."

"Right. And that's exactly why Rhonda started the Morning Munchies program at the church—so children would have a safe place to go and get a healthy meal before school started."

There obviously was no program for that in Bellepoint's small school system, which was another stark reminder that Ella's lifestyle in the city was totally different from how this town functioned.

"It's a great program," she said. "And expanding it to include aftercare is needed. We're going to make the money on the auction, Seth. And then Rhonda's dreams can be fulfilled."

He gave her a slow smile then, but the action in no way encompassed how she knew he felt about this. The auction had been his wife's brainchild—a goal she'd wanted to build on—and with her death, Seth wanted to see that goal through. Ella understood that and commended him for wanting to keep his wife's legacy alive. And while it could have been cause for contention or envy, Seth's obvious love for his wife only endeared him to Ella more. Would she ever find a man to love her so deeply, to cherish her and her memory long after she left this earth? After all she'd been through, was that even something she wanted?

She wouldn't find the answers to those questions today.

Seth stayed to chat with her a few moments longer before he had to leave for a chapter meeting, and then she found a table where she could sit down and get into her research. But hours later, when she'd returned to the comfort of her childhood bedroom once more, she sat at her desk with pencil in hand and sketched a picture of two children—a boy and a girl—playing on the playground. If those children resembled her and Seth, that was her little secret. Just as her crush on Seth had once been.

"Tree number fifteen is titled 'Christmas Island.'" A dreamy look filled Ella's eyes as she stopped in front of the next tree.

The trees were positioned in rows of five in the center of the large fellowship hall on the church's lower level. At the front of the space, just inside the entry doors, a platform had been set up. On Christmas Eve, the choir would stand there to perform the hour-long concert. Rows of chairs were already positioned in front of the stage to provide seating for the guests. On the other side of the spacious room, six-foot-long tables were being set up. They would be covered with long white tablecloths and on the night of the concert and auction would be filled with delicious desserts and festive beverages.

Members of the church moved about hanging garland, stringing popcorn, and fluffing bows to be taped wherever they needed to be. Christmas filled the space with a happy holiness that crowded Seth's chest.

"There are flowers on the tree," he replied, returning his attention to the creation in front of him. "Big, colorful flowers that you don't normally associate with Christmas."

Beside him, Ella held a clipboard in one hand, a pen in the other. Her hair was in a ponytail draped over one shoulder held by a sparkly red, green, and white hair tie that his student Devon had given her. Devon, along with his parents, were members of the church and they'd all come to help with the final preparations for this weekend's event. Seth was surprised to see her happily accepting the accessory from his student and even more elated when he saw her quickly affix it to her hair. Exactly when Ella had fallen deep into the Christmas mood, he couldn't say, but he was immensely pleased to see it.

"If you lived in the Caribbean, you might associate these flowers with the holiday. Claire, the artist who came into town late last night, is from Trinidad. She decorated this tree with her Afro-Caribbean heritage in mind."

With that information, he decided the theme made a little more sense. Deep burgundy flowers as well as lavender and coral ones hung from the branches of one of the Fraser fir trees. Bright green, clear, and gold bulbs filled in the spaces between the flowers and puffs of burlap ribbon. Sprigs of palm and what looked like a few handmade ornaments added a burst of life. Even the dark wicker stand the tree was settled in played to the theme, and Seth couldn't help but nod in appreciation. "Okay, I can see that. It's different, but nice."

"It's already getting bids and we just put it up on the website late this afternoon when Claire finished with it."

"Is she still here? I'd love to meet her and thank her personally for agreeing to help at the last minute."

Ella shook her head as she bent down to adjust one of the empty boxes that was wrapped in brown kraft paper and tied with tropical ribbon to serve as a gift under the tree. "No," she said and then stood to face him. "She had to get back. She's got a meeting tomorrow with another gallery. I called them this afternoon to give her and her work a glowing reference."

"That was nice of you," he said.

She shrugged. "It was the least I could do. Now come on. I have two more to show you and then we're down to three that need to be decorated before we leave here tonight."

They made their way down the aisle. "'Fruit Basket' is number sixteen," Ella said.

Seth couldn't help it—he laughed. "Really? There're orange slices, tangerines, apples, and grapes on this tree."

"I know! Isn't it cool? I love how the artist sprayed the branches so they look snow-covered. It just makes all the colors of the fruit and these dried roses pop." She reached out to touch one, and Seth stared at her fingers moving from that one to the next. "Remember when we were out at the farm? It had snowed the night before, so the trees looked just like this."

Of course he recalled being at the farm with her. Teddy had acted out, and they'd ended up on the ground laughing. It was one of the best days he'd had in a very long time. There'd been more really good times with Ella in these past couple of weeks. Memories he knew he wouldn't forget, even after she left Bellepoint again.

They took stock of the rest of the decorated trees—a flamingo-themed tree; a black, white, and red checkered one; a Jack Skellington one; a rainbow-themed tree; a purple and silver one; and so many more—and continued to the end of the aisle where he had to pause and take out his camera.

"The Grinch!" He chuckled and shook his head. "I need my own picture of this one," he said and then turned so that he was standing with his back to the tree. "C'mon. This theme thing was your idea, so you've gotta get in the picture with me."

"You're so silly," Ella said and laughed. "But I told you this was a great idea." And with that I-told-you-so out of the way, she leaned close to him.

"Wait, I need both of us and a good chunk of the tree in the picture," he said and wrapped an arm around her shoulder before pulling her closer. "There," he told her, and as his arm held the phone away from them, he continued, "Say, 'Cheer up, dude. It's Christmas!'" When she didn't repeat the words but glanced at him with a grimace, he laughed. "Sorry, we've been practicing for the play at school, so I've memorized all the lines. The kids have added a little of their own flair to the script."

She laughed and leaned in even closer before saying, "Cheer up, dude. It's Christmas!"

Seth snapped one selfie and then a second one. He lowered his arm holding the phone but didn't drop the one around her shoulder. "If I don't get a chance to tell you this during the next few days when we're bound to be buried in preparations and other Christmas activities, thank you."

"What are you thanking me for?" she asked, her face just inches away from his.

"For making this a really wonderful Christmas."

A slow smile spread across her face, and Seth felt as if she'd reached inside his chest and actually squeezed his heart, the pressure was so intense. "Then I should definitely be thanking you for making this Christmas more than I ever thought it could be."

"Hey, you two. These trees aren't going to decorate themselves," Jordan quipped as he walked up, struggling to carry three boxes at one time.

"Oh, don't mind him," Max said, coming right behind Jordan. She had bags in her hands but smiled gleefully as she glanced at Seth and Ella. "He's just grumpy because they ran out of oatmeal raisin cookies."

Noting the way his sister's gaze lingered on them, Seth let his arm fall from Ella's shoulder and took a step away from her. He could see what Max was thinking by the lift of her brows and that smile that never wavered. It was a look of hope, of possibility. He recognized it well and had felt those same fleeting emotions here and there during the past weeks. Those feelings had often been followed by something else, and having that heavier emotion creep through his body this evening wasn't an option. So to tamp it down, he took a few steps away from Ella until he could grab one of the boxes from Jordan.

"Which tree are we decorating first?" Seth asked Ella.

She glanced down at her clipboard. "Um, tree number eighteen. Oh yay, it's one of the concolor firs I like."

Without further conversation, Ella moved around the small group and led the way to the empty tree.

"Okay, this one is titled 'Christmas with My Love.'" Her voice had lowered slightly at the last words as she stared down at her clipboard a few seconds longer than was probably necessary.

A loud thumping interrupted the moment, and they all turned to look at Jordan, who'd dropped the boxes to the floor.

"It should be called 'Cement Blocks on a Tree,'" he grumbled. "Those ornaments weigh a ton."

"Maybe you just need to spend a little more time in the gym, buddy," Seth joked and put his box down beside the other two. "You know, instead of thinking you can hoop."

Jordan smirked. "Oh, you got jokes, huh?"

"All right, let's not get distracted," Max said. "I've got a date later, so I don't plan to be here all night."

"A date?" Seth and Jordan asked simultaneously.

Max, who wore gray pants, black boots, and a fluffy gray-and-white sweater, looked up at them before shaking her head. "Yeah, I've got a real hot date and his name's Snowball."

"Snowball?" Ella asked with a frown.

"He's Mrs. Grantley's Pomeranian," Max replied with a chuckle. "She's away for the next two days visiting her sister before Christmas because she refuses to be away from her house on the holiday. But her sister is allergic to dogs, so Snowball is spending a couple nights with me."

"Oh," Jordan said with noticeable relief. Then he cleared his throat. "That's, uh, nice that you take your work home with you."

Seth saw that his friend was now avoiding making eye contact with him and had bent down to open one of the boxes instead.

"Yeah, that's what you do when you live in a town the size of Bellepoint and don't have any semblance of a personal life." Max set her bags down and began pulling stuff out of them too.

Ella nudged Seth and gave him a questioning look before

glancing from Max to Jordan. Seth got her inquiry and wondered the same but then quickly dismissed it. There was no way Jordan liked his sister. And as much as he wanted to see Max happy, he'd never gotten the impression that she'd even considered the possibility that Jordan could bring her said happiness. Now he felt all kinds of uncomfortable at the thoughts flickering through his mind.

"Okay," he said, rubbing his hands together. "This one has a red-and-white theme."

"It looks like a Valentine's Day explosion," Max said as she pulled out rolls of glittery red-and-white striped ribbon.

Ella knelt beside the box Seth had opened and pulled out a smaller, clear plastic box. She opened it and retrieved a red bulb dusted with white flecks and featuring a huge snowflake on one side. "This is lovely," she whispered.

Seth reached into the bigger box and pulled out a plastic bag. "This," he said with a frown, "is a mushroom."

Jordan reached into one of the boxes he'd carried and pulled out a bag with more red-topped mushroom ornaments and then another with red plastic candy canes. "She's in love with mushrooms and candy canes?" Jordan asked, his face scrunched in confusion.

Ella's laughter sounded around them, or at least that's how it felt to Seth. The warmth in the sound cloaked him and gathered him close until he trembled slightly. He prayed it was slightly and that, unlike the odd looks and conversation that had transpired between Jordan and Max moments ago, nobody else had witnessed it.

He was being ridiculous, he reminded himself as they continued to unpack the boxes and place the ornaments and bulbs, ribbons and lights on the tree. There was nothing romantic going on between him and Ella. Hadn't they already squashed that notion earlier this week?

Moving around to the other side of the tree so that he could see neither Ella nor anyone else for the moment, he recalled the night before last and the moment when he and Ella had stood on that porch admitting to each other that they'd once had secret crushes. When he went home that night, he thought about that exchange on repeat. How could he have not known she liked him? Especially when he'd been into her since the start of ninth grade when she came to church wearing a long pink skirt and white blouse. She'd worn her curly hair in one ponytail then too, but it was shorter and piled on top of her head in what he imagined was the softest Afro puff.

There was something about that day, as he'd watched her walk around the sanctuary during the offering and then sit in the same row at the back she occupied every Sunday after that. When service was over, she'd stood outside of the church waiting for her aunt. The sun cast a golden sheen on her deep mocha complexion. Her nails were painted white and her slender fingers gripped the small pink purse she held in front of her. There were pearl studs at her ears and when she smiled . . . well, she'd smiled that day. Because Wendell Cherry walked up to her and said something that made her laugh.

Seth dropped the white frosted bulb he'd been about to put on the tree.

"Oh, be careful." Ella came around to the side of the tree where he stood. "Don't break them."

She picked up the bulb while he stood there like a broken-hearted teenager all over again. "Sorry," he managed to mumble when she put the bulb on the tree.

Ella shook her head. "No worries," she said and then stepped back from the tree. "It's fantastic. Fun, whimsical, and romantic. I can see exactly why the sponsor titled it 'Christmas with My Love.'"

Seth wasn't looking at the tree. He was staring at Ella when he whispered, "I can see that too."

At a little after nine that evening, Seth reminded himself again that there was nothing going on between him and Ella. She'd convinced him to join her for a movie night when they finished decorating the trees. Once they arrived at her aunt's house, he agreed to watch some romantic holiday movie—currently the main couple, a prince and the woman he'd hired to be his daughter's nanny, were locked in a greenhouse by said daughter. Their commentary throughout the movie had proven that, of the two of them, Ella was definitely more of a romantic, as evidenced each time she sighed at the way the prince looked at the nanny. Seth was more entertained by the all-knowing and slightly condescending butler, who also had a little love match going on with the housekeeper.

"Oh, that reminds me of Aunt Addie and Mr. Oscar," Ella said as they sat on the couch staring at the television.

"What reminds you of them? The staff sitting in the kitchen having dinner?"

"No." She reached out a hand to give him a playful slap on

the shoulder. "You saw her note when we came in. 'Having dinner at the ranch with Oscar.' They're dating," she said, her tone a little dreamy.

She'd been talking that way the entire time they were watching this movie, and Seth admitted to himself that he liked it. He liked it a little too much. "Oh yeah?" He shrugged. "Everybody likes being out at the ranch at this time of year. I mean, you saw it—it's like a down-home Christmas with all the traditional decorations and lights and that homey feeling."

"You're right." She nodded. "It did feel really homey there, even though right now, only Mr. Oscar and Jason are living in the main house."

"I heard Mr. Oscar had been married while he was in the service, but when he came back to Bellepoint, he was alone. He'd had some medical issues with his leg, too, for a while, but mostly he'd come back to help take care of his dad and the ranch."

"That's sad and uplifting at the same time."

"Christmas can be that way," he said, and their gazes held for a few moments.

Then, to break the awkwardness of the moment—awkward on his part because in that instant he wanted nothing more than to kiss her again—he leaned forward and reached for something on the coffee table. "What's this?"

Ella leaned toward the table too, but she grabbed the bucket of half-eaten popcorn. "You know what it is. It's my delicious movie-watching snack that you turned your nose up at and refused to eat."

He chuckled. "One, I didn't refuse to eat that messy concoction. I tasted it and then couldn't get my fingers to stop sticking together, so I abandoned the effort." He looked back over his shoulder in time to see her stuff a few kernels of the popcorn she'd drenched with fudge and caramel syrup into her mouth.

"And two, I was talking about this," he said, ignoring how cute she looked with one leg tucked under her on the couch.

Sitting back with the sketch pad in hand, he flipped it open. He noticed the book when he'd first entered the living room and he knew exactly what it was because he saw one just like it in her room the other night when he went up to hide her shopping bags from Ms. Addie. But now, he wanted Ella to tell him about it.

For a second, she seemed to pull back a bit, her hand moving slowly as it returned to the bowl and eased another kernel of popcorn into her mouth. She had a bunch of napkins tucked next to the pillow of the couch on her other side—her sly admission that her favorite movie-watching snack was indeed messy—and she yanked one out to wipe her fingers.

"I used to love drawing," she said and set the bowl of popcorn on the couch between them. "As an only child, I had to find ways to entertain myself. I mean, Mama was great. We read together and cooked together. And of course, there was the singing. Mama loved to sing."

"My mother says she had the most beautiful voice in the choir," he told her. "She said whenever your mother had a solo, the Holy Spirit arrived and applauded."

His words encouraged a soft, wistful look to appear on her face and he wondered if Ella could sing like her mother. He'd heard her humming along to songs as they played on the radio during their ride out to Grant's farm, and then again earlier tonight when she and Max had challenged him and Jordan to sing every lyric of "The Twelve Days of Christmas." But that had been a rousing fun time, not a clear expression of a voice he sensed she'd locked away with all the other memories of her mother.

"I loved hearing her sing, but I didn't like being in the choir as much as she did. A month after I moved to Bellepoint, Aunt Addie took me to the youth choir rehearsal. And I did what I knew she expected of me for the first few months, but then Ms. Phyllis saw me sitting in the back of the church drawing one Sunday. I had her for art that year. Ms. Phyllis was wonderful at encouraging me and teaching me to embrace my talent. Then one Saturday morning I was getting dressed to go to choir rehearsal and Aunt Addie came into my bedroom. She picked up all the sketch pads I had around the room and opened them up on my bed. She said, 'This is what I want you to spend your time on. The talent that God has given you.' I didn't go to choir rehearsal that day or any other day after that."

"I saw the sketches hanging in your room upstairs," he said. He wondered if he should tell her more about what he thought when he was in her room, but he wanted to take a little more time to figure out what was going on here. Now, he flipped through the pages. "These are really good."

In her bedroom, he'd seen pictures she most likely drew during her childhood. Whimsical things, childlike things. Tonight, he found himself staring into the mischievous eyes of his dog bouncing through Christmas trees on one page. The Christmas tree in Town Square on another. The barn at the Mountaintop Dude Ranch on another.

"Why aren't you using this talent?" he asked. "You're so very good, Ella. Why are you so focused on sharing someone else's art with the world, but not your own?"

She reached over and eased the sketch pad from his hands.

With it in her lap now, she stared down at it, flipping through the pages just as he did. "Drawing was always cathartic for me. It filled all those gaps that were left by grief and loneliness." She traced the outline of Teddy's face and body in one of the many pictures she'd drawn of him. "It got me through some of the toughest moments of my teen years." Pausing to take a deep breath and release it slowly, she looked at him again. "But when I graduated from high school, I knew it was time that I took control of my life—that I dictated how I move through this world. I didn't stray too far from my artistic nature, studied hard, and campaigned for the job as curator. When I got that position, I felt accomplished. I'd done it, even without having my biggest cheerleader, my mother, by my side."

Seth felt those words deeply. He knew exactly what it was to need an anchor, something that would keep him from drowning in the pain of losing Rhonda. He'd chosen Christmas, Teddy, and the fulfillment of Rhonda's dreams. "I can understand that," he said.

She nodded. "Because it's what you do also," she said. "I see it in how passionate you are about this auction and taking care of the children. You didn't go away to try to become a singer because you wanted to be here, to share your musical talent with this town. Rhonda solidified that in you. She came along and added a piece to your puzzle and the two of you started great works together."

This wasn't how he thought this conversation would turn out. He'd hoped to talk to her about her drawing and maybe share with her an idea he had about that. But now those old swirls of pain circled in the pit of his stomach as he listened to her words. Words she'd spoken in a soft tone tinged with her grief as well.

"We're some pair," he said with a huff that was meant to keep the urge to cry at bay. "Two people still stuck in pits of grief and pain but caroling and decorating Christmas trees to cover the real torture beating around inside us."

She reached for his hand and Seth laced his fingers through hers. For endless moments they simply stared down at their entwined hands.

"I'm glad you came back, Ella," he whispered finally.

"I'm glad I did too," she replied.

They watched the rest of the movie in silence, except for at the very end when the nanny left the castle to return to her home in the US and the prince went to get her. Ella's sigh of contentment and the smile that followed pushed hard at something in his chest. So hard he gasped and recovered by commenting on being glad the couple had found their happy ending.

That night, after he arrived home and was taking Teddy out for his final time of the night, Seth thought about all the things he'd felt tonight with Ella. All the emotions that warred with the guilt he hated harboring. The feelings had seemed familiar and yet different. Seth had been in love before, and he thought Rhonda was and always would be the love of his life. But then Ella came back, and now his mind—and, he feared, his heart—was opening to another feeling. A deeper, more redeeming feeling than he'd ever experienced before. It both scared and exhilarated him, and kept him up much later into the night than was wise for him, or for Teddy, who'd parked himself at the foot of Seth's bed and refused to move.

CHAPTER 13

Biscuits and sausage gravy with a side of scrambled egg whites for you," Max said as she removed the plate from the tray she carried and set it down on the table in front of Jordan.

It was a little after seven in the morning on Thursday, and Seth had accepted his friend's text invite to breakfast. Jordan had sent the message around ten last night, after he called Seth twice, but Seth didn't answer either call because he was at Ella's watching a movie and eating gooey popcorn. The memory had him smiling.

"Oh, so you're excited to get your shrimp and grits and side of hash browns?" his sister asked sarcastically. "Just know that you're taking the early morning shift tomorrow since two of the servers are on vacation."

Not willing to admit the real reason for his smile, Seth only nodded. "You got it," he said and reached for his fork.

When Max walked away, he bowed his head to bless his food. Jordan did the same and they both mumbled "Amen" at the same time.

"I can help out around here if your parents are short-staffed," Jordan said. He picked up his knife and fork and began cutting the two palm-sized biscuits smothered in Seth's mother's home-made sausage gravy.

Seth knew from plenty of Saturday morning breakfasts at the Hamil home that his mother's sausage gravy was savory and delicious. But coupled with his dad's homestyle biscuits, they were a quick recipe for a long nap immediately following the meal. Since he had to be at work by eight thirty, he didn't have time for such a glorious morning. He was already in need of a nap after the restless night he and Teddy both had.

"You're not busy with work?" Seth asked after forking a bit of the creamy cheese grits into his mouth.

Jordan shook his head while he chewed. "Just sent off for approval the final drafts of that vacation home for the NFL star and his new wife." He picked up his napkin to wipe his mouth and continued, "But I don't suspect I'll hear from them until after the new year. I mean, he's deep in the season, so I know the last thing he's thinking about is a new house, but his wife will want to keep moving forward with the plans as soon as the holidays are over since she wants the place ready for their summer stay."

"Did you make many changes since the last time I saw the plans?" Seth asked. "That place looks like it's gonna be phenomenal. The views of the mountain and the lake are out of this world."

Jordan drank from the glass of orange juice he'd ordered. "It is, man. I'm jealous, 'cause the view from my place isn't half that great. But no, not many changes since you last saw it. A few more windows to the family room and some added space to the kitchen. Oh yeah, and the wife contacted me a couple days ago to say she wanted the second pool and outdoor kitchen."

"You said she was gonna want that option." Seth tasted the

home fries, letting the onions and other spices his mother added to the diced potatoes fill his senses. He loved breakfast food.

"Well, she's expecting their first child and said they're planning for a big family, so she wants to be sure they have all the living and entertainment space they'll need for the future."

"Smart move," Seth replied.

"Speaking of growing families," Jordan said, "how are things going with you and Ella?"

Seth finished chewing the mouthful of shrimp and grits, praying he didn't choke on the quick turn this conversation had taken. "How exactly does me and Ella connect to growing families?" he asked before taking a drink from his glass.

He'd decided against coffee or any flavor of hot chocolate this morning as the two were likely to remind him of Ella, and Seth was certain he'd thought enough about her last night.

Jordan chuckled. "C'mon, man, it's me you're talkin' to. Not your mother or Max."

Seth frowned. "Did one of them tell you to talk to me about this?"

"Nah," Jordan replied. "And I'm a little offended you'd accuse me of doing their bidding."

"You'd do anything my mother asked you to do, especially if it included a personally home-cooked meal." Seth said the words jokingly, but they were true, and not just because of the food. Jordan was adopted at birth, and his adoptive parents traveled internationally extensively. So when he came to MBU for its acclaimed architecture program and he and Seth forged their bond, Jordan decided to stay in town. He ran a small boutique architecture firm out of Bellepoint, advertising mostly via word of mouth and a little bit of strategic online placement.

Jordan pointed his fork at him. "Don't hate on my relationship with Mama Gail," he said and then forked more of his food into his mouth.

"Then Max told you to say something to me, didn't she? I've told her and Mama I'm not ready for any type of romantic involvement a million times. Why don't they listen to me?" By the way Jordan's expression sobered, Seth could tell his tone had held every bit of exasperation he felt right now.

"Stop," Jordan told him pointedly. "Your family loves you and you know it. And for real, man, we've all been worried about you."

"Worried about what? I'm doing just fine. I'm socializing, working, doing all the things I did while Rhonda was alive. I kept the dog who still betrays me with every other person he sees on a daily basis. I'm still active in the community, and every once in a while, I manage to beat you at basketball. How much more normal can my life be?"

"Look, I'm the last person to dictate what 'normal' looks like. But what I do know is that you've been different since Ella came back."

Seth grabbed his napkin and wiped his mouth before sitting back in his chair. "How?" he asked with a shrug. "I'm doing all the things I normally do. Work, church, home."

"I heard your students pulled you up at school about dating Ella," Jordan said. "And on Sundays, you're looking up from the music box a lot more than usual. Staring out into the congregation as if you're hoping to see someone. And if by 'home,' you mean taking Teddy to the Christmas tree farm to spend the day with you and Ella rolling around in the snow, yeah, I'd say you're creating a new normal."

Seth opened his mouth to ask how Jordan knew all those things but let his lips close slowly as he remembered where they lived. He dragged a hand down his face and sighed. "It's not like that," he said. "It can't be."

"Why?" Jordan asked.

The one word seemed to drop between them like a lead weight, and Seth startled at how instantly stressed it made him feel. "Rhonda was my first love," he said quietly. "I mean, I liked Ella a lot when we were young, but I was just a kid then. I had no idea what love felt like or how it looked in real time."

"Your parents are a great example of what love looks like," Jordan said, his tone more somber now. While Jordan's parents had given him every material need, they'd lacked in the emotional department—a fact Jordan tried not to dwell on too much.

"You're right about that," Seth said. "They're why I know that what I had with Rhonda was so special. You don't get those chances more than once."

Jordan rested his elbows on the table. "But what about creating new opportunities? What if Ella coming back is like some kind of sign?"

"You don't believe in signs," Seth said with a wry chuckle. "You once told me you had to make your own destiny because nobody else was going to do it for you."

With a slight nod of his head, Jordan drummed his fingers on the table. "Stop tryin' to quote me, man."

They shared a moment of humor, even though they both realized how serious this topic was.

"She was everything, Jordan. I don't know if you can understand that. Sometimes it still blows me away. Every single thing that I'd looked for in a woman, Rhonda had, and we were plan-

ning to do so many things together. We just needed more time."
He crunched the napkin in his hand and tossed it on the table,
gritting his teeth against the pain surging inside him now.

"I know you loved her," Jordan said, holding Seth's gaze. "I
saw how the two of you were together, and I envied the joy that
seemed to follow y'all around like your own personal sunshine.
But listen to me, Seth. Rhonda wouldn't want this for you."

Seth looked away at the sound of the chimes at the door.

"She wouldn't want you trying to fight against something
that you know in your heart feels just as right as when you were
with her," Jordan continued.

Seth returned his gaze to his friend and shook his head.
"Nothing is the same as it was with Rhonda. Nothing ever will be."

Jordan didn't even blink at Seth's intensely spoken words.
"Doesn't mean you have to settle for nothing forever. She'd want
you to be happy, Seth. Your family and I want you to be happy."

"But what makes you so sure I'm not? How do you claim to
know so much about how I feel about Ella when I just told you
about her a couple weeks ago?"

Jordan sat back in his chair now, letting his hands fall into
his lap. "Because you asked me for Dex's number, and when I
wanted to know why, you immediately replied, 'I want to help
Ella.' You wouldn't do that for just anybody."

Dexter Holcomb was another one of their frat brothers. Even
though Dex had moved to New York right after they graduated,
he still paid his annual dues and contributed in whatever way
he could to their national and local chapters.

"She could be so much more," Seth said without thinking.
"I just want her to know that there are opportunities out there
that she hasn't explored."

"Because you're falling in love with her," Jordan said, a slow grin appearing.

Seth desperately wanted to deny his friend's words. He wanted to slam his palms on that table and yell throughout the restaurant so his family could hear him as well that this wasn't happening to him. Not again. Loving someone the way he'd loved Rhonda could only lead to more heartache, especially because Ella's life wasn't here in Bellepoint. She wasn't staying, not for him or for any other reason. Last night, the idea to pack up his belongings and his dog and head to the city with her had crossed his mind. Would she even want that? A man following her to the city just to be with her? Or would she insist he had a life here, a life too different from hers? How many hours had he tossed and turned in his bed last night trying to figure out the answers to those questions?

And he still had no answers. But he knew better than to attempt that yelling-denial thing. For one, his mother would go ballistic if he made such a scene in the restaurant, and second, Jordan was right—his family and his best friend knew him far too well. It was because of that last part that Seth found himself giving Jordan a wry grin and a shake of his head.

"You're not funny, man," he told him, but once again he and Jordan chuckled. "I seriously don't know if things could work between me and Ella. It'd be a long-distance thing and . . . I just don't know."

"Have you asked her?"

"No," he replied and was just about to say something else when his phone buzzed in his pocket. Reaching for it, he saw Ella's name appear on the screen and wondered if fate was indeed tempting him.

"Go on and talk to your girl," Jordan said with another grin before getting up from the table. "I'm going to ask Max for more orange juice."

Seth answered as soon as Jordan was away from the table. "Good mornin', Ella. Let me guess: your stomach hurts after eating all that gooey popcorn last night." It was amazing how his mood had lightened at seeing that she was the one calling him.

"No, Seth, we've got a big problem," she said. Her tone, unlike his, was filled with despair, and every part of Seth froze with dread.

Ella paced her aunt's living room for what felt like the billionth time today. It was just after four on Thursday afternoon. Eight hours after Ms. Nancy had called, interrupting Aunt Addie's morning coffee ritual. Her aunt didn't waste a moment knocking on Ella's bedroom door to wake her with the news that last night's frigid temperatures had caused some of the church's ancient pipes to freeze and burst, subsequently flooding the basement kitchen and part of the fellowship hall.

From that moment on, Ella's temples had been throbbing and her stomach twisting with a wicked combination of worry, defeat, and brewing anger over a situation she'd despised for longer than she could remember.

"Girl, you gotta sit down before you wear a hole in my carpet," Aunt Addie said, snapping Ella out of her thoughts.

She dropped down onto the couch as if her aunt had physically pushed her and let out a heavy sigh. "What're we gonna do, Aunt Addie? Mr. Paulie said he got a few of the guys from the lodge to come over and move the trees up to the sanctuary before any of the water could reach them. But we can't have the auction up there. The trees are probably all up and down the aisles and there's no way to run all the cords safely and discreetly for the lights. Not to mention, where will we have the refreshments now? The concert? There's even a reporter from a major newspaper coming down tomorrow with her photographer to take pictures and cover the event live on their Facebook and Instagram pages."

"You're gonna worry yourself into a fit, Ella. Just take a breath. Everything's going to work out just fine. Have faith."

Ella let her head fall back against the couch and groaned. "What's faith got to do with busted pipes and water damage? Do you know how much is riding on this auction? You asked me to help and there's just been one issue after another—first a sponsor pulling out and now this."

"Well, now, when that sponsor pulled out, those talented artists you know stepped right in and filled those spaces with gorgeous and creative trees," Addie said. "And didn't Seth call just about a half hour ago to tell you he had good news?"

Ella shook her head and glared at her aunt through half-opened eyes. "What's he gonna do? Host the event at his house? Or his parents' restaurant? There's nothing Seth can do. His good news is probably that they want to postpone the event." And that would solidify her failure.

She'd lost her job, ended up in this small town for Christmas on a committee that she knew nothing about, and was now bringing her bad luck straight to those wonderful children who would benefit from the expansion of the before-and-after-school program. How had all this happened? The jinx! She groaned again. It stalked her like the worst nightmare and she wanted to scream her rage and helplessness, but instead she closed her eyes again and kept her lips shut tightly.

Aunt Addie had to be growing tired of her whining all day long about this. Well, to be fair, it had stopped for about an hour and a half when Ms. Nancy and Ms. Helen came over for lunch to talk about backup plans for the event—of which there were none! The three women had instead treated the time like a regularly scheduled lunch date and begun chatting about other times things had gone wrong with events at the church, laughing at the mishaps and recalling the joy when those events still proceeded and ended up better than they'd planned.

"You know, every time we make plans, God just laughs," Ms. Nancy had said.

Aunt Addie followed that up with her own laughter. *"Yes, indeed He does."*

Although that wasn't exactly what the scripture said, Ella had heard the saying plenty of times in her life. It meant that God had the last say—that things would be as He said no matter what any of them thought or planned. Now Ella rubbed her temples, feeling edgy at not knowing exactly what God's plan was for this auction.

When the doorbell rang, she sprang up from the couch and almost fell over the coffee table as she bumped it on her way to the hallway. She could hear her aunt mumble something behind her, but she didn't pause to figure out what that was. Pulling the door open, she was a little out of breath when her gaze met Seth's. It was quite possible that aside from the fact that she'd just run to open the door, the sight of him in navy-blue slacks and a turtle-neck sweater, topped with a black leather jacket and warm smile, might've elicited the same reaction.

"Hey," she said and waved for him to come inside.

A chilly gust of wind followed him and she happily closed the door behind him.

"Hey," he said and turned to face her. "Get your coat."

"Wait, what? I thought you had some good news about the event."

"I do," he told her. "I need you to get your coat and come with me."

"Hi, Seth," Aunt Addie said when she came into the hallway.

Seth turned and immediately went to her aunt, leaning in to kiss her cheek. "Hi, Ms. Addie. No worries. Everything's going to be just fine with the event."

Aunt Addie reached up and patted his cheek. "I believe it will," she said. "I believe *everything* is going to work out just as it should."

The way she emphasized the word "everything" had Ella narrowing her gaze at her aunt. She'd lost count of how many not-so-subtle hints her aunt had thrown out this week about her and Seth becoming a couple. Ella was ignoring them altogether because trying to deny something her aunt had set her mind to had always been a futile task.

"Um, why exactly am I getting my coat?" she asked.

But before Seth could reply, Aunt Addie did. "Because it's cold outside, dear. Now go on up and grab your jacket, hat, and gloves in case it starts to snow again."

Seeing Seth shrug while grinning from behind her aunt did nothing to calm the headache that had been attacking her all day. But again, she recognized when it just made more sense to go along with the program. Moments later, she was dressed warmly and stepped out onto the porch with Seth.

He reached for her hand just as she was about to speak.

"I'm gonna ask you to trust me," he said. "Just for a few minutes more. I promise I'm going to explain everything."

"Well," she said, staring into the kindest eyes she'd ever seen on a man. "Since you've asked me so nicely."

Grinning, he leaned in and dropped a kiss on her lips so fast she didn't have a second to think whether it was a good idea or not. The way he slowly pulled back from the contact said he hadn't thought that action through either. Yet it didn't stop him from moving in again—albeit slower this time—to touch his lips to hers. This time Ella closed her eyes and joined in the kiss, enjoying the warmth that quickly spread through her.

It felt like sunshine on a cloudy day, like moonlit walks and rainy days by the fire. Like a circle of safety and compassion that stole her breath. Trust him—that's what he'd asked, and he followed that with the sweetest, most potent kiss she'd ever experienced. How was she supposed to react to this? How was she supposed to continue denying what was standing right in front of her? Holding her close now, with a silent promise to never let her go.

She was the one to ease back then, clearing her throat before saying, "We should go . . . um, to wherever it is that you're going to explain everything."

He took a visibly ragged breath in and let it out slowly. She knew that feeling well and was still grappling to control the whirlwind of emotions storming through her own body at this moment. Which was why she'd needed to break their contact.

Seth could never promise not to let her go, not if Ben could propose and then look her in the eye and say he was going to Honduras without her. And when her mother had lain in her hospital bed and closed her eyes the final time. Love didn't keep anyone here with her, and that reality took a chunk of her heart each time she hoped it would.

They got in the truck and fifteen minutes later, Seth pulled into a parking lot across from a building that looked like it also could've served as a strip mall. She waited because she knew he would come around and open the door for her, and when he offered his hand, she took it and stepped down from the truck. They walked hand in hand to the door. She was so anxious to find out what was going on that she didn't bother to consider whether their hand-holding should've continued or not.

They came to the double glass doors in the center of the space, and that's when she noticed the midnight-navy-and-gray Theta Psi Mu coat of arms on the door, Seth's fraternity's chapter name in block letters beneath it. After her conversation with him about his fraternity at the housewarming, she'd felt compelled to do some online research, and in addition to learning more about their deep commitment to community and brotherhood, she also discovered things like their official colors, coat of arms, and corresponding symbols for the organization. None of that, however, could answer Ella's most pressing question at the moment.

"What are we doing here?" she asked, unable to hide the anxiousness in her tone.

"Trust me, remember?" he said and released her hand to open the door.

At the nod of his head, she moved inside, noting the glossy dark blue floors and the light gray walls. A nod to their official colors, she realized, as her gaze continued around the space to the modern black desk and chair and a larger 3D depiction of their coat of arms on the wall behind it.

After giving her a few seconds to look around, Seth took her hand again and led her down a long hallway. There were several closed doors along the stretch, with placards indicating what lay beyond each door: the offices of the fraternity's president and fiscal officer, a tech room, a storage area, and meeting rooms. At the end of that hallway was another spacious area with glossy floors, this time with the fraternity coat of arms in the center of it. There were a few tables along the walls in this space, each one holding statues, awards, or framed photos of the members of the Pi Pi chapter.

Seth continued to move them toward another set of doors— these were glossed light pine with wide handles that he pushed to grant them entrance. When Ella stepped into this space, she gasped.

"What . . . ," she started to say but paused to catch the breath that was sticking in her throat. "What . . . did you do?"

She continued to walk, recognizing that the floor setup matched what they'd had in the fellowship hall at the church. Folding chairs were lined in rows to face a partially covered plat-form. She passed the chairs and entered the festival of trees— after decorating last night, she, Seth, Max, and Jordan had decided that's what they'd call the twenty decorated trees.

"We knew the church wasn't going to be an option for the event, so we started making calls around town. I was on the phone so much during my classes today, the kids were giving me the 'no cell phones in class' speech. And Mr. Paulie grumbled so much when my frat brothers and I showed up to move the trees that he and his friends had just hauled up to the sanctuary. You don't even want to know how irritated he's gonna be for the next couple of weeks." Seth chuckled from behind her.

Ella looked back to ask, "Why didn't you call me? I would've helped."

He nodded. "I know," he said. "But Jordan and Max were at the restaurant with me when you called. The minute I got off the phone with you, they were the first people I told and they both offered to help. So we got with my parents and hammered out a list of places where we could possibly have it. As you can probably guess, there aren't that many options in Bellepoint big enough to accommodate the event. And the ones that had the space couldn't do it for some reason or another."

"Again," she said, this time pushing her hands into her pockets as she faced him, "why didn't you call me? I could've . . . no, I would've made the calls. You had to work and your students are right about classrooms not being a place for cell phones. I'm on the committee too, Seth; you should've told me what you were doing."

He nodded curtly. "The way you told me you were calling your artist friends in to help sponsor the trees?"

She sighed and accepted that verbal jab. "Fine," she said. "We're even." That didn't mean she liked what he'd done, but it did mean she wasn't going to keep harping on it. "This space is amazing. What other types of events do you have here?"

"We've hosted lots of fundraising events here. In the summer, we have a weeklong camp for children interested in STEM. Frat brothers in the field come from all over the US and offer classes and special projects. And next year we're hosting our annual conclave."

"Oh, I'll bet that's something to see," she said.

"Well, the bulk of that program is meetings for the brothers only, but there are a few functions that we allow invited persons to attend. I think I could probably figure out a way to get you an invitation, but only if you don't appear on Santa's naughty list this year."

She laughed. It came quick, bubbling up from somewhere deep inside her and bursting free in a way that reminded her of how she'd felt these past couple of weeks. Free to feel whatever she felt about her mother's passing, free to experience the Holy Spirit moving within her at church services or whenever she was in the church doing what she knew was the Lord's work. Free to enjoy sandwiches and gingerbread cupcakes at Beaumont's, free to join Max and Brooke for drinks and girl chatter, free to sketch with the same adrenaline rush she'd gotten when she was just a little girl.

"I think I can promise I'm not on that list," she said when she was finally able to.

"You sure?" he asked, but he was also grinning. "Because while you were grabbing your coat earlier, your aunt told me how stubborn you used to be, and how you could pout until she had to threaten that your face would get stuck in that position."

"What? She did not tell you that!" Stunned at being betrayed by her aunt, of all people, Ella cracked up again. "I'm not that little girl anymore."

"No," Seth said. "Neither of us are those same people."

Suddenly the moment was more serious, and she cleared her throat before turning to walk down the aisle of trees. She didn't want serious. Not right now. She just wanted this moment to enjoy these beautiful trees and the hope that had seeped into her heart while she was planning for them to be presented to the town. "We've got to get more decorations," she said suddenly and turned to find that Seth was right behind her.

He placed his hands on her shoulders to keep her steady and she looked up at him.

"More decorations?"

"Yes! The entire fellowship hall was decorated. This space isn't. We have to Christmas it up!"

His forehead crinkled. "'Christmas it up'?"

"Yeah," she said and play-slapped at his arm. "You know what I mean. We need to get all the decorations and bring Christmas into this space. I have to call Brooke and Max and get them to come down here tonight so we can get started. But first, you and I have to go shopping."

"Shopping?" he asked and then followed up with a groan.

CHAPTER 14

"F"or years I've disliked Christmas," Ella said as she and Seth walked down Main Street at just after seven on Thursday evening. "It wasn't really a dislike—maybe *indifference* is a better word." Although that didn't really seem to encapsulate her feelings on the holiday either.

"Why?" Seth asked.

They were both carrying bags of decorations that they'd picked up from the various shops on this street. There was another street—Scholastic Lane—a block over that featured more specialty shops that Ella couldn't wait to visit.

She sighed, resigned to continue sharing this most painful part of herself with him at this moment. The night sky was clear, bright stars visible in the deep indigo space. Of course, the air was frigid, but around them the shops were alight with twinkle and cheer, Christmas carols played through the town speakers, and people milled about, shopping and chattering. There was a hint of festiveness in the air, and it had been far too long since Ella had really allowed herself to appreciate such a thing. That realization, coupled with all that had happened today, had her figuring that maybe she just wanted to purge the negativity that had lingered inside her all this time.

"The jinx," she said slowly and glanced over to see his reaction.

He didn't laugh, nor did he frown in disbelief. Instead, he nodded and replied, "You mentioned that before when we were at the tree farm. Wanna explain it to me now?"

"I probably should've then, so you wouldn't think I was the superstitious sort," she said and took a deep breath. "The jinx is what happens whenever I wish on a Christmas star, or just around Christmastime in general."

They walked a few more steps with Seth waving or returning a verbal greeting to someone who passed them on the street. When Janel Miller waved, Ms. Phyllis's granddaughter who had spoken to Ella briefly about the day care center she hoped to open, Ella felt excited to have someone in the town to speak to as well. That meant she was making connections here, unlike when she'd lived here before. When she traveled around town during the past two weeks, she'd actually had things to talk to people about—the auction, of course, but also the books she was searching for at the library and what she should try next on the menu at Beaumont's. She'd even taken another trip out to Mr. Oscar's ranch when he asked her to recommend some artwork for the walls in his home office.

"So you think about this jinx at Christmas, and that's why you don't want to celebrate?" Seth asked, resuming their conversation.

"No, I mean, I've never really not celebrated Christmas. I still bought gifts and showed up for the holiday events at the gallery. But I hadn't gone to church in years and I certainly wasn't working on any Christmas tree auctions." She sighed. "I didn't even decorate my house."

He wasn't asking as many questions as she thought he probably wanted to ask. Of course he'd be pleasant like that and give her the floor to say all she needed to say. That was a part of Seth's charm, the way he listened intently and made meaningful contributions once he knew the whole story. She appreciated that whenever he responded to her, it was free of any judgment or chastisement, even when she knew he held vastly different views from hers on some topics.

"My mother had this thing that she did each year when we decorated. I got to put the Christmas star on top of the tree, but we both made a wish on that star. It could be for whatever we wanted in the next year." There was a tugging in her gut at the words, but it was nowhere near the suffocating pain she normally felt at this memory. "The Christmas before my eleventh birthday, I wished for a pony, but a few months later, my mother passed away. I was so angry and so hurt, I decided right then that I'd never wish on a Christmas star again." Another deep breath and the tugging eased. "Last year, I thought maybe it was time to put the old hurt behind me. Things were going well in my life—my career was on track and I'd just gotten engaged."

He stopped walking then, and she had to look back to see what the problem was.

"You were engaged?"

She sighed heavily. "Yes. Ben. He was a jerk. I'm not even gonna pretend otherwise," she said. "We were engaged and I wished for a fairy-tale wedding. He got a job out of the country and left me here." When she shrugged, Seth closed the space between them.

He cupped his hands to her face and repeated her words. "He was a jerk."

Ella smiled as her heart melted. "Thanks."

Seth let his hands fall from her face and travel down her arms, until he could take one of her hands in his as they began walking again. "So you started to think you were jinxed again?"

She nodded. "I found out my gallery was closing last month, and I thought, 'Oh no, here we go again,' even though I hadn't even wished for anything. Then I got here, and the next thing I know I'm on this committee, and stuff starts going wrong there too. I was like, really? Is this what my life's going to be like forever?"

"Life's gonna be life," he said and shook his head. "With or without wishes. It's just the way it is."

"Well, thank you for that bit of encouragement," she said, but she smiled because deep down she knew he not only meant well but was absolutely right.

"I'm just sayin' we can't run from whatever life has in store for us. It'll find us anyway because that's the path God has for us. And sometimes that path is meant to swerve to teach us to trust in Him more."

"You sound like Aunt Addie," she said.

"I know—you told me that before. But that doesn't mean it isn't true."

"So you have faith that you'll love again. That you'll get married again and have those children you want who'll keep Teddy company?"

The silence that fell was instant and dreadful. She wanted to take the words back, screaming at herself inwardly for saying them so flippantly.

"I didn't think I would," he replied finally.

Now it was her turn to stop walking, but since their hands

were entwined, Seth stopped instantly too. "What do you think now?" she asked.

"I don't know," he said. "What do you think now?"

They stood there in silence for a few seconds, both contemplating their answers, when a couple of laughing children ran out of the store they were in front of and bumped right into them. Ella almost dropped a bag and Seth stumbled a few steps away from her. But they laughed along with the children who'd gone just a little bit past the store before turning back to chime in unison, "Merry Christmas!"

Grinning when he came closer again, Seth said, "C'mon, let's go inside this store since it's obviously the fun place to be."

They'd been in many stores tonight and Ella had enjoyed them all. She wandered around, touching and examining most of the trinkets, specialty gift items, and decorations they had. This store was called The Collective, and as her flat dress boots clicked over the dark wood-planked floors, she let herself be once again sucked into the treasure trove of items on display.

The Collective reminded her of an antique shop she'd once visited in the city, with its myriad shelves stuffed with all sorts of Christmas items. There were snow globes, music boxes, miniature fiber-optic Christmas trees, and more gingerbread houses in different sizes and themes than she'd ever seen. "This place is amazing," she said.

Seth didn't respond and when she looked around, she saw that he'd wandered to the other side of the shop. She continued alone, feeling a lightness that had evaded her for years. Classical music played here, but she could tell it was a rendition of a Christmas song and found herself humming along to what the words should be. They really didn't need many more decorations.

Brooke had texted to let her know that Ms. Nancy and Ms. Helen had brought a couple of boxes over to the community center. They decided to all meet there tomorrow morning—the last day before Saturday's main event—since it was getting late tonight, and Ella agreed. Especially since she and Seth were still shopping.

She'd just walked over to a table at one corner of the store that was piled with Christmas stockings. They were knitted in an argyle pattern—green ones with white and red, and red ones with green and white. She had one in each hand trying to decide if Aunt Addie should get the red or if she should, when an ornament appeared in her line of sight.

"Here," Seth said as he stood beside her now. "Why don't you try something new this year?"

"Something new?" she asked, her voice cracking on that last word. She couldn't look away from the ornament he held. At first glance they were simply angel's wings, nothing elaborate or especially Christmassy, but as she continued to stare, she noted the details. The wings were white lace, two pearls in the center, and the string that held them was another pattern of lace, looped so the ornament could be hung on a tree. Plain, simple, delicate, and, when she reached up to run one finger along its edge, soft.

"This year, you could put this on the tree," Seth continued. "Not to make a wish but to celebrate this new phase of your life that next year will bring. Your new job, your newfound joy in Christmas, all those new fuzzy socks you picked up a couple stores ago." He grinned after that last part and Ella released a shaky chuckle too.

"I told you I don't like my feet to get cold. Fuzzy socks are the best to get through these East Coast winters and the blistering summers when the air-conditioning is on full blast in your house." She meant every word and loved the dozen pairs of Christmas-themed socks she'd purchased. She even admitted to herself that she was likely to wear them throughout the year instead of keeping them until this time next year. "Besides, those socks are long and have the treads on the bottom to keep you from sliding all over the wood floors."

"Just go ahead and admit you're obsessed with fuzzy socks, Ella. I won't tell anybody," he replied. Then he placed the ornament in the palm of her hand.

He took the stocking she held in her other hand and put it down on the table, then grasped that hand in his. "I also don't blame you for the feelings you've harbored over the years. You had a valid reason to feel sad and betrayed. Believe me, I can totally relate. But I also know that Christmas isn't meant to heal those wounds or to wash them away like they were never there. Instead, it's a time to revel in the hope of peace and happiness to come. Of a joy that was promised to all the world on that night in Bethlehem.

"We deserve that joy, Ella. You and me. We've been through a lot, but we can have a new start. We can take this time to try again."

She sucked in a breath because the emotions swirling through her at this moment threatened to strangle her. Her eyes filled with tears and her hand trembled in his at the weight of his words, the truth in them and the undeniable feeling that this was exactly what her aunt had told her. It was fate.

In this moment, she was standing here surrounded by everything Christmas imaginable, and Seth—the guy she'd crushed on for longer than she ever allowed herself to like another man—was standing here with her. Not only that, but he was also offering her something . . . something she thought she never wanted to feel again.

"I don't know what to say," she admitted. She should have words like he did—declarations, propositions, anything. But no, she had nothing except the quick patter of her heart and the shaky laugh that bubbled up as she began to nod. "This is beautiful, Seth. Thank you. I'm gonna hang it on the tree at Aunt Addie's," she told him.

He smiled and nodded his agreement. "I thought of you when I saw the lace. It reminded me of the curtains in the window of your bedroom. When we were young, I used to ride my bike down your street. I always knew when you were home because you opened the curtains. When you weren't home, the window would be covered in lace."

"Okay," she said and eased her hand out of his. "I'm going to say that might've been a little bit stalkerish." She moved her fingers to mime a small amount and watched him grin and roll his eyes.

"Yeah, I know that now. And since I never told anybody what I did, that action couldn't be corrected. But the boy only knew that the girl in that room was special and someone that he really wanted to get to know better."

And just like that, her heart was melting again. "How do you do that?" she asked.

"Do what?"

"Make me feel like that young girl with a crush that was bigger than her whole world every time you look at me."

It was his turn to be speechless, but that didn't last long because a salesperson appeared to ask if they needed help.

Seth followed her to the cash register and purchased the ornament for Ella, and thirty minutes later Ella stood in Aunt Addie's living room alone with the ornament in hand.

Multicolored lights danced around the tree while all the bulbs and ornaments her aunt owned hung from the branches. Garland hugged the tree, swirling from the bottom to the top where her aunt had placed a frosted Christmas star. The moment Ella saw her aunt take that star out of its box, she'd looked away. Had busied herself with other decorations in the box across the room. And each day since they'd decorated, she'd walked in and out of the living room, admiring the tree a little more with every passing, but never looking up to that star. It still bothered her, haunted her in a way that only grief and disappointment could. But tonight, she stared at it with every fiber of her being, shaking at the intensity of the emotion moving through her.

"I'll always love you, Mama," she whispered. "But I think it's time for something new."

She stared at the angel's wings and imagined they were her mother's way of smiling down on her, agreeing that it was time for a change. The thought made her smile as she moved her fingers lightly over the delicate lace once again. It was so perfect, just like Seth.

How many times had she dreamed of them together? Of him holding her hand or kissing her the way he had in these past weeks? Of them laughing together, working together, and growing together? Once she left Bellepoint, she'd never dared to dream that way again. Never let her heart lead her mind to what might be best for them.

"We deserve that joy, Ella. You and me."

That's what he'd said tonight, and she agreed.

"Okay," she whispered and hung the angel's wings on one of the highest branches she could reach without getting the step stool. It looked almost ethereal amid the glow of the lights, and her heart beat a little faster. "I'm giving this one more try." And with those words, Ella closed her eyes and made a wish.

On Saturday night, Ella clapped her hands, rocked from side to side, and sang "Joy to the World" along with the full church choir. Seth and Hilliard had worked together to arrange Whitney Houston and the Georgia Mass Choir's version of this classic song for the adult and youth members of the choir to sing, and they were rockin' it. Everyone in the community center hall was on their feet, clapping and singing.

Mama Gail sang the lead and Aunt Addie directed them. Words couldn't explain the rush moving through Ella's body as she recited the lyrics. She knew it was the joy that the Holy Spirit was filling her with and that it couldn't be accurately explained, only felt in the deep recesses of her soul.

She wore an emerald-green pantsuit, a shimmering red camisole beneath the jacket, and black pumps. Seth had attempted to wear something close to the festive colors without wearing green or red pants that he swore would make him feel like an elf. Ella had laughed so hard at the visual his words created yesterday when they were here putting up the decorations. She knew that whatever he decided to wear, he would look handsome, and she wasn't wrong. He wore black slacks and a fitted black turtleneck with black boots. The dour outfit came to life with the red crushed-velvet jacket that looked as if it had been made especially for him.

As she watched him playing the keyboard now, she dreamed of more Christmas Eves like this one. With them all gathered together, celebrating the true meaning of Christmas alongside their families and friends.

"Feels almost like old times, doesn't it?" Ms. Phyllis, who'd been standing next to her, asked. "I remember when I used to be up there with the choir singing. At the church, though, but still." She sighed wistfully. "Oh, how I loved the Christmas programs and all the hymns that come at this time of year. Just warms my heart to see you young folk stepping into your calling here and in the town."

Ella only smiled and continued to sing, but Ms. Phyllis's words hung in her mind long after the song was over and the concert had concluded. Everyone moved throughout the hall now, either visiting the dessert table or walking through the rows of trees to admire them. A group of children, a few of whom she knew were from Seth's class—Devon and two of his friends—had pulled some of the folding chairs over into one corner where they all sat. She grinned because she recalled doing the same thing when she was younger.

"What do you suppose they're up to?" Max asked when she and Brooke joined Ella.

"Nothing good," Ella replied with a shake of her head. "I mean, nothing that'll get any of them into legal trouble or anything, but I'll bet they aren't discussing which one of the trees they like the best."

Brooke laughed. "Absolutely not! There are only two girls

in the group with four boys, so I'm betting those two girls have their sights set."

"And the boys, as always, are totally clueless as to why the girls are sitting with them in the first place," Max added.

The three of them laughed, and that's how Jordan and Seth found them when they approached.

"They're probably laughing at your bright red jacket," Jordan said, pointing his thumb in Seth's direction.

"Nah," Seth said, stopping in front of them and posing like he was in front of a camera. "They know this is the money shot right here," he continued, giving them what she figured he thought was his sexy, smooth look. "Or no, get this one. This is for the cover of GQ." He turned to the side, pushing his jacket back as he slid a hand in the side pocket of his slacks.

Max groaned. "Oh puh-lease!" She laughed at her brother.

But Brooke clapped. "I think you might have something there, Seth. 'The softer side of a music teacher' could be the cover title."

Ella only grinned because he did look good. But she wasn't about to tell him that—his ego was inflated enough tonight with all the compliments that had come flooding in right after the concert. The pastor, his wife, and other members of the church and community weren't the only ones who'd enjoyed the music. Ella spotted Nina and Ricky from the newspaper talking to Seth as well, but she hadn't had a chance to ask him what that was about.

"Talk some sense into your friend," Seth said to Brooke. "She doesn't know anything about style."

That wasn't exactly an accurate statement, and Ella was almost certain Seth knew that because Max looked phenomenal in an off-the-shoulder, knee-length red dress. Of course, she'd probably been freezing her toes off outside, but in here she had all the heads turning. Especially Jordan's. Ella had seen him staring at Max quite a few times tonight and wondered if Max had any idea how into her this guy was. Ella thought she'd picked up on some tension between them that first night she met Jordan at Beaumont's, but she'd been so frazzled by the sponsor dropout issue that she hadn't paid enough attention. But the night they were all together decorating the last trees, it was clear Jordan liked Max. Not only in the way he looked at her but in how he jumped in to help even when Max didn't need it—suggesting he was dying to be near her for any reason. Ella wondered if Seth knew, and how he felt about it. Although it was none of his business since Max was an adult, but she knew how guys could be about their sisters. Or rather, she'd seen secondhand how they could be since she was an only child.

"You like my jacket, don't you?" Seth surprised her by slipping an arm around her waist as he asked.

They hadn't talked about making their relationship public. To be honest, they hadn't actually talked about the change in their relationship. Yesterday had been full of running around from the church to the community center to Beaumont's, to pick up sweet potato and apple pies, to Sweets Bakery, to pick up the frosted sugar cookies made in the shapes of music symbols and Christmas trees specifically for the event. They'd eaten on the go, snacking on sandwiches Mama Gail had given them when they were picking up the pies and then, later on, hot chocolate and coffee cake Seth had insisted they stop at BB's to purchase. By the time she returned to Aunt Addie's, it was after ten in the evening and she was too exhausted to do anything other than climb into bed.

"I think you look festive and handsome, Mr. Hamil," she replied and tried to ignore the curious look coming from Brooke. Jordan and Max shared a knowing glance, but Ella looked away from them to focus her attention on Seth. "This jacket was an excellent choice," she told him.

"And so was this suit," he replied. "I love this color on you."

She tilted her head. "You mean Christmas colors?" she asked and chuckled.

"Not many people can pull off this combo, but you look equal parts professional, on theme, and beautiful."

Ella prayed she wasn't blushing.

"I'd actually lean more on the side of beautiful," he added before dipping his head to touch his lips lightly to hers.

Well then, they were definitely taking their relationship public, she thought as she took another kiss just before Brooke squealed.

"Fifteen minutes until bidding closes," Brooke announced. "I'm gonna go over and check with Ms. Nancy and Ms. Helen. They were taking the in-person bids. The online bids will be much easier to tally, but I think you two should make the announcement at exactly nine o'clock. At least that's what I told the reporter you were going to do."

Ella nodded her agreement.

"The reporter and her partner have been moving around the room all night, both holding up their phones and recording," Max said.

"I know!" Brooke chimed in. "I keep checking to see if we're trending yet. That would be so amazing."

Yes, that would be awesome, even though Ella didn't think she could be happier than she was at this moment. Everything had turned out so wonderfully, despite the hitches in their plans and the emotional roller coaster she'd been on for the past few years.

"This whole event has been amazing," Seth said, but he was looking at Ella instead of the other people around them.

She felt his words swirl and settle in the thumping of her heart. "It has," she admitted.

"Come on, you two. As much as I'm liking the two of you all booed up, you should get over to the counting table with Brooke," Max said. "And I'll go round up the reporter and her assistant so they'll be ready for the big announcement."

"I'll go with you," Jordan replied and looked at Max. "You know, in case you need help rounding them up."

That was the moment Max caught a clue. Ella saw it in the way her eyes widened and then narrowed just as quickly. Max seemed unsure how to play the situation, though, and didn't speak for a couple of seconds.

"You could invite them back for the frat's upcoming charity event for the children's hospital," Ella said to Jordan.

When Jordan glanced at Ella, it was with a smile of appreciation. Max, on the other hand, tossed her a quizzical look but said, "Come on if you're coming" as she walked away.

"What was that all about?" Seth asked.

Ella took his hand and began following Brooke across the room. "I'll tell you about it later." When they weren't near Jordan or Max, in case her suspicions were correct and Seth felt some type of way about his sister getting involved with his best friend.

Half an hour later, applause rang out through the large space. Confetti machines that she didn't know the fraternity had reserved shot red, green, and white flakes into the air as they announced that the Christmas tree auction had earned $42,519. Of course, that was before they subtracted their expenses and shipping costs to be incurred in sending the tree boxes to each of the twenty highest bidders, but that still put them well over the $30,000 they were aiming for, and Ella felt as if her chest would burst with pride.

Seth immediately turned to her, lifted her off her feet, and spun her around. "We did it!" he said repeatedly.

She could only grin and hold on, her excitement matching his, and as soon as they stopped spinning, she locked her arms around his neck and pulled him down for a tight hug. "Thank you so much for all you've done to make this a wonderful Christmas." She'd said it before—they both had—but she was so filled with joy that she couldn't hold the words in.

When she came back to Bellepoint a couple of weeks ago, she'd never even considered seeing Seth again, let alone working with him in any capacity. But since the first moment she ran after him outside the coffee shop, there hadn't been a day that she didn't think about him and wonder, *What if?* Well, now she didn't have to wonder anymore. She was in Seth's arms and it was exactly where she wanted to be.

Ella had slipped her cell phone into the front pocket of her pants so she would be able to check the online bids throughout the night. It startled her just now when it buzzed, and she jumped back from Seth as if she'd forgotten it was there. "Oh. It's my phone. Duh!"

She reached into her pocket and looked at the phone screen. "Oh my! It's Pamela Tramonte."

Seth frowned. "And who is Pamela Tramonte?"

"She's the curator at the museum where I interviewed," she

said. "I've got to go into the hallway so I can hear." She started to walk through the hall and pushed through the double doors that would take her into a quieter area.

She swiped her hand across the screen to answer. "Hello?"

"Hi, Ella. This is Pamela Tramonte from the Steven Werner Gallery. I hope I'm not catching you at a bad time."

"Oh no, no. It's no problem. I mean, I'm at a church function, but it's okay. I stepped outside to take the call."

"I know it's Christmas Eve, too, so I'll be quick. I wanted to let you know that we've concluded our interviews and that we'd love to have you join us at the gallery the first of the year."

"Oh wow!" Ella's heart pounded in her chest at the sound of those words. "Really? I mean, thank you so much."

There was a chuckle on the other end of the phone and Pamela continued, "I could take that as an acceptance, but considering the timing of this call, I'm going to wait until Monday morning to email you the official offer letter. It'll outline all the details regarding salary, benefits, and so forth."

"I can't believe this," Ella said. But that wasn't entirely true. Wasn't that the reason she'd gone to the library to do extra research? She believed that whatever career opportunity was meant for her would come to her, and it had. She was grinning widely but made herself tamp down the excitement so that Pamela wouldn't regret offering her the job.

"The board was very impressed with your credentials," Pamela continued. "One of our board members is also a close friend of the former owner of the Liberty Gallery, and they had nothing but good things to say about you. So we're very excited to have you join the team. That is, if you decide to take the position."

"I'll review the offer letter as soon as I receive it," Ella said. She was sure there were questions she should be asking or something more professional she should say, but honestly, she was just bowled over with excitement tonight. There was so much happiness swirling around her that she felt like she was floating.

"Great," Pamela said. "And again, I apologize for calling you at this time of night, and on Christmas Eve at that. I just wanted to give you a heads-up and hopefully an early Christmas present."

Ella nodded. "An early Christmas present indeed," she said. "Thanks so much again, Pamela. And have a merry Christmas!"

Pamela wished her a wonderful holiday as well and Ella disconnected the call. Then she broke out into a dance, turning in a half circle before catching herself the moment she realized Seth was standing close by.

"Oh my gracious," she said, a hand going to her now wildly thumping heart. "I didn't know you were there."

"Sorry, I just wanted to make sure everything was okay," he said and took a step closer to her.

She closed the distance between them with more hurried steps than he'd used. "I got the job!" she said and then giggled. "She called me on Christmas Eve to offer me the job! Can you believe that?"

"Yeah," he said with a slow nod. "I can. You're great at what you do, Ella. I never doubted for one moment that you'd get this job or whatever job you applied for. I always believed in you."

Well, now tears sprang to her eyes. Nobody, except her mother and her aunt, had ever said that to her. She'd never expected to hear it from anyone else, but hearing it from Seth at this moment had all the feelings for him she'd tried desperately to fight floating to the surface. "Thank you," she said softly. "I feel so overwhelmed right now—with how wonderfully the choir sang tonight and the success of the auction—so this was just the icing on the cake."

He nodded slowly. "I bet it is."

He stuffed his hands into the front pockets of his pants as he stood there staring at her. His shoulders were more rigid than they were a few minutes ago when they were in the hall hugging and congratulating each other on a job well done with the auction.

"Are you okay?" she asked. "Did something happen with the auction while I was out here? Did we not make as much as we thought? I knew we should've found an accountant to handle all the money stuff."

Now he was shaking his head. "No. No. All of that's fine. I mean, it's a good idea for us to do a closer count and subtract all of our expenses and fees next week, but right now, we're good. The auction is good, is what I meant to say."

Even his tone was different, something she hadn't noticed until this very moment.

"So what's going on? Why are you talking to me like I'm a stranger all of a sudden?"

"You're not a stranger," he said and stepped closer. He eased a hand out of his pocket and touched a finger to her chin. "I'll never think of you as a stranger, not after this time we've shared."

"Good," she said, but she wasn't totally sure she was buying that everything was okay. Maybe all the excitement and celebration had him thinking about his wife again.

She hadn't stopped thinking about her mother, but she was able to focus on all the good that was happening tonight. Seth was usually so much better than she was at doing that, and she hardly ever saw him feeling down with his grief. That didn't mean it wasn't there—she knew that from experience.

"Do you want to leave now? We can go back to Aunt Addie's. I baked some brownies earlier and Aunt Addie made two different flavors of Christmas punch for our dinner tomorrow. You can be a taste tester." She grinned because she already knew which flavor she preferred.

He dropped his finger from her face and cleared his throat. "Uh, no. That's actually what I was coming out here to tell you as well. I need to go home and check on Teddy. He didn't go out again before I left and it's been about four hours, so I'd better go take him out before he decides to forget all the housebreaking we've worked so hard on perfecting."

"Oh," she said, missing his touch and the eye contact he'd broken as he already started to turn away. "Well, do you want me to come with you? I don't have to go right home. Aunt Addie rode with Mr. Oscar, so he can take her home." And she'd never been to Seth's house.

That fact hadn't bothered her until right this moment.

"No," he said without any hesitation. "I'll see you in church tomorrow."

She almost said "oh" again but felt the echo in her mind and bit the word back. "I'll . . . uh, I'll see you in church tomorrow."

And just like that he walked away. No kiss. No hug. No . . . nothing.

CHAPTER 15

Ella was leaving.

Seth had known this moment was coming, so he shouldn't have been shocked, and yet the second he overheard her on the phone and saw her dancing with joy, his heart had plummeted.

Thirty minutes after he left the community center, Seth dropped his house keys in the bowl by his front door and leaned down to release the leash from Teddy's collar. The dog took off into the kitchen to find his water bowl. Seth had been right about one thing—the walk was needed. Teddy had almost bolted out the door when Seth first arrived home.

What Seth was sadly certain he'd missed the mark on was Ella. He took off his coat and hung it in the closet before going into his living room, where he stopped and stared at the Christmas tree. Traditional versus themed. That was one of the first arguments he and Ella had just a couple of weeks ago. Had it really been such a short amount of time that she'd been back in his life? Why did it feel like so much longer, and why did he think it hadn't been long enough?

Folding his arms over his chest, he continued to stand there, his gaze fixated on the blinking lights and the way they danced off the shiny bulbs. When he was a child, he used to lie on his back so close to the tree that Max had once joked they should put a bow on his head and pretend he was a gift. The memory had his mouth lifting in a small smile. He obviously wasn't a gift to anyone—not this year anyway.

But he'd begun to think, he'd begun to hope, that after all those nights he dreamed of being with Ella, maybe now was finally their time. Timing was everything. Seth had learned that long ago. As his family traveled from state to state, and for a brief period out of the country, for his father's career, he always knew there was a time and a place for everything. It helped to think that way when he was struggling to find his place in each new location. That time was for that place, and so he adapted because that was what he needed to do. When they came to Bellepoint, he was certain that this place was for him. He'd counted himself blessed that the members of his family thought the same thing.

Then Ella had come into his life. She walked into their fifth-grade classroom, and the fatigue Seth had been feeling from sneaking to stay up late the night before to watch a wrestling match on television had immediately vanished. Sunlight poured through the classroom windows, hitting her skin and softening the edges of fear he knew she felt. She clutched her notebook tight to her chest like a shield against anyone who didn't want to accept her. Seth knew that action well—he had done it so many times before they'd settled in Bellepoint. And when she walked to take the seat Mrs. Holback had directed her to, Seth stared at the back of her head for the duration of the class.

For the years that followed, he did just about the same thing where Ella was concerned, watching her in whatever classes they had together or whenever he saw her in church. He had a full plate of sports, music lessons, and helping out at the restaurant, so he didn't often see her outside, which was why he used to ride his bike past her house as much as he did. With a huff, he thought once more how creepy that sounded now that he was an adult. If he ever had a son, he'd be sure to tell him that was a no-no, regardless of how much he liked the girl.

And Seth liked Ella . . . a lot.

The heaviness in his chest was familiar and yet different. It was more disappointment than loss, a prelude of sorts to what could've been a much deeper heartache, he supposed. If there was anyone Seth could've seen himself loving again, it was Ella. But she had a life; she had a career. He'd known that from the moment she approached him about having her cup of coffee. Another grin spread slowly, regardless of the sadness now gripping him. She had been so spirited that chilly afternoon. Insistent and confident but still polite. Almost brutally so. She'd intrigued him from that very moment. And when he realized who she was—he shook his head with the memory—he'd known he was lost. Again.

What was it about this woman that always grabbed him by the throat and held on for dear life? Until the moment she walked away.

That last part had him sighing and turning away from the tree. He walked through the living room then, passing the dining room until he was at the back of the house in his home office. He spent a lot of time in this space, grading papers or preparing lesson plans. Messing around on his keyboard, singing into the space in a way he rarely did in public anymore, besides church. Switching on the floor lamp by the door, he moved farther into the space until he could drop down into the chair behind his desk. There was a recliner on the opposite side of the room, where he sat when he listened to music.

He rested his elbows on his desk and dropped his head into his hands. Why was he so gone for this woman? He knew this couldn't possibly work. She lived in the city and his life was here in this town where his family had roots and history—where he'd built a life for himself. Ella was never going to fit into that life. She worked with expensive pieces of art, traveled in circles where people drank champagne and drove fancy cars. He enjoyed his mother's beef stew and snickerdoodle hot chocolate. His dog was goofy and a part-time traitor who rode around in the back of Seth's pickup truck with his face to the wind. This wasn't her world and he'd known that.

So why had he been so irritated earlier when he heard she'd gotten that job? He even told her that he knew she would get the offer. And he did. There wasn't anything Ella couldn't do. She'd shown them all that by deciding not to attend MBU as most of the Bellepoint young adults did. Instead she'd gone to a great school on a full scholarship, before going on to run an entire art gallery. She was boss lady personified, and he couldn't compete with that. No matter how much he'd started to love her again.

What he also couldn't bring himself to do was ask her to stay here in Bellepoint. And do what? There were no art galleries here, although she could open one on Main Street. He was sure tourists would enjoy that. But would Ella? What else would she do here? No, asking her to stay wasn't an option. Could he go with her? He could teach anywhere, and he could continue his dedication to his fraternity—they had local chapters all over the world. Teddy would learn to like the city. His dog had already proven he really had no loyalty to place or person. Would Ella want that? A man following her just to have a place in her life? Or would she feel rushed and crowded? They hadn't talked about what this new development between them would look like, and he thought they could do that in more detail after Christmas, but then reality happened.

With a heavy sigh, he lifted his head and sat back in his chair. It was on wheels, so the quick action moved it a short distance. He dropped his hands to his lap and stared up at the ceiling. When the surface offered no new answers, he stood and walked over to built-in shelves that held his music collection. His recliner was positioned in this corner, with the record player he actually used on a specially made stand on its other side. He'd been listening to his CD player last night after he came in from being with Ella all day. He'd wanted to listen to *A Swinging Christmas* and imagine her hearing it as a child. What each song would've meant to her then and how it still impacted her life now. He pushed the Play button again tonight and waited while the first piano keys were struck on the first track before taking a step back so he could sit in the recliner.

A cracking sound interrupted the music, and when he shifted again, the sound increased. Realizing he was responsible for the sound, he instantly looked down and lost his breath. Jumping back, he fell to his knees, his eyes glued to the cracked CD case. With shaking fingers, he pushed the plastic aside to pull the cover of the CD free and stared with blurry eyes at the colorful paper with that silly unicorn on the front. He had flashes of the Christmas he'd sat in the living room happily pulling items out of the shimmering green gift bag Rhonda had packed them in. They were both sitting on the floor opening their gifts to each other with the glee of two little children. She waited excitedly while he pulled out all the tissue paper she'd stuffed in the top of the bag. Then there were a couple of tries before he got to the best gift ever—the CD.

Tears flooded his eyes at that memory. Guilt clogged his mind and applied pressure to his chest. What was he doing? Pining over one woman when he hadn't finished mourning the loss of another. He choked out a sob as the weight of the guilt he'd carried around for almost two years came surging to the forefront. Music still played in the background, and at some point Teddy came into the office and plopped his big body down right beside Seth. When Teddy rested his head on Seth's lap, it reminded him that Teddy had lost her too. He dropped a hand down to pet his dog while in his other hand, he still gripped the broken CD cover.

He had no idea how long they sat like that or when the tears stopped flowing. All Seth knew was that this moment had a been a long time coming, and deciding where he went from here wasn't going to be easy, but it was necessary. Because as Jordan had told him, Seth didn't have to settle for nothing forever.

At almost midnight on Christmas Eve, Ella sat on her aunt's couch holding a glass of white grape punch with cranberry ice in one hand. She'd been home from the auction for a couple of hours but had gone straight to her room when she first arrived. It was her intention to go straight to bed. Her body was exhausted from all the running around she'd been doing these past days. But her mind obviously had other plans, because try as she might, sleep had evaded her.

When she finally had enough of tossing and turning in her bed and figured her next flip would have her rolling right onto the floor, she got up, put on her robe and slippers, and came downstairs. As she had so many times as a child, she walked straight back to the kitchen in search of a snack. The two jugs of Christmas punch Aunt Addie had made were on the top shelf of the refrigerator chilling for tomorrow, along with other containers of the salads that she and her aunt had prepared ahead of tomorrow night's dinner. But at the very front, her aunt, bless her heart, had placed a slender tumbler filled with the punch Ella told her she liked the best.

After she fixed her glass, Ella made her way to the living room. She stopped to plug in the lights on the tree before going to the couch and taking a seat. Now she crossed one leg over the other and took a sip of the fruity and refreshing beverage. A pang of disappointment that Seth hadn't come over to share this drink with her resonated, and she let out a soft sigh.

What happened between them tonight? One minute he seemed perfectly fine—they'd been hugging and celebrating and had even shared a couple of really sweet kisses. And then his mood totally shifted, and the next thing she knew, she was watching him walk down the hallway of the community center until he was out of sight. It was the oddest and most frustrating sensation she'd felt in a very long time.

Not that she didn't have other things on her mind tonight and could use the time alone to put those things into perspective— that was certainly something she needed to do. But she still couldn't stop wondering what had changed his mood.

She took another sip and recalled a quick exchange she'd had with Jordan just as they started packing up to leave.

"*I know he seems like he has it all together all the time, but things aren't always as they seem,*" he'd said.

For a moment she didn't understand, but then she nodded. "*We both have a lot to work through,*" she'd replied. "*And I know grief wasn't easy for me to deal with, so I don't expect anyone else to have a smooth time with it.*"

"*I don't think that's all he's struggling with right now,*" Jordan said, and she was tempted to ask him more questions to find out exactly what Jordan knew about his best friend's feelings for her specifically, but she decided against it.

When it came time to find out how Seth felt about her, she wanted the words to come from him. Besides that, was she really hoping for some deep sentimental confession of feelings from Seth? Just as she'd noted earlier this evening, they went from working on this event together to feeling comfortable enough with whatever this personal thing between them was to kissing each other where any and all of Bellepoint could see them. Considering the rumor mill in this town, that was a big deal. But was it a big enough deal to think it meant something lasting, perhaps forever?

She shook her head quickly at that thought, as if the effort would wipe it away from her mind. "Forever's a long time," she whispered.

Her mother was gone forever. She'd thought she was going to be with Ben forever.

Those facts carried her gaze to the Christmas tree and that star resting confidently at the top. Wishes that didn't come true.

With another heavy sigh, she finished her punch and reached out to set the glass on the end table. Then she stretched out on her back and continued to stare at the tree.

She hadn't come to Bellepoint thinking about making another wish or hoping that it would come true. Yet here she was
again, waiting expectantly. It occurred to her then, with the
quickness of the blinking lights, that this was not how it worked.
Just because she wanted something didn't mean she was going
to get it.

Yes. No. Or wait.

Those were the answers God gave to prayers. Aunt Addie had
been right about that. Wishes had to be included. What if she
was supposed to wait for this current wish to come to fruition?
What if the answer was no? Either way she had to be okay with
it. There could be no more pouting and sacrificing happiness in
other areas of her life just because one thing she wanted wasn't
meant to be. A no didn't mean her life was over. It just meant
that her path was destined to go in another direction.

Her gaze fell to the angel's wings. Earlier this morning she'd
gotten out of bed and found her sketch pad once more, and
from memory had drawn the ornament. After the auction and
Christmas were over, she planned to purchase a frame for it so
she could hang it in her bedroom in the city. She wanted a daily
reminder of how special that particular ornament was to her
because she knew it would be packed away once the decorations were taken down. Sure, she could just take it with her and
keep it out at all times, but she felt like those angel's wings were
right where they belonged here in Bellepoint. Did that mean she
belonged here too?

Again, it had never occurred to her that on this trip she'd
be considering whether or not to move—either to Pittsburgh
for a new job or back to Bellepoint. She was looking for a job
and hoping she'd find one by the first of the year, and that

had happened. Was that because she'd had faith? If she were truthful with herself, she'd admit that for the last few nights, she hadn't prayed for that job at the gallery. No, what Ella had prayed earnestly and fervently for since she'd been in Bellepoint was the clarity to see what her next move should be. Wasn't that the Steven Werner Gallery? Hadn't she been seeking out a new job as curator in another museum?

Lifting an arm, she let it drop over her forehead as she groaned. "Adulting is for the birds," she mumbled. A low-key headache had started to brew as she lay here unsuccessfully trying to figure out all the answers.

At some point it occurred to her that she just didn't know the answers and that perhaps she should let go of the notion that she alone could control the outcome.

"Now faith is the substance of things hoped for, the evidence of things not seen."

The scripture replayed in her mind as she continued to watch the lights blinking happily on the tree. The star guarding the top of the tree as the symbol of things hoped for, and the angel's wings as the evidence of things not seen.

CHAPTER 16

On Christmas morning, Seth sat in the front pew at church. He had played the first part of the service—the procession, morning hymn, and first choir selection. Now Hilliard played the sermonic selection, "O Holy Night." The senior musician also sang the song in his rich tenor voice.

With his legs partially spread, Seth leaned forward and rested his elbows on his thighs. He lowered his head as he listened to the lyrics. This would forever remain one of his all-time favorite Christmas songs. While he enjoyed the composition and the playing of the song, mixing the sound from the traditional organ with the more contemporary keyboard, he loved to hear it sung so much more.

Behind him and throughout the sanctuary, he could hear members of the congregation expressing their enjoyment of the song as well. A random "Amen!" and "Sing, Hilliard!" were shouted along with a few claps of encouragement. Seth nodded his head to the rhythm, absorbing every word and letting the lyrics sink into his every thought, to filter and guide his emotions. Focusing on the service, on each song that was sung, each scripture read, each testimony given, had been feeding him in a way he needed so desperately.

To say he'd had a rough night would be an understatement. It had been one of the worst Christmas Eves he could remember. And yet this morning when he opened his eyes and realized that by the grace of God, he'd made it to his bed finally and hadn't still been on the floor in his office crying, he knew that all he could do was rejoice. The sun was shining, although he knew more snow was forecasted for later this morning. Everybody loved snow on Christmas, him and Teddy included. So he'd climbed out of bed and headed to the shower before going downstairs to brew some coffee.

While he'd waited for it to brew, he thought randomly of Christmas punch and wondered which flavor of Ms. Addie's was Ella's favorite. The thought brought a hint of a smile as he dragged his hands down his face. What was he going to do about Ella?

The question had gone unanswered as he'd entered the sanctuary, and now, as he sat being ministered to by the music, he still felt unsettled where she was concerned. Where he felt an unwavering peace was in regard to the death of his beloved wife. Somewhere during the time that he'd sat on the floor in his office, shedding tears he suspected he'd been holding in since sitting in the hospital room for those last minutes with Rhonda, he felt an enormous weight being lifted from his shoulders. It was the weight of grief, he knew, and it was gone. He figured some would say he'd traveled through all the stages, even though he had no clue what the stages of grief actually were. When living it, he hadn't thought of searching for a checklist. He only wanted to be able to function each day, and he had done so. But up until a few weeks ago, only a semblance of him had gotten to this point. This morning, he felt like he was whole again. Not that he loved and cherished Rhonda any less, but he could be grateful for the season of his life that she had been with him and still feel steady enough to enter this next season without her, or her memory, holding him back.

The song was over too soon, and afterward he sat back against the pew and prepared to hear the pastor deliver his Christmas sermon. This was always a special message to Seth and the rest of the congregation, he was sure. He glanced back quickly to one of the last pews in the sanctuary, where Ella sat. Brooke was beside her today, both of them looking up toward the pulpit after turning to the scripture the pastor had cited as his reference text. She wore a burgundy dress today, her twists pulled up into a neat bun. And she'd smiled at him when she caught him looking at her earlier in the service.

This time he was wise enough not to stare so long as to get caught. The last thing he wanted was for her to call him creepy or stalkerish again. A chuckle bubbled in his chest at the thought and he turned his attention back to the pastor, who'd begun speaking.

The pastor wasn't even a third of the way into the sermon when Seth felt his phone vibrating in the front pocket of his dress pants. He reached for it and pulled it out, fully intending to decline the call and continue enjoying the service, until he saw the name on the screen.

Then he was looking around the sanctuary again, trying to see where Ms. Nancy, the usher general, was. She would've taken a seat in the back of the church because it was preaching time, but her gaze would still be wandering throughout to catch anyone moving unnecessarily or taking attention away from the sermon, according to her rules. He spotted her in the last pew in the sanctuary, doing exactly what he thought she would be—looking around at everybody else. He eased out of his seat, keeping his body bent low as he made his way to a side door and slipped through it as quickly as he could. If Ms. Nancy was going to come after him—as she'd done so many times before during his teen years—she'd have to find him first.

He moved quickly down the stairs and into the fellowship hall—which by now was free of water but still had damage to the floor—to answer the phone before it stopped ringing.

"Hello?"

"Hey, Seth. Merry Christmas, man!"

"Dex, hey, man. Merry Christmas!"

"Sorry to be calling you back on Christmas morning, but I'm at the airport heading to Aspen for some skiing into the new year with my family."

Seth walked with the phone to his ear. "Yeah, Jordan said you'd gotten married and you have, what? Two kids now?"

"Yup, two sons and another baby on the way. Haven't even announced that one to our family yet," Dex said. "We're just taking this week to ourselves and then we'll tell everyone when we get back."

"That's what's up," Seth said and nodded. Family vacations and new baby announcements were things he'd always dreamed of having for himself. "Well, I won't hold you up. I sent those sketches to you via email just to get your thoughts. But you can hit me up after the first of the year if you think it's something."

"Nah, man, it's no problem. That's why I'm calling," Dex said. "As soon as I received the pictures, I sent them over to a colleague at another agency and he flipped over them. He's super interested in talking to her about representation."

"No kidding?"

"I'm calling you on Christmas morning, ain't I?"

Seth chuckled. "Yeah. That's amazing," he said. And it was perfect. The more good news that Ella received at Christmastime, the easier it would be for her to let go of the notion of being jinxed in any way.

"So my assistant is going to be back in the office for a few hours the middle of next week, and she's going to send you an email with all the contact information so you can forward it on to your friend. The ball's in her court, but like I said, my colleague is really interested."

"Thanks a lot, man. Next time I'm in New York, I owe you dinner," Seth said.

"I'm gonna remember that," Dex said before wishing Seth happy holidays again and disconnecting the call.

Seth slipped his phone back into his pocket and felt like dancing the way Ella had last night. Luckily he didn't, because when he turned, it was to see his sister standing there with her arms crossed over her chest in her Max-has-something-she's-about-to-say stance.

"Hey," he said and straightened his jacket before walking toward her.

"Hey," she said and raised her brow in question. "What was that all about?"

"Nothing," he replied.

"Nothing? Who do you owe dinner in New York? And before you answer, let me tell you that it better not be a woman." She shook her head. "You better not have been leading Ella on all this time. Not after I saw the two of you last night all hugged up like high school sweethearts."

Yep, Max had something to say.

He huffed. "It's nothing like that."

Max narrowed her eyes at him. "Nothing like what? You're not leading Ella on? Or I didn't see what I know for sure I saw between the two of you last night? As a matter of fact, everybody in the room saw it last night. Mama called me first thing this morning to talk about it because Daddy wouldn't let her say anything to me or you while we were there last night."

His mother hadn't said anything to him about it this morning when she came into the sanctuary and he hugged her and wished her a merry Christmas. That meant his father had given her a time when she could say something, and that time was most likely once he got to her house this afternoon for dinner.

"Can we not do this here?" he asked, anxious to get back to the service. Because once it was over, he planned to tell Ella the good news.

"Why not? There's obviously something going on with you, and I want to know what it is."

"There's nothing going on." Although that wasn't totally true. There was something going on and in the last few minutes, he'd realized just how good that something was.

"With you and Ella, right?" Max pressed.

She was his sister and Seth loved her. He'd do anything for her, but right now he really wanted her to let this go. "Can we just get back upstairs before he's finished preaching? We can talk when we get to Mama's. I promise I'll answer all your questions then, no matter how personal they are."

He made the mistake of trying to walk past her, but Max grabbed his arm and he turned again to face her. "I'm not patient enough to wait till later. I want to know what's going on right now, because I've been holding my thoughts in about this situation all night long and I'm gonna burst if I don't get it out."

He shook his head but had to laugh—only his sister could be this borderline rude and intrusive, and he still felt nothing but love for her. The bigger part of this was that Seth knew where this heavy-handed concern was coming from, and he held a good chunk of it for Max as well. He was just much better about keeping his on the low.

"Why'd you run out of there last night?" she asked without waiting for him to say if it was okay to continue the conversation or not. "Ella looked really upset when she came back into the hall."

Ella had appeared confused when he left her standing in the hallway, so he could imagine that had morphed into irritation.

"I shouldn't have left like that, but there were some things on my mind I needed to sort through. Things that have been going on that I've been grappling with and trying to figure out."

"Things like falling for Ella but feeling guilty because you don't want to betray the memory of your wife?"

Seth sighed heavily and moved his hand over his chin. "Yeah," he said because there was no use denying it now. "I didn't know how to separate the two or how to tell Ella what I was feeling."

"Why don't you start by talking to her the same way you're talking to your sister?"

The sound of Ella's voice from behind him had Seth simultaneously feeling joy and regret. Joy that she was here so he could tell her the good news and regret because—just as he had last night—she'd overheard a conversation that may have caused her hurt or more confusion. He narrowed his gaze at his sister because she had to have seen that Ella had come into the fellowship hall and hadn't bothered to stop the conversation. Max only looked at him expectantly.

"Go," Seth said in a low, no-argument-needed tone.

Like a petulant child, Max pursed her lips and walked away.

When he turned this time, it was to see Ella standing with her hands clasped behind her back. He wanted to run to her and hug her, to repeat his apology for being such an idiot last night, but he accepted that she might not want him to touch her at the moment. So instead, he closed some of the space between them. Not so much that he crowded her, but enough so that their conversation was just between them and not whoever else might come into the fellowship hall.

"I'm sorry," he said without preamble. "I reacted badly to your news last night and I'm so sorry."

She blinked as if she was surprised that was the reason for his abrupt departure. "But you were the one who said I'd get the job. You said you never doubted I would get the offer."

He nodded because she was absolutely right. "I did believe it. From the moment you told me you were looking for a job, I knew you'd have no problem finding one. You've never had a problem achieving your goals, Ella. Look at how you walked out of Bellepoint, obtained a degree in a highly specialized field, and then landed an amazing job. You built the life you wanted and I'm extremely proud to say that I know you. That we used to be in the same class."

"That you burned a hole in my book bag with acid," she replied with the slightest tilt of her lips.

"Yeah, that too." He almost smiled, thinking that her quick jab was a sign that she wasn't as irritated about last night as

Max had implied. But he knew there was more between them. A hill of things that needed to be climbed and settled before either of them could walk away from this comfortably . . . or move forward together.

"I've spent these last weeks promising you I'd show you the real meaning of Christmas and watching you embrace every aspect of this holiday, mind and soul, without much help on my part. I got so caught up in how good it felt to see you on a regular basis again that I just lost track of . . . everything," he said, feeling a little bit more of the weight he'd carried being released. "There were hours in a day that I didn't think about what else I could do to keep Rhonda's memory alive. In the evenings, when I went home to Teddy, I didn't wonder if that would be the day that I wouldn't want to walk into the kitchen and see Rhonda standing there. I just stopped wondering," he said.

Tears filled her eyes and he watched her shaking her head slowly. "It was never my intention to take your wife's place, Seth. I could see from the start how much you loved her, and I am the last person to tell you how to deal with your loss."

"That's just it," he said and reached out a hand to touch her before letting it fall back to his side quickly. "You aren't taking her place. I mean, when we . . . if we . . ." He stopped and took a slow breath in and then out. "What I'm trying to say is that there's room in my heart for you. A space that's all yours. That, truth be told, has been yours since that day you walked into Mrs. Holback's classroom."

She gasped and then used a knuckle to stop the tears before they could flow down her cheeks. "Seth," she whispered.

"No, let me finish. Please." He was standing closer to her now, couldn't keep himself away a second longer. "I'm not asking you to do anything you don't want to do. I'm just asking you to consider us in whatever form that can be. Pittsburgh's not that far, a four- to five-hour drive. I can be there on weekends. You can come here on weekends. I want us to . . . We can make this work. I have faith in these feelings that haven't wavered in all these years, that there's something . . . We can build something together, Ella."

"Seth, the job—"

He didn't let her finish that sentence. "Right! The new job. Well, I hope you won't get angry with me all over again when I tell you this, but I did something."

Now she looked at him suspiciously, her head tilting slightly. "You did something?"

He nodded. "That night when I took those bags up to your room, I sort of took something out of your room too."

"Seth!"

"I know, I know. I'm creepy, stalkerish, and a thief. I need prayer. I know," he said with a half smile. "But hear me out. I sent a few of your sketches—the one of gingerbread men dancing along the counter toward the pie, the one of Ms. Addie sitting in her recliner, and the one of the Christmas tree with the star on the top—to a frat brother who's also a book agent in New York." He cleared his throat. "Ella, he just called me. That's why I was down here in the first place. He sent the sketches to another agent who I guess represents artists and illustrators or whatever. But his colleague is very interested in talking to you about representation. Now, I know you said your drawing was just cathartic—" His next words were cut off when she stepped closer and placed her hand over his mouth.

"I . . . I didn't realize I'd drawn that tree," she said, her words quiet and wavering like the new tears that had formed in her eyes. "I never forget it. Ever. It's always in my mind, with that gold star at the top just where Mama always put it." She shook her head as the first tear fell and dropped her hand from his mouth.

Seth grabbed that hand and used his free one to wipe the tear from her cheek.

"If you had asked me for those sketches, I wouldn't have given them to you. I would've insisted that my job was as a curator. It's what I trained to do." She took a deep breath and looked up at him. "But last night . . ." She paused and blinked. Her brow furrowed. "Last night, when I was lying on the couch staring at those angel's wings and telling myself that it would be okay if my wish didn't come true this time, that I could still have faith, I felt this calm come over me. And in that calm, I realized that I wasn't using all of my talents and that I owed it to myself to do that. To follow that path and see where it leads."

He was watching her as she talked, saw a spark of something enter her tear-filled eyes, and felt his chest tighten with emotion. "So you wished for clarity in your career and it came true," he said. "Your wish came true, Ella!"

But even as he was growing excited, she was shaking her head.

"No," she said quietly. "I wished for happiness in every aspect of my life because all this time I've had things, Seth. I've had the job I thought I wanted and the life I thought I was supposed to lead, but neither of those things had ever made me happy. Not like I was when I was here with you—when I was doing things that were fun and that made me feel happy on the inside and out. So this morning, before I even went down to have coffee with Aunt Addie, I got online and researched drawing classes. There's a professor I met from all those art department functions I attended during college who's now teaching specialized drawing courses. I enrolled and will start in mid-January."

"What? You're not taking the job? You're going back to school?" He didn't know whether to be happy or give in to confusion. They were both pretty good at confusing each other.

"I'm going to offer to do some virtual consulting work for them, but no, I'm not accepting the curator position and I'm not moving to Pittsburgh. I'm going back to my apartment in Philly. I have savings that can support me for a few months while I take the classes and explore what my next steps are going to be." She squared her shoulders. "But I'm not the person I was when I came here a couple of weeks ago. I've learned to let go of some things and to let other things in."

For a second, he wondered if now was the time he could wrap his arms around her and spin her around the way he had last night when they learned they'd met their financial goal. "That's wonderful, Ella. I'm really proud of you. No matter what you do."

"Thanks, Seth." She stepped closer to him then, lifting her free hand to cup his cheek. "I'm proud of you too. For being such a rock for me when deep down you were still crumbling. I'll never forget that. I'll never forget you."

"Well, that would be pretty hard to do since I plan on doing just like I said and driving up to Philly every weekend to stand on your doorstep."

"Oh," she said with a smile. "You're not going to ride your bike this time?"

Seth grinned and wrapped his free arm around her waist before bringing the back of the hand he still held to his lips to kiss lightly. "Nah, Teddy can't fit on the bike with me."

Ella laughed and leaned into him.

"Seth." She breathed his name before lifting her gaze up to meet his. "My wish did come true this time. Not only did I rediscover my joy of drawing, but I also discovered my love for you."

Seth pressed his lips to her forehead and breathed the sigh of relief he'd been holding in for what seemed like forever. "I love you, Ella."

He had no idea what was going on in the sanctuary now, or anywhere else in the world, for that matter. All Seth knew was that he was holding the woman he loved and that at this moment, she was happy and loved him too.

EPILOGUE

O scar was so surprised when Seth and Jordan announced that their fraternity brothers would be making it an annual event to come out here and decorate," Aunt Addie said as she added the miniature post office to the Christmas village she and Ella were setting up in the family room of the main house at the Mountaintop Dude Ranch.

Ella moved around at the far end of the platform, fighting to adjust some of the trees between the houses she'd placed there. "He said it was a unanimous vote at their last chapter meeting. And I heard Jordan talking about adding on a couple more cabins."

"Oh yes, we're excited about that. This place is such a local treasure, we need to do what we can to preserve that history and to make it sparkle for the next generation to enjoy."

Ella paused at her aunt's words. It had been almost five months since Aunt Addie and her new uncle Oscar had been married in a beautiful ceremony on the far eastern side of this property, by the lake. She'd never seen her aunt as happy as she'd been this past year, being "properly courted," as Aunt Addie had told her on each occasion she'd asked about their relationship. For the first part of this year, Ella and Seth had taken turns traveling on weekends—him to Philly and her back here to Belle-point. By the time school had let out for the summer, they'd decided that Seth and Teddy would spend a few weeks in the city with Ella. Those weeks had turned into two months, until her aunt had announced her engagement and wedding that followed just three weeks later. When Ella returned for the wedding, she'd returned to Bellepoint for good.

"I think that's just wonderful," she replied when her aunt caught her staring wistfully at her.

"Well, you're doing a lot for the new generation as well," Aunt Addie said and stood back to check the positioning of the post office building, which she obviously didn't like because she quickly picked it up and put it someplace else in the Main Street area of their village. "Gail and I stopped by Janel's new day care center with a special Thanksgiving lunch last week. The place is looking really good, and Janel said she was almost to capacity with children."

"After talking to Seth about the lack of day care facilities in Bellepoint for children of working parents, I knew I wanted to look into that further. And once I had a chance to speak to Janel about her initial plans being thwarted because she couldn't get approved for a small business loan, I figured there had to be another way. Looking into grants that Bellepoint's small school system qualified for was quite a task, but once we found a few, it was game on! We didn't stop until we perfected those applications, and now Janel's dream has come to fruition. I love to see it!"

"We do too," Aunt Addie added. She moved the post office again and Ella bit back a grin.

"My gracious, Addie, are y'all still working on this Christmas village?" Uncle Oscar asked when he came into the room carrying two more boxes. We've still got a few rooms in the house to get finished. The crew outside are coming along pretty good."

"Really?" Ella asked. "When I was out there last, Max and Jordan were about to go to war over a string of lights. That's why I switched teams and came inside." She chuckled, but the tension between Max and Jordan had kicked up a notch during the time Ella had been in Philly taking her drawing classes. Neither she nor Seth knew exactly what had gone down between them; instead they all tried to steer clear of the impending implosion.

Uncle Oscar shook his head and came over to wrap his arm around Aunt Addie's shoulders. "Yeah, Seth bailed on them too. He's doing the main living room now."

Ella would never get tired of the way her aunt looked at her uncle, or the way he looked at her. In those few seconds that he'd touched her, they'd both forgotten that Ella was even in the room. Their gazes held, smiles sending private messages to each other. It was the sweetest thing to see and her heart filled with joy for them. This little scene also made her feel like a third wheel, so she eased away from the table and exited the room.

The ranch had started to feel like a second home to Ella in the months that she'd become a permanent resident in Bellepoint again. That decision hadn't come easily. The idea of taking formal drawing classes had come to her so quickly, and she'd felt compelled to act on it even when Aunt Addie insisted she was a wonderful artist without them. But Ella had wanted the formal training. She'd wanted to learn more about the craft she'd planned to fully embrace, especially once she had a chance to speak with Seth's friend's colleague. Troy Franklin had turned out to be an amazing agent who'd gotten Ella her first illustration deal with a new children's book series. The first book was set to be released next week and Ella was hosting a release party at Aunt Addie's house—which was now her house.

The theme for the party was Toyland since the first book in the series was titled *Every Me I See* and was about a girl in search of dolls that looked like her in every store she visited.

"I have to say, for someone who just a year ago didn't like decorating, you've been on a roll today," Seth said when she walked into the living room and immediately joined him near the humongous balsam fir tree Moses Grant had delivered early this morning. "I've seen you doing something in every room of the house and outside."

She shrugged, recalling exactly where she was emotionally last year and how far she'd come to be at a place of peace this year. "Just trying to make sure everything gets done out here. This is going to be a busy month with the release party next week—we're going to have so many children moving in and out of that house." She chuckled. "That reminds me: I have to check on those inflatables for the front yard."

"You mean those enticers that will keep Teddy running around trying to attack them for hours," he said and grinned.

Ella and Teddy had become the best of friends. Since she worked from home most of the day, Seth dropped Teddy off at her house each morning when he was on his way to work. In the afternoon, when Ella needed to get over to the church where she worked part-time at the new after-school program, she dropped Teddy off at Max's shop, where Seth would pick him up later.

They had a great little routine going, and lately Ella had begun to wonder what she'd ever done without the two of them in her life.

"He's gonna be fine. I'll have a talk with him and he'll know to leave them alone," she said and picked up an ornament from one of the boxes on the chair and placed it on the tree.

"Good luck with that," Seth said and moved around to the other side of the tree. "He seems to listen to you more frequently than he does me, so you might have a chance."

"Teddy's a sweetheart. You just have to remind him of that. Oh! I almost forgot. We moved the next auction committee meeting to Thursday evening, right before choir rehearsal. Brooke said she has some great new graphics to show us for this year's Christmas tree boxes." Last year's auction had gone so well that they'd immediately started preliminary plans for this year. Ella and Brooke took the lead on developing a complete marketing strategy for this year's event, so they'd been able to start the search for sponsors the week before Thanksgiving, and the mailing list they'd built from last year's online bidders had been receiving monthly newsletters since October, but that would now shift to weekly.

"That's fine. I'm not really looking forward to choir rehearsal anyway," he said.

She moved until she was standing beside him again. He'd just put another bulb on the tree when he dropped his hands to his sides and stared at her. "Why?" she asked. "Because you're singing a solo next Sunday?"

He frowned. "How'd you know that?"

"Max said she heard you practicing when she stopped by your house to drop Teddy off last week. And I know that Hilliard and your mother have been on you about singing more." She, on the other hand, had never pressured Seth about his singing. He was adamant that becoming a famous singer wasn't his calling, but he also acknowledged how much he enjoyed it from time to time. Ella respected that and was ready to cheer him on whenever he picked up a microphone.

"Max talks too much," he said with a smile. "And nothing stays a secret for long in Bellepoint."

"Now that's the truth," Ella said. The pastor had announced her book deal during a Sunday morning fellowship service only days after Ella had signed the contract. She'd known that had come from her aunt Addie calling everyone she knew to shout how proud she was of Ella.

"Okay, I think this is finished," he said, taking a step back to look at the tree that was packed with lights, colorful bulbs, ribbon, and the huge flower ornaments Aunt Addie had bought at an after-Christmas sale last year.

"Yeah, it looks good," she said. They were going out to Grant's this weekend to get a tree for her house and one for his house. While her aunt was firmly on the traditionally decorated tree side, Ella had already decided she wanted a really happy tree and had opted for a candy land theme that would go perfectly with the release party decor.

"Hand me that box over there with the topper in it, please."

"Sure," she said and turned away to retrieve it. The minute her hands touched the silver box, she froze.

Memories flipped through her mind like a movie reel.

"It's all done now, Mama."

"Not quite, baby," Mama said. *"You know what's the last very special part of decorating the tree?"*

Ella did know and she hurried over to the bin that held a red velvet box. Ella knew to handle the box with care and she lifted it out of the bin, moving as slowly as she possibly could. She took a deep breath, then let it out in a whoosh as she eased the top from the box. The gold star inside glittered and glistened as if it were brand new. Her fingers moved over it, going from one pointed peak to the next.

"Do you know why the Christmas star is so important, Ella?" Mama had come up behind her, touching a hand lightly to her shoulder as Ella nodded. "Yup. It's where all the wishes come from."

Ella let her fingers slide over the box, purposely keeping her breathing even as her mother's voice settled over her. Oh, how she loved her mother and everything that she'd taught her, and while her heart still ached for the loss, she rejoiced in knowing that their time together had been perfect and magical.

"Here," Seth said as he stood beside her. "Why don't you try something new this year?"

"Something new?" she asked, her voice cracking on that last word. She couldn't look away from the ornament he held. At first glance they were simply angel's wings, nothing elaborate or especially Christmassy, but as she continued to stare, she noted the details. The wings were white lace, two pearls in the center, and the string that held them was another pattern of lace, looped so the ornament could be hung on a tree. Plain, simple, delicate, and, when she reached up to run one finger along its edge, soft.

She'd framed her drawing of the angel's wings Seth had given her and it had hung in her bedroom at her house in Philly. When she moved to Bellepoint and after Aunt Addie had packed all her pictures and mementos, Ella had hung the picture in the foyer of the dusty-blue craftsman house where she'd grown up.

This was Uncle Oscar's tree topper. The box didn't look like one she'd seen with Aunt Addie's stuff last year. And Ella didn't know if there was a star, an angel, or even an elaborate bow that went atop this tree. All she knew was that with it was the spirit of hope, of possibilities and of love. She inhaled a deep breath and released it slowly. Then she carried the box over to where Seth stood and handed it to him.

"I want to hang it," she said. "Let me just find the step stool."

She wandered out of the living room and into the dining room, where she'd last had the stool as she'd hung garland around the entryway. Returning to the living room, it was to see that Seth had removed a beautiful Black angel from the box. The wings were gold and looked as delicate as the lace ones of her now favorite ornament. "Oh, that's lovely," she said and heard the lightness in her tone.

"It is nice," Seth said. "Here, let me help you."

She set the stool close to the tree and Seth placed a hand to her hip to steady her as she stood up on it. "Okay, hand it to me."

He passed the angel up to her and her fingers shook momentarily as she held it in her hand. Ella stared down into the serene face of the angel, the warm brown eyes and high cheekbones, the curly hair and pert lips. "Lovely," she whispered once more before she reached up to settle the angel on the top branch.

When she was sure it was on firmly, Ella turned to step down off the stool, but Seth grabbed her hand and held her there.

"What—"

The words died in her throat as she looked down to see the

open black box that he'd placed in her palm. He moved slowly, like they were in some weird freeze-frame scenario, going down on one knee.

"I've been carrying this around in my pocket for days, trying to find just the right time," he said, his voice a bit gruff, his gaze intent. Then he cleared his throat. "I wish that this love we've shared throughout the year would continue to grow. That our bond would continue to be strengthened. That our faith continue to hold steady in the days, months, and years to come."

She gasped. "Oh, Seth."

"I wish that the girl I fell for so long ago and the woman who captured my heart and brightened my world would forever find all the joy and peace she deserves." He smiled slowly, and Ella felt as if her heart would explode with love for this man.

"I wish that Ella Wilson would agree to become my wife."

Tears were already flowing, the hand that held the box with a brilliant diamond ring staring back at her shook, but all she could think about was claiming this happiness. Not waiting to see if another wish would come true but living in this moment and believing that each moment to come would be just as joyous and fulfilling.

"Yes," she whispered and nodded as she repeated, "Yes!"

Seth's grin was huge as he stood. He took the box from her hand and removed the ring. And when he slid that ring on her finger, he looked up at her and whispered, "You're my every wish come true."

His hands went to her hips to lift her down off the stool and Ella wrapped her arms around his neck. Their lips touched in the softest, sweetest kiss right in front of that lovely Christmas tree.

DISCUSSION QUESTIONS

1. Which characters did you like best? Which did you like least?
2. Which character did you relate to, or empathize with, the most?
3. Was Ella and Seth's connection believable? If so, at what point did they click for you?
4. Did reading this book bring back any special Christmas memories for you?
5. Have you ever had your faith tested the way Ella's was? How did you deal with it?
6. Do you think it was fair for Seth's friends and family to encourage him to be with Ella?
7. What do you think happens with Aunt Addie and Mr. Oscar after the book's official ending?
8. How did the setting impact the story? Would you want to read more books set in Bellepoint?
9. Which scene has stuck with you the most?
10. If you could ask the author anything about this book, what would it be?

SNICKERDOODLE
HOT CHOCOLATE

Prep time: 10 minutes
Cook time: 10 minutes

Yields: 2 servings

3 cups half-and-half cream
1 bar (3 ½ ounces) 70% cacao dark chocolate, chopped
2 oz. milk chocolate, chopped
2 tsp. caramel (plus more for rim and drizzling)
1 tsp. ground cinnamon (plus more for cinnamon sugar)
1 tsp. vanilla extract
¼ tsp. ground nutmeg
¼ tsp. salt
1 tsp. sugar (optional)
Optional: Sweetened whipped cream, snickerdoodle
    cookies, and cinnamon sugar

Directions

1. In a medium saucepan over medium heat, heat half-and-half cream until it begins to steam and bubbles form at edges.
2. Add dark and milk chocolate, caramel, cinnamon, vanilla, nutmeg, and salt. Stir constantly until all chocolate is completely melted.
3. (Optional) Pour 2 teaspoons of caramel into a small bowl. In a separate bowl add 1 teaspoon of cinnamon and 1 teaspoon of sugar, mix. Dip mugs in the caramel and then in the cinnamon sugar.
4. Ladle hot chocolate into mugs, then top with whipped cream, sprinkle with more cinnamon sugar, and garnish with a snickerdoodle.

ABOUT THE AUTHOR

Lisa Fleet Photography

Lacey Baker, a Maryland native, is a wife, mother, nana, and author. Family cookouts, reunion vacations, and growing up in church have all encouraged Lacey to write heartwarming and inspirational stories about the endurance of family and finding love. She is the author of the Crescent Island series and Hallmark Channel Original Movie novelizations: *A Gingerbread Romance* and *Christmas in Evergreen: Bells Are Ringing*.

Connect with her online at laceybakerromance.com
Facebook: @laceybakerromance
Twitter: @laceybakerbook
Instagram: @laceybakerbooks
BookBub: @laceybakerbooks